Morgan rode his risers, aimi all around him. He was sev an anti-aircraft gun, sounding like a big bass drum from three quarters of a mile to the south, opened fire on the formation of planes. A mobile job, thought Morgan, concealed under camouflage netting. There was a fiery flash from the same C-46 they'd been aboard and a few seconds later the ka-whump! of the explosion carried to him, muffled by the distance. Then a high keening whine as the big plane went into a slow, almost graceful nose-diving tailspin, trailing black smoke like a grim streamer from its tail. The big plane disappeared into the dense green of the swampland and seconds later a red fireball rose into the sky, bright as the sun. A thick black pillar of smoke snaked into the air, marking where the C-46 had gone down.

The accompanying fighter planes banked around and dived into a strafing run at treetop level. The anti-aircraft gun fell silent. The fighters flew off to rejoin the remaining cargo planes, which by now were receding black specks in the pale blue sky.

Morgan landed with bone-jarring impact. He rolled once and came up running onto the wide shoulder of the dirt road. He hurriedly shrugged off the parachute harness and sprinted over to join the platoon, who were gathering nearby, their rifles ready, every man eyeing the dense, green wall of swamp.

Further up the road, it sounded like no more than half a mile, an exchange of weapons fire could be heard.

José completed a fast headcount. "It looks like we're all accounted for. We made it!"

"Good for you," said Morgan. "Welcome to hell."

For James Reasoner

THE CASTRO DIRECTIVE

For Barb & Al —
Steve's "JFK Novel."
Hope you enjoy it!
In friendship
& with Best Wishes,

STEPHEN MERTZ

Steve

CROSSROAD PRESS

PROLOGUE

In 1961, the Cold War showed no sign of thawing.

U.S.-Soviet relations were severely strained. In fact, the world teetered on the brink of nuclear war. An American military spy plane had been shot down over the Soviet Union, and the Berlin Wall would be constructed within the year. In a speech at the United Nations, the Russian leader, Khrushchev, got so angry that he took off his shoe and beat it on a table. "We will bury you!" he threatened.

In Cuba, ninety miles south of Key West, Florida, the Socialist revolution of Fidel Castro was in its eighteenth month. The United States had initially welcomed what looked like a democratic Cuba, but a rude awakening came within months when Castro established military tribunals for political opponents and jailed hundreds. Thousands of Cubans fled the country. U.S. assets were confiscated and Soviet-style collective farms established. When the U.S. broke relations with Cuba on January 3, 1961, the Castro government formalized its alliance with the Soviet Union.

In Washington, the Kennedy administration, less than ninety days old, viewed these developments with alarm. The small island nation was considered a beachhead of Soviet expansion into the western hemisphere. America and her allies were determined to stop the spread of communism around the world...

CHAPTER 1

The only sound for the past ten minutes had been the lapping of gentle swells against the low, black-painted hull. The V-20 speedboat rode the swells one hundred yards offshore. Sleek, sixty-three-feet in length, the launch bore no name or markings. A gun pit amidship mounted a .50 caliber machine gun. A squat wheelhouse was topped with a short radar mast and folding radio antenna. Moonlight dappled the ocean, making the black water shimmer like polished dark glass. At thirty minutes past midnight, there was no trace of a breeze. The warm air was heavy, oppressive. Inland, beyond the beach, trees and vegetation were an ominous, inky smudge.

Two men stood behind the V-20's wheelhouse.

Riley said, "There it is." He was a muscular black man of indeterminate age, sporting a battered skipper's cap, a white T-shirt and a pair of blue denims.

Lehman saw it, too: the pinpoint of a flashlight flickering on and off, three times, from the blackness of the beach.

"About time." He snorted his irritation. "Ten minutes late." Lehman was in his middle forties; a short man, powerfully built, also wearing denims, with a light sport jacket over a black T-shirt.

Riley returned the signal with his flashlight.

"Sometimes it pays to be careful. This boy meeting us, he knows that. I know it, too. The Ruskies delivered ten new patrol boats to Havana last week. I haven't lost a delivery yet. I'd hate for you to be the first."

A rowboat materialized from the shadows. A single occupant could be discerned manning the oars, closing the distance toward the launch with powerful strokes. The sound of the oars through the water carried clearly.

Art Lehman absently patted his pocket for the wallet he knew was there. His wallet contained a Canadian passport identifying him as an employee of a company in Cuba that was secretly owned and operated by the Central

Intelligence Agency. The wallet also held a fake work permit and the two thousand Cuban pesos he had been issued before leaving Key West. Lehman had been in espionage for a long time. Too long, he sometimes thought. First in the OSS during the war, when he had regularly been air-dropped behind Nazi lines, then as a field agent after the wartime Office of Strategic Services was transformed into the peacetime CIA, operating in dangerous, shadowy corners of the world, hellholes from Algiers to Vietnam, from Hungary to Guatemala. Lehman knew more than a dozen ways to kill a person without a weapon, though he rarely went unarmed, and an equal number of ways to persuade an unwilling person to talk. He could lose himself in most crowds and was adaptable to all the ordinary habits of any country he happened to visit.

The bow of the rowboat kissed the hull of the launch with a muted thump.

Lehman exchanged a handshake with Riley. "Thanks for the lift."

"Anytime. Watch yourself, company man."

Lehman made the easy step down into the rowboat.

The black man was already gunning the twin 1500 horsepower Hudson Invader engines. The launch swung around and away, rapidly gaining speed, creating swells that rocked the little rowboat. The engine sounds faded into darkness.

Lehman estimated the young Cuban rowing the boat to be no more than twenty. He was casually dressed in an open-necked shirt and khaki slacks. The moonlight limned a wiry build and clean-shaven features.

Working the oars without effort, the young man returned Lehman's unconcealed scrutiny. "I am Diego Vasquez."

"I know."

They spoke in Spanish.

"Ah, no names. As you wish, *señor*."

"I don't wish. The name on my passport says Lehman, so that's my name. You're late."

"My apologies, *señor*. The government radio broadcasts nightly with warnings of an invasion by the Americans to overthrow the Castro government. The Revolution Defense Party is everywhere, worse than before. Neighbor spies upon neighbor. I had to be careful."

"That's what Riley said."

"The man who brought you here, is that his name? I have been bringing you people ashore like this for almost a year. But until now, all the ones from Key West have been Cuban."

Lehman stared toward the beach and saw nothing but the darkness. The gloom beyond the beach crackled with a cacophonous symphony of night birds and insects. The smells of the swamp grew stronger, overpowering the saltwater air with an over-ripe stench of decayed vegetation and stagnant swampland, making the darkness heavy and oppressive, enveloping Lehman's senses like a smothering, damp blanket.

Insertion was always one of the most dangerous points of any mission. Once you were in country, you could hopefully rely on your training, your survival instincts; sometimes you could even depend on the people you were supposed to work with. But getting in was always the tricky part, when you didn't know if you were stepping onto solid ground or stepping off a cliff. This was when that intangible element, plain old-fashioned *luck*, came into the equation.

He said, "At this stage, the Agency feels it's important to have a man on the ground with you people in country."

"I think you will find that our sabotage operations have been most successful." The young Cuban spoke with pride. "Only last month a major refinery outside Havana went up in flames. The arms and explosives your government provides us have been put to good use. So, you are here because the invasion will come soon, yes?"

Lehman slapped a mosquito feeding at the back of his neck. "I don't know. I'm here to coordinate the regional cells of your underground so that you people are fully prepared to offer support. I'm just a guy they send in to do the dirty work before the shit hits the fan."

They were almost ashore. Diego stepped from the boat into ankle deep water and guided the rowboat onto the beach.

"I live less than a mile from here with my mother and sister. You will stay with us?"

Lehman joined him on a strip of sand that was black in the light of a quarter moon. The surf whispered at their feet.

"For tonight. Tomorrow I'll need you to help me get to the people I need to meet. There's a lot to be done in a very short time."

He unbuttoned his sport jacket to allow easy access to the .38 revolver he wore in a concealed shoulder holster. He swatted at another mosquito and started to look around, inland. He hadn't been to Cuba since before the revolution, when the gaudy casinos of Batista's Havana had provided suitable rest and recreation for a divorced, childless agent between assignments.

Blinding light flooded the beach from high voltage searchlights.

He jerked up an arm with a curse, shielding his eyes from the glare, momentarily unable to see a thing. His stomach became an icy knot and his throat was suddenly dry. So much for good luck. *Be cool,* he told himself. *Stay calm. You can get out of this.* Blinded as he was by the row of lights, he heard rather than saw a line of men charge onto the beach; the padding of their boots on the sand.

When he began regaining his vision a moment later, he saw that he and Diego were surrounded by militiamen in fatigues, wearing berets, aiming their rifles at him and Diego.

Lehman said, "You're not a part of this, are you, son?"

Before the young man could respond, a Cuban Army officer stepped forward and swiveled the butt of his rifle in a short arc that caught Diego in the stomach. Diego collapsed to his knees, bent over in pain, gasping for breath.

Lehman sighed. "No, I guess not. Guess you just weren't careful enough."

Two men emerged from behind the searchlights.

Lehman's attention was drawn immediately to the more impressive of them.

Fidel Alejandro Castro Ruz was thirty-five years old. A tall man of great bulk, somehow big without an inch of fat to him. His towering physique was encased in a perfectly tailored whipcord olive-green campaign uniform, open-necked. He wore a campaign cap. Horn-rimmed glasses adorned a heavily bearded face. He chewed on an unlit cigar and two more unwrapped cigars peered out from his left breast pocket. A pistol in a web holster rode at his hip. His black boots were highly polished. He walked with a swagger and in fact carried a short swagger stick at his side.

Lehman tried to keep his voice steady, hoping not to reveal his complete surprise. "Well, well. *El Premier.* The Commander-In-Chief himself. Quite a welcoming party."

The bright lights danced off the silver star of *Commandante* that was pinned to Castro's collar. "Do not flatter yourself, *señor.* Snaring you is a satisfactory bonus. But it is your friend, Diego, that we are most interested in." His hard brown eyes glared at the young man. "Traitor. Major Medina has been after you for some time and now that we have you, you will tell us everything we wish to know about your counter-revolutionary activities."

Diego propped himself up onto one knee and started to rise, his breathing returning to normal. "I will tell you nothing."

"We shall see. Take him away."

Militiamen roughly led Diego off to beyond the row of lights which, Lehman now saw, were mounted on a pair of vehicles parked facing the beach beyond a stand of palm trees. His attention turned to the man who stood beside Castro.

This one was as nondescript as Castro was flamboyant; in his fifties, wearing a dark suit and tie, his hair thinning on top, a moustache carefully trimmed above a thin-lipped mouth. This man appraised Lehman and spoke with a slight smile. "Let me try to read your mind, Señor Lehman. You recognize me, do you not? You are debating with yourself the advisability of acknowledging that you know who I am."

Lehman snorted gruffly but the surprise within him was yielding to a chill at the base of his spine that he recognized as fear. *They knew his name! They knew he was CIA!*

"Don't know what you're talking about, pal. I was brought ashore illegally and you guys caught me. Now what?"

The man's smile grew smug. "You do know who I am. I can see the recognition in your eyes. I am Doctor Ernesto Rivas, one of the leaders of the Democratic Revolutionary Front in Miami. You are thinking that right now, I should be in Miami with the exiles, plotting the overthrow of my *Commandante*."

Lehman decided not to waste time sparring. His luck had run out, but not his options. He said to Castro, "With Doctor Rivas in your pocket, you must know just about everything."

Castro nodded, taking the cigar from his mouth to study it idly. "Everything except for the time and place of your planned invasion of my country."

Lehman told himself, Don't let them see the fear. Play this hand out. You can still walk away. This isn't endgame.

He said, "I hope you're not going to torture me," and he heard the tremor in his voice. He added, "I couldn't tell you a thing. Nobody has that information. You'd be wasting your time."

Castro returned the cigar to the corner of his mouth. "I am aware of that. You will appreciate then why apprehending you in the process of capturing Diego Vasquez is of small consequence to me. I have no real need of you, you see."

Castro nodded and two militiamen sprang forward to grab hold of Lehman by each arm. Their officer patted him down and relieved him of his concealed pistol and of a knife worn at the ankle beneath his trousers.

Castro drew his pistol, a Mexican Obregon .45.

Lehman said, "Now wait a minute," and he felt his heart begin to hammer against his rib cage, and his voice quavered more than before. He licked at his dry lips. "You've got no use for me, you said so yourself. Why don't you throw me in the calaboose? Name your price. Cut a deal. You know who to talk to. My people will pay to get me back."

Castro's beard twitched, the corners of his mouth curling with the hint of a smile. "Ah, but I do have a use for you, gringo." He handed the pistol to Rivas. "Doctor."

Rivas accepted the gun. He held the pistol as if quite comfortable holding a firearm. His eyes were no longer amused, but deadly serious.

This is a bluff, Lehman told himself, but the chill at the base of his spine, the fear, spread through his body and for some reason he became acutely aware of everything around him even as his eyes centered on the gun.

From the direction of the swamp, a night bird cawed.

Lehman's body tightened. His muscles bunched up. The militiamen held him firmly in place.

"Now wait a minute, Doc." He was unable to prevent the words from spitting out breathy and too fast. "Uh, don't guys in your profession take an oath or something about doing everything in your power to *save* life?"

Rivas raised the pistol without hesitation. "In your case, *señor,* I will make an exception."

Panic flared through Lehman. There were no more options. His luck had run out. He was going to die on this stinking beach in the moonlight. *Christ, he was going to die!* He gave one mighty, ineffectual wrench in the grasp of the two men holding him.

"*Wait!* Don't do it!"

The gunshot cut off his rising scream. He was kicked free from the militiamen under impact of the bullet and sprawled upon his back, arms out-flung, and his mouth frozen in the *O* of a silent scream.

There came a fluttering from the swamp, frightened birds taking wing.

Rivas handed the pistol back to Castro. "I see now, *Commandante,* why you ordered me to accompany you tonight. The ultimate test. Was my loyalty in question?"

Castro holstered the .45 and casually withdrew a cigarette lighter from his pocket. He took his time lighting his cigar. "You have served me well, Doctor."

Rivas nodded with deference. "It has been my privilege to best serve the Revolution by posing as one who would plot against you."

Castro said, "The exiles and the gringos trust you implicitly. But that is what concerned me, you see. You have spent this past year with my enemies, living in Miami as one of them, gaining their friendship and trust. An invasion of our island is clearly imminent. I have set up militia posts at every conceivable invasion point. But it remains imperative that we find out where their main force will strike and when. You will appreciate, Doctor, how implicit must be my trust in the one I expect to relay this vital information to me."

"Of course, *mi Commandante*. And have I passed the test?"

"You have. Splendidly. Have a cigar."

"Thank you, *Commandante*." Rivas lighted the cigar with his lighter. "The CIA toys with the exile leadership. They view the entire Cuban population of Miami as a security threat. But I assure you, when I learn of their plans, I will convey that information to Havana without delay."

Castro erupted with an angry oath. He kicked the dead man at their feet. The blow sounded like a boot striking a sack of grain.

"I have harbored hatred in my heart for the gringos since the days when we were but a handful in number, fighting half-naked to survive in the mountains, hiding from Batista's death squads. The Americans delivered the bombs and the ammunition for Batista's army and air force. I will never forget or forgive that."

Rivas nodded, exhaling a long stream of smoke. "Good men died horrible deaths for no greater crime than to dare to fight for a government of their own."

"I swore then," said Castro, "that the Americans would pay. And now comes their new President who says he will not *tolerate* our Revolution ninety miles from their shore, as if our sovereignty is not a right but a favor they would grant us. I anticipate extreme personal satisfaction when they launch their invasion, Doctor. It is my natural destiny to reach the apex of power. Men of greatness have it in them to affect the course of history. I will humiliate and defeat those who would destroy me: the exiles in Miami, the Cuban mercenaries trained by the Americans to spearhead the invasion, and the counter-revolutionary scum in our country like Diego

Vasquez. But most especially, I will humiliate the new gringo *Presidente* in the eyes of the world."

Rivas heard something unusual, and realized that Castro was urinating upon the corpse.

CHAPTER 2

John Fitzgerald Kennedy, who at forty-three years of age was the thirty-fifth President of the United States, sat in the rocking chair next to his desk in the Oval Office of the White House. The desk was bare except for a telephone, a row of buttons at its base, and two buzzers. On the floor in front of the desk was an oval rug with the Presidential seal in the center. The walls of the office were a soft off-white. Late afternoon sunlight poured through the curved, inch-thick bulletproof windows. An expensive but conservative tailor-made blue pinstripe suit clothed the President's lean, six-foot frame. His thatch of chestnut hair was dry but carefully coifed.

Agent Tal Garrett stepped discreetly back and waited after handing the President a sheet of onionskin containing a decoded message.

Garrett was a sub-chief in a department whose budgetary details were buried deep in General Accounting. At fifty-one, his was a chunky, deeply creased face topped with a wiry salt-and-pepper crew cut. Broad across the shoulders, he worked to stay in top physical shape through a daily regimen of exercise, though this had not deterred the spare-tire of middle age around his waist. He'd given up smoking a month earlier and that had only added another seven pounds in addition to making him more irritable.

He stood between the two other men in the office who sat in armchairs facing the desk. Robert Kennedy, the President's younger brother and Attorney General, was to his right. General Curtis Atwater—ruddy of complexion, late-middle-aged, in full dress uniform—sat to his left.

The President wore his reading glasses. When he set the paper aside on the desk, his eyes were somber. He stood and turned to gaze out through the glass doors that opened onto a portico overlooking the Rose Garden. He said nothing. Garrett happened to know that the President wore corrective shoes and a cloth brace beneath the quietly stylish suit. Kennedy had been injured in 1939 while playing football at Harvard, and famously re-injured when his PT boat was rammed during the war. The President's back had undergone a disk operation in 1944 and another in 1954, to no lasting benefit. He was said to be in nearly permanent discomfort if not pain.

Robert Kennedy rose from his armchair. The Attorney General was nine years the President's junior, but with his equally stylish tailored suit and dry-combed thatch of chestnut hair, there could be no doubting the strong family resemblance. He read the onion skin before handing it to Atwater.

"Our man never made it past the beach."

Atwater read the message. He leaned forward to replace it on the desk. "Only select members of the Democratic Revolutionary Front leadership knew Lehman's destination and ETA."

Garrett said, "If the Cubans have a spy inside the exile leadership in Miami, things could unravel very quickly. This entire project could run out of control."

The President returned to his rocking chair. He jerked out the tail of his monogrammed shirt and vigorously cleaned his glasses. "I wonder if something isn't trying to tell us how ill-advised this invasion is. The CIA cooks up a hare-brained scheme for Eisenhower and I inherit it, whether I like it or not."

"Unfortunately," Robert said, "you did promise during the campaign to get tough with Castro. That island of his is a communist foothold in our hemisphere. The trade embargo has only driven Cuba closer to Moscow."

The President tucked in his shirttail. He slipped his reading glasses absently into an inside breast pocket and tapped the fingers of one hand upon the arm of his chair with a restless energy.

"I know, I know. Dammit, our whole campaign was based on charges of Republican inactivity in the face of advancing Communism. But Bobby, you know that I've never felt comfortable with the level of risk involved in this operation."

Early in 1960, the Eisenhower administration had authorized the training and arming of a Cuban "army of liberation," under the direction of the CIA, to be trained for a landing in Cuba. This plan was based on the "Guatemala model" of 1954 when, in one week, the CIA had overthrown the duly elected Marxist government with one hundred and fifty exiles, firing barely a shot, and a handful of World War II P-47 fighters flown by American pilots hired by the CIA. This plan called for the recruitment of Cubans who had fled to southern Florida after Castro's rise to power and a secret CIA training facility in northern Nicaragua, where commandos were drilled by U.S. personnel in the tactics of guerilla warfare. Nicaragua insisted these were its defense forces.

Throughout late 1960 and early 1961, there was continuous and intensified sabotage within Cuba. Light planes dropped incendiary bombs. Terrorists struck in Havana. The central tactical aim was to disrupt the Cuban economy before the spring sugar harvest. But what had begun as a typical guerrilla operation, involving men who carried their own weapons, had somehow evolved into a military operation that called for the landing of a brigade of fourteen hundred troops and a platoon of tanks.

A section of Cuban territory would have to be secured by indigenous Cuban forces, at which point a provisional government with a U.S. representative would fly there from Miami to land on a secured air strip and declare themselves a government in arms, whereupon the U.S. fleet, lying offshore, would then come in with aircraft and 15,000 Marines. It was anticipated that the populace of several provinces would arise, particularly in western Cuba. The political prisoners in the Isle of Pines would be released and join the invading brigade. It was thought—or hoped—that Castro's own troops would defect and join the invaders. With the help of local volunteers, the CIA expected the Brigade to double in size within four days.

General Atwater cleared his throat. "You gentlemen know my position, and I am not alone in my pessimism, I assure you. No force the size of Brigade 2506 is going to overthrow Castro. The plan is impractical. The force is inadequate. In addition to being a violation of treaty obligations, Mister President, there are those of us who find it extremely doubtful that the Cuban people will arise in the face of the landings. Our intelligence sources in Cuba are limited and operating under severe handicaps. By the time the information reaches us, it's extremely sketchy. The entire command control structure is inadequate. And if all of that's not enough, well, the Soviets are feeling cocky too. Our armed forces are below strength. If we move on Cuba, Khrushchev could well move on Berlin."

The President's eyes were thoughtful. "General, I am not disregarding what you say, and I appreciate that open intervention runs contrary to our traditions and to our international obligations. That's why I'm reserving the right to cancel this right up to the end. Our hand in this must be concealed. We must maintain plausible deniability."

Robert glared irritably at the General. "This project has already cost millions and is more than a year old. The Brigade is fully trained and ready to fight. Another couple of months and the Soviets will have totally re-armed Castro's army and the Brigade won't stand any chance of success."

Atwater ignored Robert and addressed the President. "That brings us back to our Cuban spies. We know Castro has eyes and ears all over Miami. But if he has a mole planted inside the exile leadership and another inside the Brigade in Nicaragua, we're in big trouble."

The President nodded. "At our last meeting I asked you to find us a man we could assign to investigate this. Who have you got for me?"

Atwater reached for his briefcase, which rested against his chair. He withdrew a manila folder; a military 201 personnel file.

"I had seven department heads run complete file searches for the type of man we're looking for, a soldier with combat experience who knows how to conduct an investigation and maybe something about espionage. Not your average GI's job description."

"Average won't do for this," said the President. "We need a man of extraordinary capability. We need the best you've got."

Atwater handed him the file. "Here's the only name that consistently ranked among the top two names on every list."

The President began to gently rock his rocking chair. He leafed through the file at arm's length, not bothering with his glasses.

"Sergeant Michael Morgan. Born Milwaukee, Wisconsin. Thirty-eight years old. Twenty years active duty. Ranger-Commando. Son of a police officer. Enlisted in the Army right after Pearl Harbor. Action in the Pacific. Guadalcanal. Saipan. Iwo Jima. A Purple Heart and two Bronze Stars. Drill instructor after the war. Korea. Special Forces." The President nodded. He was a speed-reader, capable of scanning and absorbing twelve hundred words per minute. "Looks like he's been to every hot spot on the map. Eastern Europe. Central America. Asia." Kennedy chuckled at something in the file that caught his eye. "Interesting nickname he's earned himself: Graveyard."

"He's put his share in them," said Atwater. "As you can see from his commanders' evaluations, he prefers to make his own rules. He's not a by-the-book man. In fact, Graveyard Morgan has a reputation for being the exact opposite."

"So I see. What about his private life?"

"Married to his high school sweetheart. One child, a grown daughter. The wife lives in Miami. She's filing for divorce. The daughter also lives in Miami and works part-time as a society reporter for the *Herald*."

Robert Kennedy frowned. "Home in Miami? Wife filing for divorce? Won't that complicate things?"

"For Morgan maybe," said Atwater, "but not for us. Hate him or love him, there's one thing every C.O. he's ever served under does agree on. That soldier gives one-hundred-and-ten percent on every mission he's ever been assigned."

The President turned to Garrett. "What do you think, Tal?"

Garrett had been listening closely. "With everything going wrong this close to the wire, sir, I'd say he sounds like he's the man we're looking for."

Kennedy closed the file and set it on his lap. "And right now he's in the central highlands of South Vietnam, training Montagnard tribesmen to fight the Viet Cong. That's one hell of a mess over there and the deeper we get into it, the more we're going to need men like Morgan. North Vietnam is predicting that the South will be theirs by the end of the year. But Morgan does seem to be the man we're looking for. What do you think, Bobby?"

Robert said, "Graveyard Morgan," and smiled at the sobriquet. "Yes, he *sounds* like the man for this job."

The President drew a deep breath and exhaled slowly. "General, I want Morgan yanked from his present duty assignment ASAP. I want him in Miami within seventy-two hours."

Atwater was already on his feet. He said, "Yes, sir," and left the office.

Kennedy turned to Garrett. "Tal, you're on the next flight to Miami. Learn whatever you can from your people down there assigned to work with the Cuban exiles, anything that doesn't feel right. Set things up for Morgan. And of course I'll want to size him up personally."

"Yes, sir."

Robert said to the President, "And we're on schedule for our flight south to meet with the exile leaders in Miami. The First Lady and your children are already there, down at your father's estate, as cover. A nice, quiet family pleasure trip."

The President said, "I wish. Gentlemen, this one is for all the marbles. The highest stakes we've ever played for. With Russia involved, backing Castro the way they are, we could be facing another world war."

CHAPTER 3

The shriek of low-flying jets heading north yanked him from a fitful sleep. For an instant, bathed in cold sweat, Morgan had no idea where he was. Then the shrill whistling receded and the ice picks of sound ceased stabbing his ear drums. He sat up on his bunk. He was bare-chested, clad in fatigue pants. He laced up his combat boots. He was alone in the hooch he shared with three other GI's who were presently somewhere on duty. He thought, I should be with them.

Morgan was a tall man, well-muscled, his dark hair shaved military close on the sides but was unruly on top. Scars from old wounds were in evidence across the upper half of his body. He grabbed the M-16 carbine from beside his bunk and went out to the latrine.

The mercury hovered near one hundred degrees. The sun was an angry fireball seen through the gauze of a humid haze. Special Forces Detachment A-110 occupied barren acreage that had been cleared from the jungle. Drab and squalid. No color except for a coating of red dust that blanketed everything. Machine gun placements lined a perimeter of concertina wire beyond which a killing field had been hacked from the wall of jungle. A morning mist clung to neighboring hilltops. The air was alive with the chatter of birds, monkeys and insects.

Morgan finished his business at the latrine and started back toward the hooch when he saw the Montagnard tribesmen. Deo Tra and his team stood just outside the front gate. Morning mist swirled about them, making the hill men look like visions from a dream.

Deo Tra stood at the head of a patrol comprised of seven Monts whose modern Army-issue assault rifles and ammunition pouches contrasted with their traditional tribal garb. Diminutive size and musculature was offset by fierce demeanor and primitive features. Their teeth were stained black, filed to points.

Deo Tra beckoned to him. Deo Tra held a five-foot-long spear with sacred markings of the Rhade tribe, adorned with gaudy ceremonial war feathers. Morgan started to angle in that direction.

A gruff voice said sharply from behind him, "Hold on there, Yard."

Gilbert and his shadow, Hanney, approached from the direction of the comm shed. They wore fatigues without name tags or rank. Assigned under cover of the Program Evaluations Office, U.S. Overseas Missions, the Central Intelligence Agency was in command here. Gilbert was Agent in Charge. He was thirty years old, burly with a square-cut face. His sweaty skin was mahogany brown from years spent under the Asian sun. He positioned himself directly between Morgan and the front gate.

"Where the hell do you think you're going?"

"To speak with my team."

Gilbert said, "They're no longer your team. You're through here, Morgan. The chopper from Saigon that's hauling your ass out is due any minute. You stay put."

Hanney added, "You had your chance to kiss them Stone Age aborigines bye-bye." His breath smelled of stale beer.

Morgan started to walk around the CIA men as if they weren't there.

Hanney closed in. He had the build of a bruiser, sloping big shoulders and a dull-eyed face. He clutched Morgan by the left arm, above the elbow.

"Hold it, hotshot. You haven't been dismissed."

Morgan braced himself to take Hanney down but when their eyes met, Hanney saw something that made him release his hold on the arm. He stepped away.

"I'll be here when the chopper touches down but while I wait, I'm going to visit with my friends."

Gilbert spat upon the ground. "The hell with you. Go ahead. I just don't get it." He regarded the tribesmen with disdain. "Bet those savages carve out the hearts of their victims and eat them raw, for Chrissake."

Hanney's laugh was a sneer. "He spent too much time with them savages."

Morgan walked to the front gate, feeling their eyes on his back.

He said to Deo Tra, "My friend, you should be on patrol."

Deo Tra extended the spear. "First this, then we go." Missionaries had taught Deo Tra the rudiments of English years before. "We will fight and slay the Viet Cong, using weapons and training brought us. You are a warrior, Graveyard Morgan. You are one of us. Let this spear always remind you of this."

Morgan accepted the spear. "I will never need reminding but thank you, my brother. Thank your men for me." He turned to the men of the patrol and lifted the spear to indicate his acceptance. They murmured and nodded in approval. He said, "I shall seek always to remain worthy."

The noise of an approaching helicopter drew their attention.

One of the new Bell Light Observation bubble-fronts, small and maneuverable, recently purchased by the South Vietnamese from the US, rotored in; a small, unarmed helicopter not designed for combat but for ferrying personnel about. It touched down in the center of the compound. The rotors' backwash created a sandstorm of red dust.

Deo Tra said, "Goodbye, Morgan. May your god protect you."

The Mont took point and led his team single-file along the narrow dirt road that cut away from the front gate, into the jungle.

Morgan returned to his hooch long enough to throw on and button up a fatigue shirt and grab his duffle bag. He took one last look around the hooch. Four bunks and footlockers. A comfortable male untidiness, an empty beer can here and there, battered paperback books and the Playmates his buddies had scotch-taped to the walls.

He said, "So long, shit hole."

He approached the chopper, carrying the spear with his duffle bag, the M-16 slung over his shoulder. The sandstorm had subsided. The young Viet pilot was holding the engine at low idle.

Gilbert held open the diminutive chopper's Plexiglas side door. He raised his voice to be heard above the engine noise. "On your way, soldier. Those orders yanking your ass out of here came straight from the top. HQ won't stand for your maverick crap the way I've had to."

Hanney, standing beside him, snickered. "Good riddance to bad trash. A whole lot of changes coming down and your leaving is just one of them."

Morgan hesitated just short of boarding the chopper.

He said to Gilbert, "What does he mean by that?"

"He doesn't mean anything. Get out of here, Graveyard."

Morgan turned to face Hanney. "What did you mean, a lot of changes? What's it got to do with me?"

"It means," said Hanney, "that we're getting rid of you and those Mont savages on the same damn day and there's not a damn thing you can do about it."

"What's he talking about, Gilbert?"

Gilbert's eyes were cautious. "He's talking about us losing to the goddamn Viet Cong. Saigon is pressuring Washington for a military escalation. My mission is to cooperate with the gooks toward that end."

"I still want to know what the hell you're talking about."

"Soldier, your mission was to train and advise. That mission is completed and you've been reassigned."

Morgan said, "Those Monts are civilians with families. I trained them to fight for you, not die for you."

Hanney stepped forward. "Board the chopper. That's an order," and he made the mistake of jabbing an index finger into Morgan's chest for emphasis. Morgan extended the tribal spear between Hanney's ankles and executed a sharp twist. Hanney toppled with a startled cry and splashed into a puddle of red mud left from yesterday's rain. Sputtering, he propped himself on his elbows, covered with mud. Morgan placed a boot sole on Hanney's chest, pinning him in the muck. The point of the tribal spear glinted in the sunlight when Morgan brought it around and placed its point at Hanney's throat.

"What is going to happen?"

"What the hell do you think is going to happen?" snarled Gilbert. "You're no damn babe in the woods. You're big, bad Graveyard Morgan. You figure it out."

Morgan applied pressure to the spear point. It pricked Hanney's throat, drawing a ruby red droplet of blood that sparkled, discernible through the mud. Hanney stopped struggling in the mud.

"Now wait a minute! Take it easy, you crazy son of a bitch."

Morgan said, "Tell me, Gilbert, or you're short one ass kisser."

"Let him up, Morgan. Don't do this."

Another prick of the spear point.

Hanney emitted a frightened, feminine squeal.

"Okay, okay," said Gilbert. "There's nothing you can do about it. I didn't issue the order. The gooks in Saigon developed intel that a VC unit is in place to wipe out those Montagnards in an ambush today and we're going to let it happen. The gooks want a high body count to convince Washington how desperate they are for assistance and, well hell, look I know it sounds brutal—"

Morgan took hold of Gilbert by the collar and thrust him atop Hanney in the mud puddle.

"I ought to kill you both."

Morgan boarded the helicopter. The young pilot had been observing the unfolding drama with alarm. Morgan unclipped the pilot's seatbelt. He said, "Sorry, pal," and he flung the kid from the bubble-front and took his place behind the controls. He revved up the chopper's engine.

Gilbert was rising from the mud, drawing his pistol. "Hold it right there!" He was shouting at nearby GI's, gesturing wildly with his pistol. "Stop him! Stop him! He's hi-jacking the chopper!"

None of the GI's responded. Hanney was kneeling in the puddle, wiping mud from his eyes. Gilbert was angling around for a shot. Morgan increased the RPM's of the rotor blades, stirring up another sandstorm that blotted out everything behind swirling dust.

He worked the control stick. The diminutive helicopter lifted off, banking north over stark green jungle in the direction taken by Deo Tra's foot patrol. The narrow dirt road disappeared from sight here and there beneath the panoply of trees and vegetation that blanketed the terrain blurring by beneath him. The patrol would follow the road for one-and-a-half klicks until they came to a game trail, a shortcut to the malaria treatment center in the village of Ho Duc, another three klicks distant.

Then Morgan saw the VC.

A force comprised of no less than twenty figures, details of their appearance indiscernible at this distance, could be seen in position along the trail, lying in wait under cover of the thick foliage no more than a quarter klick ahead of Deo Tra and his men,.

Morgan flew the chopper in low. There was no place to land. The tree line bordered either side of the road. He buzzed the startled Monts who vanished into the undergrowth. The helicopter swooped around for another pass and then another, giving the Montagnards ample opportunity from their concealment to identify the markings on the chopper's underside.

At last Deo Tra emerged from cover to stand squarely in the road. It would be impossible for him to recognize Morgan from down there. The rest of the patrol would be aiming their rifles at the helicopter. Morgan reached out and waved his arm in wide circles, pointing down the road in the direction of the waiting ambushers who had disappeared from his line of vision. Deo Tra looked in that direction, and then raised one arm, holding his rifle high to signal his understanding.

Morgan resumed flying over the dirt road.

The Viet Cong again came into view again. Black pajama-like uniforms. Straw hats. Each VC was armed with a rifle except for a point man who wore only a sidearm. This would be the military advisor from Hanoi, leading peasants from nearby villages and hamlets, who were inspired by the communist North's promise of land and an end to the political corruption and repression of the US-backed government in Saigon.

At first sight of the approaching helicopter, the VC opened fire on it.

Bearing straight down on them, Morgan positioned his M-16 through the open side window with his left arm while piloting the chopper with his right. His left thumb flicked the rifle's selector switch to automatic and he made a strafing run with the M-16 hammering. The Viet Cong scattered, a few standing their ground and returning fire, others toppling under the auto fire. The helicopter soared past them.

Morgan brought the bubble-front around for another run. Through the flight noise could be heard the metallic chings of the fuselage taking fire. Then the helicopter lurched violently, its speed decreasing sharply. The drone of the transmission above and behind Morgan ended. Abrupt silence.

The control stick vibrated wildly in his fist. White smoke was billowing into his slipstream from the slowing rotors. Every gauge on the instrument panel went to zero. Morgan slung the rifle across his back and shoved forward the lever to his left that controlled the pitch of the rotors. Autorotation of the blades from the helicopter's forward momentum would keep it on course, airborne for perhaps another thirty seconds, no more…unless his fuel tank exploded first.

The wounded, gliding aircraft was steadily losing what little altitude remained. The landing rails clipped the treetops. The Viet Cong were scattering to escape its incoming path…except for the North Viet officer, who stood coolly triggering off ineffectual rounds from his handgun at the bubble front.

Morgan released the control stick. He threw himself from the chopper. A short nothing of a fall broken by the wide fronds of tall trees and the interlocking branches and vines beneath that battered him as he plummeted through, knocking the wind from his lungs. But they slowed his descent.

The chopper crash-landed. The fuel tank exploded with a loud blast and an angry orange-red fireball ascended into the sky.

Morgan landed roughly upon the spongy jungle floor. He drew himself to his feet, sore from the beating the tree limbs had given him but there were no broken bones. He unslung his M-16 and swept it about, searching for targets, ready for anything.

Rifle fire from the tree line across the road began stitching the Viet Cong, announcing the Montagnards' arrival. Weapons fire from both sides peppered the crackling flames of the downed chopper, its wreckage burning at the exact spot where the North Viet officer had made his stand.

The remnants of the VC force began falling back, laying down heavy fire along their backtrack, unaware of Morgan's position until he mowed them down with a sustained burst from his M-16.

The fire fight, like most, was over that quickly.

A familiar figure came striding in Morgan's direction.

Morgan laughed. "This is a first, Deo Tra. I've never seen you smile before."

The Montagnard indicated the flaming wreckage of the chopper. "And I have never seen anything like this."

A quick headcount determined that the Mont team had suffered no losses.

"That spear you gave me," said Morgan. "It went down with the chopper." He thought of dropping Gilbert and Hanney into the mud puddle. "I did put it to good use in the short time I had it."

Another trace of a smile from the Mont. "Could we not say the same of the helicopter? What will you do now, my brother?"

"I'd better hike back to base camp," said Morgan. "There are some CIA guys I need to have words with while I wait on Saigon to send me another chopper."

CHAPTER 4

Carmen Vasquez set down the gardening trowel and leaned away from the bed of cape jasmine. She pushed back the wide brim of her straw hat and dabbed a sleeve across the sheen of perspiration that coated her forehead. She loved tending the neat rows of fragrant color, the warmth of the sunlight on her bare arms, even the smudges of brown earth that soiled the knees of her faded blue jumper.

From here, the land sloped downward and became rocky and, no more than half a mile away, began the clutter of stucco walls, buildings with red tile roofs and the dusty streets of the village of Giron, nestled against a sandy white beach and the sparkling, limitless expanse of the Caribbean. The village was dominated by the cathedral and the town hall on the village square, and by the multi-leveled tourist resort, under construction, fronting the beach. From her garden she could also see the militia barracks to the northeast beyond the road to San Blas. To the east beyond the fields of sugar cane, the swampy lowlands and the abandoned airstrip, there was the far lovelier sight of the mouth of the bay, four miles wide and thirteen miles long. A cool breeze carried the salty scent of the ocean and the songs of the gulls swooping in the distance against the cobalt blue of a clear sky.

She wore sandals and an embroidered blouse that revealed her shoulders. Jet-black hair, usually worn down, was pinned beneath her hat against the heat. She was twenty-three years old. She had been working for the past hour in the garden in front of her house that was really no more than a wooden shack with a tin roof that leaked whenever it rained.

This was the only time of day that she enjoyed. Working in her garden was her only pleasure. The person she had once been—the carefree young woman who flirted with the young men in the *zocalo* to the strains of a marimba band and had fun with her girlfriends along the arcade, and loved everything about life—had long ago become the tired, drained creature of despair that she was today. Her fitful tossing and turning at night could not be called sleep. The anxieties of constant concern that sapped her every waking hour were only made worse because her worry and concern were for those she loved most. Her mother. Her brother. She was so close to losing them both forever and she knew she was powerless to do anything to stop it. This was her curse. This was what her life had become. These stolen fragments of time, when she could be alone and peaceful and left to toil in her garden, this was her escape from worry, from despair, from time itself.

She thought she heard a rustling in the thicket of cane that bordered the property line beside her. She started to turn in that direction.

A male voice whispered, *"No!"* and she ceased the movement and returned her attention to the flowers. There was urgency in the voice, which continued no louder than was necessary for her to hear. "Go on with what you're doing, Carmen. Do you recognize my voice?"

She resumed her weeding. "Yes, Felix. I've been expecting you. My brother is in prison because he belongs to your group. I cannot say that I am happy to hear your voice."

"It's not *my* group," Felix Carriles whispered. "I am but the leader of one cell, one of many. Your brother volunteered to be on that beach to meet the gringo. I never have to assign Diego. He always volunteers."

"A lot of good it did him." She found herself working the trowel with excessive force.

Felix said, "I can't afford to be seen. We have all taken to cover after what happened on the beach last night."

She ceased her vigorous weeding. "People in the village have spoken of nothing else all day. They're holding Diego for interrogation at the militia post. A major named Medina has been sent from Havana personally by Castro to hunt all of you down."

"Medina is cruel, evil man. But Diego is strong; strong enough to withstand torture."

She felt a spasm in her stomach, a wave of nausea. "Felix, please."

"I'm sorry."

"Some things are...unthinkable, like that being done to my brother. Words cannot match the horror of my imagination."

"You will help us, will you not?"

"I will help Diego. Our family has sacrificed enough."

"Carmen, don't deceive yourself. I've know you since we were children. You would take up arms and fight in a minute if it came to that. Your father died in prison for the crime of merely speaking his mind. A man made old before his time, who wanted only to teach. They took away your family's home in Havana and drove you and your mother out here."

She stared down at the trowel in her gloved hands. Sadness washed through her. "Stop. I know what has happened to me. I know what I've lost."

"The view from here may be beautiful," he persisted in a whisper, "but you exist in poverty and now they have your brother. You serve *La Causa* best right now by kneeling in your garden and working and seeming to mind your own business, drawing no attention to yourself. But you would fight with us if it came to that."

She continued to avoid glancing in his direction. "This garden is my mother's pride and joy. It is my duty to tend it for her. Diego must have told you that he's asked me many times to join your movement, but he understood why I declined and so you must understand if you are truly our friend."

"I know that your mother is gravely ill."

"I care for her," said Carmen. "That is also my duty, first and foremost. That woman gave me life. She put my welfare before anything else when I was a helpless infant and dependent on her, and I will do no less for her now in return. If something were to happen to me, who would she have?" Her words tapered off and she gazed off across the panorama of land and sea. "I wish Diego had never told me where he hid that radio transmitter."

"He's told Medina nothing," whispered the voice from the thicket, "or there would have been more arrests. But none of us can afford to be seen anywhere near that transmitter. Have you sent the message?"

"Yes, Felix. And no one saw me. I wish Diego had never shown me where it is, or taught me how to use it."

A small, folded piece of paper had been slipped to her when she'd gone to the market that morning. Someone, she could not tell who in the bustle of the crowd, had placed the unsigned note into her hand. And she had done as the note requested. Using the code in the book Diego had left with the transmitter, she had turned on the small unit and had communicated with the Americans offshore. She first tapped out Diego's identification code and then reported the death of one of their agents and the arrest of her brother. Since returning home, she had been expecting Felix to make this contact with her.

A vehicle suddenly drove into view, the sound of its approach having been shielded from the garden by the sloping ground beyond the property line. It was a Jeep with military markings. A tall whip aerial swayed as the driver braked to a stop.

Carmen heard Felix gasp under his breath. "My God! It's Medina!"

She rose as the Major and his driver, a militiaman, approached her. She heard the slightest rustle from the canebrake.

They did not seem to notice. When they reached the garden, the militiaman positioned himself in the background, his hand on a holstered sidearm.

Medina clicked his heels and bowed from the waist, a middle-aged man, thin to the point of emaciation. He sported a pencil-thin moustache. His narrow face was severely pockmarked, his countenance stern. His fatigues were smartly starched and his boots shone in the sunlight.

"*Señorita*, do you know who I am?"

"I know who you are." Her voice was taut. "You are the man responsible for detaining my brother and now you have come to terrorize my mother and me."

His eyes were expressionless, reminding her of cold, polished chips of stone. "Your brother is a counter-revolutionary."

She drew her back straight and met him eye-to-eye. "There are worse things to be in Cuba today."

"You have sympathy with the underground?"

She said, "Our family was never better than middle class. My father was against Batista, against the corruption and the injustice. In the beginning he was for your beloved Fidel. But the changes after the revolution should have been carried out under our national constitution. The government needed to be cleaned out, not overturned. These sentiments branded my father a traitor."

"Sentiments inherited by you and your brother, obviously."

"I am proud to be my father's daughter. Reform was needed, but not Castro's reform. His reform is nothing but thievery. He confiscated the land and property of hardworking, decent people like my parents and when people like my father spoke out against this injustice, military tribunals were established. And now you come for me, just as you came for my father and my brother."

"We are looking for Felix Carriles."

"I cannot help you. I'm sorry. I know no one by that name."

He inclined his head and a smile that was more of a sneer curled his thin lips. "You will forgive me if I say that I do not believe you. I regret to say that I have the unpleasant duty of placing you under arrest. You will come with me, *por favor.*"

"But my mother...surely you know my situation here. I can't leave her!"

A flash of color caught her attention from the opposite direction that Felix would have taken. She saw two teenagers, a boy and a girl, walking along her property line, taking a shortcut from the lot behind hers, and walking in the direction of the road. They were holding hands and seemed oblivious of this unfolding drama, involved as they were in conversation, in their own world. The flash of color had been the bright red blouse worn by the girl.

Medina followed the direction of her gaze.

He said, "Who are they?"

"The neighbor's boy and his girlfriend. At least let me get someone to watch over my mother while I'm away. Please, Major. Think of your own mother."

"That was the wrong thing to say, *señorita*. I killed my mother when I was fourteen, may she rot in hell."

"Major, I implore you."

After what seemed an eternity, he nodded. "No more than a minute. I am not in the habit of granting favors, but," he bowed smartly from the waist, "in the case of one so lovely as yourself, *señorita,* I will make an exception."

She felt his eyes on her as she hurried across to the two teenagers, who paused at her approach with greeting smiles that darkened into concern when they saw the Jeep and the soldiers.

Cosme Gomez was a polite, quiet boy wearing a white shirt and khaki slacks. His girlfriend, Lupita, was very pretty. Carmen knew the two were engaged to be married.

"Cosme, I need your help. There is no time to lose."

"Of course." He was an earnest lad who worked hard with his father and uncles in the cane fields. "What can we do? Are you in trouble?"

"I can't explain now. I...have to leave with these men. I shouldn't be gone long."

"Is it about Diego?"

"Cosme, there's no time for talk. Please get your mother. She's my mother's best friend. She'll want to care for my mother until I return."

"I'll see to it at once," the boy promised.

He and the girl hurried off.

She rushed into the house with barely a glance at Medina. His appraising gaze had shifted from her to a lusting gaze after the youthful figure of the departing girl.

Carmen passed through the cramped living room/dining room area of the small house, which was appointed with homemade furniture of wood and cane. There were two bedrooms; one was Diego's, and the other she shared with her mother.

Florina Vasquez had withered away from her cancer, to become a frail scarecrow. She lay in bed with a thin sheet drawn up to her chin. Her arms were visible, spindly and scabbed. It was impossible now to tell that she had once been a professional seamstress. Her fingers were bony, talon-like. Once luxurious black hair was white and wispy upon the pillow. A crucifix adorned the wall over the headboard. There was the cloying, sickly sweet smell of death in the room and the thought crossed Carmen's mind, as it often did when she saw her mother like this, was *this* a reward for a long, hard life, well-lived? How sad and unfair.

She sat on the edge of the bed. Her mother's eyes opened. With tender fingers, Carmen brushed into place an errant strand of snow-white hair.

"Carmen, I was dreaming."

"Mother–"

"I dreamt of that summer we spent in America." The words came faintly, raspy. "We were together again. Your father was about to be accepted to the University. I was busy with you two children." Rheumy eyes seemed to gaze beyond the bleak walls of the bedroom. "You and your brother were no more than babies. My beautiful little perfect babies. Carmen, where is Diego? He seems to have been gone for a very long time."

Carmen could not look her mother in the eye. "I'm—I'm going to see him now."

Señora Vasquez seemed not to hear. "It was so long ago, that summer in America. I thought then that our little family would stay together and be happy forever. I never thought of myself as old. I did not want my life to go by so quickly."

When she again looked upon her mother's face the eyes were closed, the breathing was feeble. "Mother, *Señora* Gomez is coming to visit. I've sent Cosme for her. I won't be long, I promise. You'll be all right." She leaned over and kissed her mother's forehead, which was cold and clammy. She started to rise from the bed and was startled to see Medina watching her from the doorway.

"Major, couldn't we stay until the neighbor woman arrives?"

"No. You will come with me now."

"I swear that there is nothing I can tell you about my brother or his friends."

"Then you will be home to care for your dear mother in due course."

"You heard what I told her, that I was going to see Diego. Can you arrange that for me?"

Medina's smile did not reach his eyes. "Of course, my dear. I promise that you will join your brother."

CHAPTER 5

A motorcade of five shiny new Oldsmobiles glided to a stop in front of the National Agrarian Reform Institute in the Miramar section of Havana. The building that housed government headquarters towered over the other buildings that lined an avenue of white sidewalks and swaying palm trees. Bearded, machine gun-toting guards leaped from four of the cars and scurried to form twin lines leading up the front steps.

Castro remained in his car for the length of time required to complete dictating a memorandum to his stenographer, an attractive young woman with lush lips and prominent breasts, whose firm figure was encased in fatigues. When he left the car, carrying a briefcase, his stride was lithe and agile despite his considerable size. He was chewing on a cigar.

The command office overlooked a courtyard of cypress trees where birds sang. Upon Castro's arrival, orderlies made haste to bend low and clean the mud and dirt from his boots. He accepted this attention as his due, without comment. With a visible show of impatience, he utilized the opportunity to relight his cigar. He had just finished breakfast at the restaurant of the Havana Libre Hotel, formerly the Hilton. While eating, he perused intelligence reports and the morning newspapers, and would now settle in for a solid three or four days of work, based out of this office. He allowed himself only the occasional nap as his schedule permitted.

Three men, wearing pressed olive-green fatigues, sat around a conference table in a room where maps of the entire coastline decorated the walls. They rose as one when he entered.

"You may sit," Castro told them, though he remained standing, as was his custom. "I presume you have seen today's papers." His voice was permanently hoarse from constant cigar smoking and speech-making.

His brother, Raul, nodded. Raul Castro was approximately his brother's height but did not possess Fidel's size. Rather, Raul's thin physique and wispy moustache suggested a vaguely effeminate manner. He said, "We've read the transcript of Kennedy's press conference yesterday. U.S. policy toward Cuba was the main topic."

Chief of Staff Major Juan Almeida sat next to Raul. He was clean-shaven and barrel-chested. "A clever bit of business. The gringo *Presidente* assures the world that he will not intervene in Cuba. But would he not go to such length to make such an issue of excluding participation...*unless* an attack was imminent?"

Raul said, "It only confirms what our spies have been telling us."

The fourth man present bore clearly the physical ravaging of years of asthma attacks and bouts of malaria during the mountain campaigns of the revolution. "Che" Guevara pounded the table angrily with his fist.

"They must be stopped. This aggression has been inevitable from the beginning. Is it not of a piece? Cutting off our oil supplies and sugar markets. Diplomatic maneuvering to isolate us from the rest of Latin America. They have smuggled in arms and saboteurs in arrogant disregard of our sovereignty, and now this."

Fidel made a placating gesture with both hands. "Do not fear, Che. Sovereignty is not a favor they grant us. It is our right as a nation. Our dream will not be stolen from us. Think of what we have accomplished in little more than two years. Our revolution would not be a reality were it not for the majority of the people being on our side. That is why these would-be invaders will be stopped. *That* is why nobody can steal our dreams, *amigos*, not even the mighty United States."

Raul said, "Most of our people have never had it better."

Because of nationalization of public services, land reform, profit sharing, rental cuts, state housing, state managed industry and rural electrification, for the first time in Cuba's history, everyone who wanted a job was working. Every child attended school. Ten thousand classrooms had been added to the educational system. Forty-five new hospitals had been established.

The revolution had been, more than anything, a revolution for economic development waged against a system of power, which had existed for decades, culminating in the iron rule of Fulgencio Batista, a harsh dictator who had dissolved all political parties after leading a military coup.

An elite group of top government officials, army officers, and wealthy family tradition had dominated Cuban society, a tradition-bound, ruling minority unwilling to relinquish its semi-feudal domination. The majority of Cubans, on the other hand, especially the peasants and rural laborers and small farmers, had lived in abject poverty, suffering under the weight of chronic unemployment, poor living conditions, disease, illiteracy and malnutrition.

Wealthy American business interests maintained the plantation system. With the power of the Cuban courts, the lower classes were stripped of their land. Cuban lands soon became largely American owned. The huge, sprawling sugar plantations in the years immediately preceding the revolution had employed over half of the rural labor in Cuba. The sugar companies owned roughly fifty per cent of the total cultivable area in Cuba. Batista kept a tight rein on the labor unions, universities and the press, all with the unequivocal support of the United States, which ignored the crushing of political opposition, the suppression of civil liberties and the terrorism thereafter. Thousands of Cubans were murdered, many more tortured or maimed. Before he was deposed, Batista and his cohorts had murdered an estimated 20,000 Cuban citizens.

Given the key role of the United States in that power structure, the revolution had inevitably led to this conflict with the U.S.

Major Almeida was staring at the maps tacked on the opposite wall. "A pity we don't have a better idea of where or when their attack will come."

Fidel studied the maps, twisting strands of his beard. "It will come in the south. Perhaps Cienfuegos, or Trinidad." He spoke confidently.

"*Jefe*," said Che, "we must also consider the possibility of simultaneous attacks. There are many points along the coast of Oriente Province that would be ideal."

Raul said, "We're ready for them no matter what they have in mind. Our defense force is more than adequate."

Almeida nodded. "Twenty-five thousand soldiers with the best equipment and training our Russian friends can provide, and two hundred thousand militiamen. Battalions stationed throughout the island at every strategic area."

Fidel paced as usual during meetings. "Very good. Raul's force to the east, Che to the west and your men, Major Almeida, defending the center of the country while I coordinate all operations." He spat angrily upon the floor. "These mercenary invaders will not last twenty-four hours."

Raul said, "All that remains is for us to learn when and where."

Che exhaled a white cloud of cigar smoke. "Our man in Miami will tell us when," he snapped a finger, "and our spy in Guatemala will tell us where."

Fidel ceased his pacing, removed his cigar from the corner of his mouth and glowered down at it. "I do have one interesting fact to share that was brought to my attention in an intelligence briefing over breakfast. The death of the American agent, Lehman, has elicited a personal response from President Kennedy. A specialist has been called in to deal with the spies they suspect we have in place."

Raul emitted an effeminate laugh. "A specialist? What does that mean?"

"One of their Green Berets," said Fidel. "A ranger-commando specialist. I don't recall the name offhand, but they sent all the way to Vietnam for him."

Major Almeida considered this with a frown. "Steps should be taken to neutralize him."

A sparkle lighted Fidel's brown eyes. "Rest assured, Major that has already been seen to."

CHAPTER 6

She awoke quickly from deep, dreamless sleep to lay there, wide-awake, staring at her surroundings. A cell with a dirt floor. A single dim light encased in a metal mesh on the ceiling directly above her.

Carmen sat up, brushing away the pebbles and filth that clung to her. The cell was ten-foot square, stone walls with a low ceiling. Its clammy dampness had settled into the marrow of her bones. She had not intended to fall asleep. So much was happening. Diego. Her mother. And now, *her* arrest...

She wondered how much time had passed since Major Medina and his soldier had led her down a flight of stairs to this dungeon beneath the militia post headquarters. Her stomach had been knotted with stabbing cramps when they'd brought her here. When left alone, she'd closed her eyes, trying to relax. She must remain levelheaded or she could do no one any good.

She suddenly realized what had awakened her. A key was turning in the lock of the cell's heavy wooden door. The door swung inward. Medina strode in. The soldier who had accompanied him earlier waited behind, holding a rifle.

Carmen rose from the floor, lifting her chin to meet Medina's stony gaze. Anger and resentment raged through her.

"You said that I could see my brother."

Medina's pockmarked face was ashen in the dimly lit cell. "And you shall. I am here to take you to him. But first, my dear, I thought it best that you fully appreciate your situation."

"Oh, I understand, Major. You have Diego but you haven't been able to break him. You intend to use me to make him talk."

Medina gave a short nod. "Your presence will surely...encourage him. We know much about your brother and Felix Carriles. And about you. For reasons of your own, you have chosen not to become involved in their counter-revolutionary activities. Very wise of you."

She indicated the close confines of the cell. "A lot of good it's done me. This is wrong of you, Major. The revolution could have been so glorious."

"With talk like that, perhaps you are one of them after all."

"How many, like my family, were victimized by the revolution for no reason? My family was no danger to anyone. My father wanted only to teach. A good, decent man."

"Enough," said Medina. "I will not debate with you. But I will tell you why you are here. Among the things I intend to learn from your brother is the location of a radio transmitter with which his group maintains contact with American agents offshore. And I want Felix Carriles, and the names of the others in the underground. It would be in your best interest to persuade your dear brother to cooperate, or things could go very badly for the both of you. Truly, *señorita,*" his voice took on an edge, "I do not wish harm to befall such a lovely creature as yourself." He turned to the soldier and snapped his fingers.

The guard swung his rifle over his shoulder by its strap and hurried forward to grasp her right arm above the elbow, using enough force to make her wince. She bit her lip and made no sound. She did not struggle.

Medina stepped aside and the guard led her from the cell, into a stonewalled corridor that felt like a dank cave. Narrow barred windows at ceiling level allowed in muted sunlight. To her left, the stairs led upward. She was led away from the stairs and shoved into another cell. The soldier stepped back. Medina entered after her.

Carmen's breath caught in her throat.

Diego sat, securely bound to a wooden chair. His chin rested on his bare chest. With a groan of effort, he managed to lift his face. His bottom lip was split. A trickle of blood wended its way from the corner of his mouth. His nose was crooked, broken. One of his eyes was swollen shut. The other was glazed. He was covered with bruises, some an angry red where the flesh had recently been pummeled and broken, others already turned an ugly purple. There were burn marks too.

A hulking black oaf stood behind the chair. Bald, scar-faced, he too was bare-chested, clad in fatigue trousers and combat boots. He had been engaged in strenuous exercise. His sweat shone like polished ivory in the vague illumination,

"Carmen..."

She bolted toward him. "Oh, Diego! *Diego!*"

Medina grabbed her arm as the guard had, and this time she couldn't hold in a sharp bleat of pain.

"I said you could see him. That doesn't mean that I will indulge you in a tearful family reunion."

Diego stared at Medina with a mixture of fear and contempt in his good eye. "Why did you bring her into this? Major, you know she has nothing to do with...what you want."

Medina tightened his grip on Carmen's arm. "But surely you understand my intention, *Señor* Vasquez." He glanced at the looming black man. "What Ramon has done to you, he will do to your sister. You would not like that, eh?"

Diego shifted his glazed eye to Carmen. "Forgive me, Carmen. I have told them nothing. I *must* tell them nothing, no matter what they do. Many lives are at stake...and the future of our country. Forgive me."

The anger within her hardened into a steely resolve. "I promise, Diego. I can be strong. Do what you must."

The semblance of a grin reshaped Diego's battered features and he said to Medina, "You see, you cannot break us."

"*You* shall see," said Medina. He nodded to the man behind the chair. "Ramon."

Ramon delivered an almost casual open-handed blow to the side of Diego's head with enough force to lift two legs of the chair.

Carmen tried to jerk her arm free. "Please, Major! *Make him stop!*"

Medina's grasp only tightened. "Ramon will stop with your brother and begin with you. And then your brother will talk."

Ramon drew back a fist for another swipe at the bound man. Then he paused and examined Diego.

"Major."

"Yes, what is it?"

"He's dead."

Carmen somehow ripped free of Medina. "Oh, *God...no!*" She lunged for the unmoving form strapped to the chair.

Medina glared at Ramon. "Clumsy idiot."

The black man's eyes studied the floor. "I'm sorry, Major. I guess he just had enough."

"Get out of my sight."

Carmen tenderly lifted Diego's face. His open eye was blank, his expression relaxed in death. She thought fleetingly of how his face used to brighten whenever he heard a beautiful piece of music. And she remembered that the last time they had spoken, they had quarreled about his underground activities. She had not even told him that she loved him.

She whirled on Medina. "Murderer."

He regarded her with cool detachment. "This changes things. A pity. But with your brother dead, I see no further reason to detain you, *señorita*. You see, I know that you do not belong to this group I seek. You may claim your brother's body at your convenience."

CHAPTER 7

The CIA had set up headquarters for the greater Miami area in a drab three-story, eleven-unit apartment house on Segovia Street in Coral Cables. Rows of anemic palm trees, topped with sickly yellow-brown fronds, separated the building from identical structures on either side. It was a neighborhood of low-income rentals, some bungalows and a few storefront businesses—a hair salon, a bicycle repair shop and a liquor store on the corner.

Traffic sounds filtered in through the open window of Sam Resnick's office that looked out over the street.

Garrett sat in a kitchen chair that faced a small wooden desk in what had been the apartment's living room. He felt over-dressed in the blue serge he'd worn on the flight down from Washington, but he didn't unbutton his jacket against the comfortable warmth of Resnick's converted office on the top floor of the building. No reason to let Sam know he was putting on weight. Langley guys took enough riding from field agents.

Resnick was in his late forties. He had thinning blond hair, a healthy tan and an easy-going manner. He wore a *guayabera* shirt, linen slacks and a pair of leather loafers. He looked like a sport fisherman, thought Garret with a trace of envy, a high-lifer fresh from the dock, from having his picture taken with the prize marlin he'd just reeled in.

There was a time when Garrett had been just like Resnick. Like Lehman, for that matter. Medium. Nondescript. Average. Those were the magic words of a successful field agent. Resnick had the sort of affable features that would be next to impossible for an untrained witness to describe. Garrett had been like that years ago, before the desk assignment. Before the middle age spare-tire. These visits into the field, made less and less as he climbed through the ranks in Washington, were always bittersweet. He didn't miss the risks, the edge-of-the-knife existence that was life in the front-line Cold War world of covert ops. But he did miss being like Resnick.

Resnick drew a half-finished bottle of scotch from the bottom desk drawer.

"I was beginning to think Washington was forgetting about us down here. Guess that last transmission put us back on the front burner."

They clinked glasses and threw back the shots.

"You've been doing a good job, Sam. What did you want, a pat on the back every week or so?"

Resnick leaned back in his swivel chair and made a face. "Good job, huh? Good as can be expected, I guess. I got the exile leaders organized, but do you know how easy that was? There's not two of those characters you can get to agree on what day of the week it is."

The Democratic Revolutionary Front represented the conservative Cuban exile forces that were determined to overthrow Castro. Garrett was well aware that it had been no small task to corral the constantly feuding factions, then fund and construct a coalition of refugee groups. Resnick was the Agent in Charge.

"You set up the Front," said Garrett. "That was your mission." He extended his glass.

Resnick poured them each another, then capped the bottle and returned it to the drawer. "So what do we have? Fifteen hundred Cubans training for a landing to overthrow Fidel. The biggest secret operation in history, with the coalition combing Little Havana for even more recruits for the training camp in Guatemala. Does Washington really think this isn't already all over Miami? These people love to talk."

"Go ahead, Sam. Let off steam."

"Well hell, we're planning a military invasion and the military isn't even in charge. The command control is totally inadequate. Oh yeah, I'm doing a great job. This whole project is out of control and it's about to blow wide open and this station is supposed to sit on the whole thing and keep the lid on. It's about time someone from up north listened to what I'm dealing with down here."

"There is a model, you know."

"Yeah, I know. Guatemala."

"Well?"

"Apples and oranges, buddy. We only squeaked by on that one. I was there, remember? The government we were overthrowing had a limited force. Castro has a two-hundred-thousand-man army and militia, and they're growing and becoming better equipped by the hour thanks to the Russians."

Garrett said, "You make it sound like it couldn't get any worse."

Resnick's eyes narrowed. "And you flew all the way down here to tell me that it's about to get worse, didn't you?"

"Afraid so. Sam, there's a spy in the coalition leadership. That's the way it looks, anyway. The President has taken a personal interest."

"Well, holy shit."

"Presidential shit, and that's the worst kind for spooks like us. We've got to straighten this out and fast."

"How about another drink?"

"No, thanks."

"Okay, me neither. A spy, huh? Shit."

"Any ideas?"

Resnick thought about it. "There are seventeen hundred new refugees a week pouring into Miami since the revolution. We've identified a number of *Fidelista* agents in Little Havana. We're using them to feed disinformation back to Cuba. But they're street level, bottom echelon."

"Think big," said Garrett. "This will be someone highly placed in the Democratic Revolutionary Front. The fact that they were waiting on that beach for Lehman tells us that much. That was a highly classified mission. Only the coalition big-shots knew about it."

Resnick said, "Aw hell, I need a drink," and he retrieved the bottle. He poured and downed another shot, avoiding eye contact with Garrett. He replaced the bottle in the drawer and let his breath out slowly. "Every man on that council has had his background gone over by teams of experts both here and in Washington. We haven't come up with anything suspicious on anybody in the leadership, or on anyone close to them. Every one of those Cubans is a diehard anti-Communist. They hate Castro with a vengeance."

Garrett said, "Each coalition member has his own staff, right? An assistant, a secretary or both. Let's start there, with the staffers. Is there anyone at that level who's signed on during, say, the last six months?"

"Doctor Rivas took on a new man last month. First time any of them have taken anyone new into the fold in awhile. The guy's name doesn't come to me offhand but I can dig it out."

"Do it. We've got a mole to catch."

Resnick stood and turned to the gray metal filing cabinet in a corner near his desk. He drew open the top drawer and began moving a finger along the file index tabs.

"I don't remember anything out of whack about the guy. He's Rivas's assistant. Okay, here it is." He withdrew a manila file folder and read from the tab, "Hector Solas." He handed the file to Garrett.

Garrett leafed through the file. "Looks okay on the surface. Says Hector Solas spoke out against the revolution in Cuba. Got himself some hard time in a Castro prison. After his release he managed to escape to Florida on a fishing boat."

"The timing's right. He could be our man." Garrett handed the file back. "It's worth a try. We need to identify and nullify our spy like yesterday."

Resnick returned the file to the cabinet. "In that case, the timing's right for us too. Doctor Rivas is giving a speech tonight at a fundraiser for the refugee groups. Solas will be there."

"Good. See to it. There is one more thing."

Resnick started tapping the eraser end of a pencil rapidly and repeatedly on his desktop. "There always is." The façade of affability was beginning to wear thin.

"The President has personally selected his own man to, uh, help us out." Garrett spoke without enthusiasm. "A Green Beret, no less, pulled from combat duty in Vietnam as of yesterday, expressly for this purpose."

"What purpose?"

"To be the President's personal point man on the spy investigation."

Resnick ceased his pencil-tapping. "I don't like it."

Garrett grunted. "What's that got to do with anything? The President wants his point man calling the shots. That's the way it is, Sam. He gets a free hand and full cooperation. Who knows, it could work. He's supposed to be one hell of a mean son of a bitch. A real maverick."

"What's the name?"

"Morgan. Sergeant Michael Morgan."

Resnick sank back against his chair cushion with a frown. "Well, that's just great." He brought a battered pack of Chesterfield's from a pants pocket and took a moment to fire up, filling the air with gray smoke. "The whole operation coming apart at the seams and I get to take orders from Graveyard Morgan."

Garrett brushed a hand back and forth to dissipate the smoke. "His reputation precedes him?"

Resnick nodded. "Supposed to be the baddest mother in the valley and a royal pain in the ass to work with because the only rulebook he follows is his own."

"Since when has a rulebook got anything to do with this operation?

Resnick said, "You got me there. They say he gets the job done, come hell or high water. Just not real tidy about it."

"Then let's hope he gets this job done before it's too late. He's landing in Miami today."

"What are my orders?"

Garrett's expression creased with displeasure. "A lot of this is going to be played by ear. Hell, I don't like the interference either, especially at this stage. But if Morgan gets an inside track, we can pick up the credit when it's done. His kind doesn't stick around when the dust starts to settle. For tonight, let's concentrate on Hector Solas. See where he takes us."

Resnick glanced at his wristwatch. "Then I'd better get across town if I want hear Doctor Rivas give his speech."

"Be careful, Sam."

Resnick plucked a small-brimmed straw fedora from atop the filing cabinet and placed it on the back of his head. "Wish I could say it's been nice seeing you again, Tal. Help yourself to the bottle."

CHAPTER 8

Morgan navigated his way through the condensed mass of humanity, toward his wife. He wore an open-neck white shirt, a navy blue sports jacket and pressed slacks with black shoes. He felt mildly ill at ease in civilian clothes. He only ever felt like he was in uniform when he wasn't wearing a soldier's uniform.

The stark, modern Miami airport terminal always reminded him of a mausoleum, with its angular concrete walls and tiled floors that echoed the lightest footstep. The waiting area at the terminal gate was crowded with family, friends and associates come to greet those arriving on the Houston flight. The air temperature was in the mid-sixties, but felt downright frigid to him after months spent in Vietnam.

This was the end of a journey that had begun more than thirty hours earlier on the other side of the world in Saigon. He had slept through much of the flight time, a sound, dreamless sleep interrupted only when he had to change planes. Right now, he felt refreshed; better than he had in a long while. A relaxing sleep was a privilege you didn't allow yourself when you were tracking Viet Cong through the bush.

After forty-eight hours at a stretch, with nothing but paranoia and bennies to keep you going, after the heat and the humidity and the physical exertion of hacking your way through the endless jungle, after your men were flat worn out and couldn't, just plain couldn't, push on for one more step, then a security perimeter would be established and then you might catch some z's, trading off with your buddies until the snap of a twig or a bird call from a treetop kicked you awake from what had really been nothing more than a fitful catnap...

Another world. That was the world he had dozed off from, to awaken in *this* world.

The temperature seemed to continue dropping with every step that brought him closer to Vera. She didn't step forward to greet him but remained where she was, surrounded by a cacophony of conversations and welcoming hugs.

She wore her chestnut hair shoulder-length, its highlights shimmering like burnished copper in the late afternoon sunlight. She looked good in a summery white dress, with a wide black leather belt, and matching high heels. Vera was long legs and a narrow waist, of sleek, firm lines; somehow she exuded a natural aristocratic bearing even though, like him, she came from a middle-class, blue-collar family. Vera was proud of her figure, and had a right to be.

When he reached her, he said, "Hi, honey," and started to lean in for a kiss.

She drew back. "Hello, Mike. I was surprised to get your telegram from Australia."

She was seven years his junior. Blue, intelligent eyes. Her prominent chin was slightly cleft, making her all the more attractive in Morgan's opinion.

"We had a one hour layover in Sydney," he said. "It was news to me too, getting yanked home so fast like this."

"It must be important," she said in a neutral voice. "It always is."

"I still don't know what it's about. Haven't been briefed yet."

"You must be exhausted." She said it politely but the chill emanating from her up close was cooler than the air temperature.

The crowd around them was thinning as people began walking in the direction of the parking lot or wandering toward the baggage claim area. The Morgans pretty much had this little corner of the world to themselves.

He tried again. "It's good to see you, hon. Thanks for coming to meet me."

She held her back straight, and lips that he remembered as being hot and pliant when passionate were now drawn into a grimace.

"I'm not doing anything nice. What I'm doing is cruel and terrible and I'm ashamed of myself already for behaving this way. And you, the returning war hero."

"What's this about?"

Remoteness touched her gaze, as if she was already someplace else. "I've decided it would be best if we just got this over and done with. I know I'm being cruel, welcoming you home like this."

"Yeah. Some welcome."

"You can take it. You face much worse every time you leave home."

She was starting to irritate him. He said, "Darling, what are you talking about?" There was a cooling edge in his voice that hadn't been there before.

She opened her purse and withdrew a business-size envelope, which she handed to him. "These are divorce papers. I was going to have the lawyer mail them for me but I feel better doing it this way…braver and stronger, like I'm doing something on my own for a change, taking another step to where I want to go."

For a moment he looked at her as if he were another man, seeing her for the first time. She was still the most beautiful woman he'd ever seen. Hers was a physical beauty of facial structure and build, a beauty animated by strength and beauty of spirit, a strength he'd seen exhibited throughout the raising of their daughter and in the sacrifice it took for any woman to give her heart and make a commitment to a professional soldier.

And now, this.

He dreamt about her when he was in those shit-pit war zones around the globe that his CIA control officers sent him to. When a man dreamed of a woman under those conditions, he could construct the perfect woman, beauty without flaw. The hair. The eyes. The lips. The body. For him, Vera was that woman. Even now as she stood before him, handing him the legal paperwork that said their love was finished.

"The last time we saw each other," he said, "you saw me off from this same gate, as I recall. Things had come to a head the night before. We agreed that I'd get my own place when I got back, if that's what you wanted. A trial separation, so we could work things out between us."

"I'm sorry, Mike. This is for the best. I'd be impossible to live with."

"What cooled you off like this?" He stared into her eyes, trying to read them. "Is there someone else? Is that what this is about?"

"No, Michael, there's never been anyone but you. That you'd even ask that shows how far apart you've grown from who I am. Part of me wants to slap your face for even thinking it after the hundreds, thousands of nights I've slept alone and sat up late worrying about you and wondering where in the world you were. No, there's no one else."

"Then what —"

"I've got to go. I'm sorry. You must think I'm a rat and I suppose I am."

He looked around them. Everyone else had gone from the gate. They were alone.

"I was at least expecting a reception from Susan."

"She's working."

"How's she doing? I know she was unhappy at the paper, just getting the social page and fashions. See, I'm not completely lost in my world. I'm the one who told her to walk if they wouldn't give her better assignments, to look for work at a TV station."

Vera's eyes softened. "Yes, you've never been anything but good to and for our daughter...when you're around. She followed your advice. She told the editor she was going to quit and why and they decided that she was too good to let go."

Everything else within him gave way to a flush of pride. "That's our girl."

The warmth of his words seemed to have the reverse effect on Vera, as if snapping her from reverie. "Susan couldn't make it to meet you because she's working. They're having her write human interest stories. She's covering a talk tonight by one of the Cuban exile leaders, to get a woman's slant on the conditions in Little Havana."

"Well, that's good news. I'm proud of her."

"I'm sure you'll have a chance to tell her that." Vera's manner became cold again. "And now I really must go. I'm sure you've got to report to someone about this latest war you've been in."

"Vietnam isn't a war," he told her. "Not yet, anyway. We're just acting as advisers, over there to train them to fight communists on their own."

"But why does it always have to be your fight, Mike? And why does peace in your world always have to come from the barrel of a gun?"

"It's your world too."

"Well then, maybe I'd like to help find another way to change it. There has to be another way. Go ahead, tell me what an idealistic fool I am."

"I'll tell you what I am," said Morgan. "I'm a soldier. That never used to bother you. That's my job. It's my duty. I go where they send me. It's what a soldier does."

"I know that, Mike. Look, this was a bad idea, me coming to meet you like this. I've never minded you being a soldier. It's who you are, I understand that. And you're the man I fell in love with."

"So what's changed?"

"You've changed. It's not like it was before. You're not like you were. It didn't happen all at once or I would have caught it and said something. It happened slowly, over the years, so I didn't know that something in you was changing until it already had changed."

"Let me get my luggage. We'll go somewhere and talk."

"No, I don't think that would be a good idea."

This time he couldn't suppress his anger. "Well, what *do* you think would be a good idea? You're not making a whole lot of sense, Vera."

A touch of sadness flitted across her face. "You become more detached with every mission they send you on. Something started eating away at you, deep inside, and maybe you don't even know what it is."

"That's crazy."

"You say you want to talk, but we won't. You'll behave as if nothing's wrong; as if you haven't built a wall around you that no one can climb over or break through. Something's eating at you and I don't have a clue what it is."

"Maybe you're wrong."

"I live with you," she said, "at least when you allow me to. Whenever you come home from one of your dirty little wars, you bring nothing with you but a brooding chill that won't leave until you do. I think it hurt Susan more than it did me when she was growing up. That's why she's so driven, why she never has time for romance, because there never was romance in her home. I don't know. Maybe you'd rather be in the jungle, killing, than be at home with your family. You've become just another stoic, violence prone, uncommunicative male. "

This time his anger flared white-hot. "And maybe you did fall in love with some Jody Boy while I was over there, and that's why you're in such a hurry to dump our marriage?"

He was certain then that she intended to haul off and slap him.

Instead, she said, fiercely, "Damn you," and threw her arms around him and hugged him hard with a little moan close to his ear from those passionate, kissable lips. Then she whirled and ran off across the terminal.

CHAPTER 9

The basement of the church was crowded. The audience represented the full range of the Cuban exile community in Miami. There were older couples, well-dressed, the men in linen suits or shirtsleeves, usually with a trio of cigars aligned in the breast pocket. The women wore their best Sunday dresses as if they had just come from attending Mass, which many of them had. There were young couples, dressed more in the American fashion, some with children who could be heard playing happily in an adjoining room.

Doctor Ernesto Rivas stood behind a lectern on a small stage, hurrying the cadence of his words as his speech approached its scripted climax, his voice reaching a crescendo, holding his audience's attention without use of a microphone.

"My friends, Cuba today has become no more than a captive of Soviet Communism. We can no longer view this struggle against Castro as but a fight between Cubans. It is more than that, my friends. This is a war to the death between democracy and communist totalitarianism. My friends, I need your help. We must band together to restore Cuba to Cubans. We must rescue our imprisoned island from the shackles of Communist foreign power. Believe me when I tell you that soon the blow will be struck, a blow to the heart of the dictator, Castro. Security measures forbid me from being specific. But your help is needed now so that our shared dreams of a free Cuba will become reality. I ask you to give what you can, freely and from your hearts. *Viva la Causa!*"

The crowd erupted in thunderous applause. The assembly room rang with every voice present lifting to echo: *"Viva la Causa! Viva la Causa!"*

Afterward, Rivas was crowded in on every side by those wishing to engage him in political conversation while countless discussions and debates sprang up spontaneously throughout the room. It was close to a half-hour before he had an opportunity to engage in conversation the two people who had accompanied him here.

Maria Quintana said, "Doctor, we've finished collecting the donations." His secretary was forty-five years old, short, heavyset with a gold-toothed smile, clad in a smart blue suit. "Everyone was most generous."

Rivas smiled warmly. "I'm glad to hear that. These are fine people."

Hector Solas, who was in his early twenties, trim and neat in a frayed, inexpensive suit, with a gentle, direct gaze that peered out from behind thick wire-rimmed glasses, accompanied her. He said, "Your speech was inspiring, Doctor. A call to the hearts and minds of every patriot in the audience."

Rivas smiled again, modestly. "Hector, please."

"Hector is right," said Maria. "May God bless you, Doctor Rivas, for your efforts in the fight against the dictator, Castro."

"None of us can do it alone. We need each other. *Viva la Causa.*"

He glanced casually over Maria's shoulder. A man across the room was pointedly staring at him. The man was stocky, hard-faced, in his forties, wearing an expensive, smartly tailored gray suit, a gaudy tie and a Panama hat. Rivas nodded almost imperceptibly. The man returned the nod and looked away.

An Anglo woman approached them. She was in her early twenties with a bright, friendly manner that immediately put Rivas on guard. She wore a dark suit with a white silk blouse buttoned modestly to her throat, and sensible flat shoes with her nylon hose. Her chestnut hair was in a stylish bob. She held a pencil and small tablet.

Rivas returned his gaze to where the man had been standing. He heard the woman say to his secretary, "Excuse me. My name is Susan Morgan. I'm with the *Herald.* I'm writing a piece on the lives of the Cuban refugees in Little Havana, and I was wondering if Doctor Rivas—"

He did not hear the rest of it, nor Maria's reply. She would doubtless accept the offer for an interview on his behalf. As leader of a prominent exile group, he was expected to generate publicity for their plight so as to influence American public opinion and government policy.

Those who remained after most of the audience had departed were mostly the younger males. Their loathing of Castro and the hope that they could do something about it was the gist of animated conversations all around him. A few of the men had engaged Hector in discussion.

The man who had been trying to catch Rivas' eye eased unobtrusively from the room.

Rivas followed one minute later.

The restroom consisted of twin urinals and twin booths, neither in use. The stocky man was just turning from the sink, ripping a paper towel from a wall dispenser and drying his hands.

The man's every movement was precise. His expression revealed nothing. "Well, Doctor, have I been seen enough?"

"Yes, Armand. You may leave now. I will meet you later. In a half hour, say, at your club."

The man crumpled the paper towel and tossed it into a wastebasket. "Good. I don't like being here."

Rivas arched an eyebrow with mild amusement. "You feel uncomfortable in a church, is that it? I would not have thought you to be a superstitious man. Do you believe in God?"

"I believe in fate," said Ortiz. "Perhaps it is you who should be fearful in a house of God, Doctor, for your transgressions. The good Doctor Rivas, who labors so long and tirelessly on behalf of the refugee community, leading the fight to destroy Castro, and all the while you're passing on their most vital secrets through me to Havana."

"Shut up, you fool."

Ortiz flicked his wrist and, as if from nowhere, a stiletto appeared in his hand.

"No one will hear us. If they do, it will be their bad luck." The stiletto disappeared back up the sleeve of Ortiz's jacket. "I'll be happy to be gone from this country. These Americans! A rude lot, always in a hurry. I miss the beaches of Havana and the beautiful ladies along the Mercado."

"You're getting out just in time," said Rivas. "The CIA had a man in the audience tonight. An agent named Sam Resnick. He stayed to the rear, but I saw him. It has begun. He's here to follow Hector."

Ortiz sneered. "Poor Hector."

"Hector Solas is a decent man. It is a pity that he must be sacrificed. But the Americans want a spy, and so we shall give them a spy."

"Anyone but you, eh, Doctor?"

Rivas studied him in the harsh florescent lights of the restroom. Ortiz was a man used to giving orders, not taking them. Rivas bristled at the man's contempt for authority, but would not provide Ortiz the pleasure of showing it. He'd be well rid of this one.

He said, "Leave now. I will arrive at your establishment in thirty minutes. Make certain you're there, Armand. It would not bode well for you were I to inform Havana that your performance tonight is less than satisfactory."

Rivas left the rest room and returned to where Hector and Maria stood, sipping from paper cups near the punch bowl.

"Well, my friends, I believe we can mark tonight as a success."

There was no sign of the young woman from the *Herald*.

Hector patted the leather briefcase he held. "Tonight's donations will go far to further our struggle."

Maria said, "Who is that man?"

Rivas followed the direction of her gaze. Ortiz was walking along the opposite wall of the rectangular room, heading for the stairs.

"As a matter of fact," said Rivas, "I passed him with a nod only moments ago, but I don't believe we've met formally."

Hector volunteered, "His name is Armand Ortiz. He manages a club called the *Paradiso* on Flagler Avenue."

Rivas chuckled. "Then I know we've never met. I've never been there, but the *Paradiso* has a most unsavory reputation."

Hector said, "The same could be said of *Señor* Ortiz. I'm surprised to see him here."

Rivas smiled. "Don't be. Even a man such as that can have political sentiments."

Maria continued to gaze at the stairs thoughtfully after Ortiz had disappeared from their sight. She said, "I know that man from somewhere. I'm not certain where, but it will come to me. I haven't seen him in a long, long time but somehow...I *know* him."

Rivas studied her carefully as she spoke, and decided to change her train of thought. "And is our sainted Maria to appear in the Miami *Herald* anytime soon?"

She smiled shyly. "I'm only one of several ladies she said she'd be speaking to. Miss Morgan wanted my phone number and said she'd call me. She was very nice." Her smile faded. "I would welcome the chance to tell her about that communist bastard, Castro."

"*La Causa* could not ask for a better spokesperson," said Rivas with his gentle smile. "Well then, I suppose we should be on our way. Hector and I shall walk you to your car, Maria. Then we'll drive to the office and deposit the briefcase in the safe until the banks open in the morning."

Hector held his jacket lapel aside far enough to reveal a pistol worn in a belt holster. "We have protection, Doctor."

"Good. Very good."

They watched Maria drive off into the night then walked toward Rivas' Buick.

"Hector, I hope this is not an inconvenience, but I have one brief stop I should like to make before we drive to the office."

"Of course, Doctor. Where do wish to go?"

"The Club Paradiso."

"But I thought– "

"I did not want to alarm Maria."

Hector's eyes were inquisitive behind the thick lenses of his glasses. "Alarm her? About what?"

"She worries about me, you know. But sadly, in a war to the death such as we are engaged in, one cannot always choose one's allies. What you said about Ortiz is quite true and he is not a personal acquaintance of mine, I assure you."

"He is working with us?"

"Dear Hector, I fear there are some things which even you cannot be privy to. But yes, you should know that *Señor* Ortiz is doing his part for *la Causa*."

"As you say, Doctor."

The pawnshops, thrift stores and cheap restaurants that lined Flagler Avenue–nearly every one of which sported a "~Spanish spoken here~" sign in the window—were closed, but the street throbbed with nightlife emanating from the bars and nightclubs that also lined the avenue. Neon illuminated this world. The street was alive. Bright colors and the latest fashions paraded by to the music of powerful gunning exhausts and the calls of young men to the women. The crack of a pistol sounded from somewhere nearby, twice, but no one paid any attention.

The Little Havana section of Miami was bordered to the east by South Miami Avenue, to the west by Westchester, on the north by Hialeah and extended south to Flagler Avenue, roughly twenty-five blocks long, twenty blocks wide, an area of less than four square miles. A world unto itself.

Rivas wheeled his Buick into an alley that ran behind the *Club Paradiso*. He turned off the headlights. The neon and passing headlights from the street behind them did not reach this far into the steep-walled canyon of the alley. Here, everything was shadow. The sounds of the city echoed as if from a great distance.

"I appreciate your indulgence of this inconvenience, Hector. I will be but a minute."

Hector Solas held the leather briefcase, containing the proceeds of the night's fundraiser, close to his side, braced under his arm. His other hand was on his pistol, which remained holstered.

"Perhaps I should go with you."

"No, really. That won't be necessary."

"Take my gun, then. A man like Ortiz can be all the more dangerous when trusted."

"I will be quite safe, Hector, though certain precautions should be taken." He unscrewed the dome light before opening his car door.

"Excuse me, Doctor, but are we certain that Ortiz can be trusted? From what I know of him...it's difficult to believe such a man would have an interest in helping us."

Rivas remained seated. "Believe it or not, Hector, the man is a vital link in our pipeline to Cuba. He contacted me tonight because important documents have come into his possession, sent to me by a General in Castro's army. I must have this information."

"I understand."

"There's more. It is of the utmost importance that you tell no one about this, absolutely no one."

"You can trust me, Doctor, of that you can be sure."

Rivas rested his hand on Hector's shoulder. "I am sure. Thank you, my friend. I will return shortly."

Rivas left the car then, closing the door so as to make no sound. He merged with the shadows that were deepest and unlatched the rear door to the club and went inside. He entered a narrow, poorly lighted corridor where the floor and walls vibrated to the pulsating percussion of a red-hot Cubano band, burning its way through a jazzed-up rumba that drove the raucous laughter and joyous shouts of a crowded nightclub just beyond the wall to his left.

He strode briskly to a door to his right and opened the door without bothering to knock. He stepped into a cramped office of bare walls.

The only light came from the golden glow of a shaded desk lamp. There was a small wet bar next to the desk, some file cabinets and the muted vibrations of the live music.

Ortiz sat behind the desk, working at his nails with a file. "Ah, Doctor. All goes according to your plans?"

"Thus far."

"Good, good. You were followed by the American agent?"

"Almost certainly. He was good enough that I was not able to spot him. But they were to have a man at the church, ready to follow Hector."

Ortiz smirked. "And your Hector has now been followed to a contact with me, a known Castro agent. You will tell the Americans that it was Hector who asked you to drive him here. *You* waited while *he* came in to see me." He pocketed the fingernail file. "Yes, very clever."

Rivas looked about the office with distaste. "I understand your enthusiasm for leaving."

"I will not miss this country," said Ortiz, "but I will miss the *Paradiso*. You see, Doctor, in some ways I miss the old days in Cuba when the hotels and casinos were filled every night, when a man could easily line his pockets from the vices of others."

"It is strange to hear a fellow *Fidelist* speak so."

"I speak frankly only because I know we are two of a kind."

"Don't flatter yourself, Armand."

Ortiz chuckled, the gravelly sound rattling around the bare walls of the office. "No, think about it, Doctor. We are both, you and I, motivated by survival and expediency far more than political ideology, are we not? I in my way, you in yours. You're on my turf now. This is where my kind fleeces our fellow man of his hard-earned wages. At least we're honest about it. We sell what people want, pleasure. We don't wrap our thievery in religion or patriotism or the egotism of the medical profession."

Rivas curled his hands into fists. His features grew tight. "That will be quite enough of that."

Ortiz plucked a matchbook from a glass bowl on the bar top and jotted a telephone number across the inside of the matchbook. He extended it across the desk.

"Here is the telephone number of my replacement. His name is Morales."

Rivas dropped the matchbook into his jacket pocket without glancing at it. "And have you followed your instructions?" He loosened his dark blue necktie. "You have told absolutely no one that I was coming here to meet you tonight?" He removed his necktie, unbuttoning the top button of his shirt as if against the closeness of the office.

Ortiz snorted. "Of course. I hardly want things to go wrong this close to my departure. But the fact is, Doctor, I am not keen on this business which is to protect you, not me. As a prominent leader of the exile coalition, are you not putting yourself at considerable risk? Do you not fear that the CIA agent following you could see that it was you and not Solas who came in here to meet me?"

Rivas folded the tie and dabbed lightly at perspiration on his brow. "Thanks to your cooperation in turning off the backdoor light, it will be quite impossible for anyone who followed us to distinguish who stayed in the car and who came inside. Do not fear, Armand. My word will be taken over Hector's. All is proceeding according to plan."

Ortiz rose and turned his back on Rivas. He reached for a bottle on the small wet bar. "How long do you intend to keep them sitting out there waiting?"

"Just long enough," said Rivas.

Ortiz heard something in his tone of voice and started to turn. Rivas swooped in from behind, wrapping each end of the necktie in a fist and lowering the necktie around Ortiz's throat. He began to strangle Ortiz who danced a frantic jig against him, his fingers clawing at the necktie. He was gasping in vain for air. His harsh wheezing tapered off as his struggles weakened.

When the tattoo of shoe heels upon the floor finally stopped, Rivas applied additional effort to the task for another minute to make certain. Then he lowered Armand Ortiz to the floor, unwinding the tie from around the throat. His nostrils twitched at the stench of the dead man's voided bowels. He stood, replacing and retying the necktie about his own neck.

He stepped over the corpse and picked up a pen from beside an appointment book next to the lamp on the desk. He scrawled *Solas* across the blank page, and a telephone number. He used a handkerchief to wipe the pen clean of fingerprints and dropped the pen back onto the desk.

Outside, Solas was waiting for him beside the car, standing with his pistol drawn.

"Doctor, I was beginning to worry. You seemed to be gone for a long time. Is everything all right?"

"Everything is most satisfactory. Thank you for your patience, Hector."

Rivas carefully steered the Buick out of the alley, onto Flagler. As he drove away, he saw in his rearview mirror that a car, parked along the block on the far side of the Club *Paradiso*, chose that moment to pull away from the curb and join the flow of traffic two cars behind.

The headlights remained at a set distance in his rearview mirror, following.

CHAPTER 10

At 0900 hours, Morgan stood waiting in front of the Palm Beach Hotel. An unending stream of people were arriving and departing from the busy main entrance, twenty yards away. Taxicabs and private vehicles came and went. Bellhops hustled briskly. The sound of traffic carried from a boulevard lined with palm trees.

He wore his Class A uniform, freshly pressed and delivered to his room that morning by the hotel dry cleaners. His orders had been to check in at the Palm Beach after arriving in Miami. An envelope awaiting him at the front desk had contained a ten-page report, entitled *Cuban Operations Report*, and a five-by-seven-inch sheet of white paper, blank except for a single typed sentence instructing him to be where he now stood. The sunshine was a comfortable, warm caress after the brutal, pummeling heat of Southeast Asia.

And yet that place, and the awareness it took for a soldier to stay alive in that environment, had not yet loosened its grip on his psyche. In the war zones that were his home away from home, sudden death could come at any time, on a day of violent action or by surprise when everything seemed wholly ordinary.

After the scene with Vera at the airport, he'd lost his appetite and so had caught more rest time after checking in last night, storing up sleep hours like a camel stores water, and had foregone having his first American meal upon his return until a breakfast of steak and eggs with a ton of coffee at the hotel restaurant this morning. Now he felt like a new man, ready to perform at peak proficiency, as if he would never need sleep or food again. He'd tried calling Susan last night and again this morning before leaving his room, but there had been no answer. She would be on the move, hard-working her way up the journalistic ladder at the *Herald*.

After breakfast, he walked through the arcade of hotel shops to this spot in the sunshine and he put his wife and daughter out of his conscious thoughts. He was not armed, but his every combat sense was attuned to his surroundings, picking up snatches of conversation, noting the ebb and flow of vehicular and pedestrian traffic. He even heard the buzz of a fat bumblebee wending its way toward a nearby flowerbed.

A late model robin's-egg blue convertible with the top down broke from a line of arriving cabs, gliding to a stop at the curb in front of Morgan.

The driver wore a dapper three-piece gray suit and sunglasses. "Sergeant, I'm Tal Garrett."

"Garrett. Nice wheels."

"It's a rental. Thought I'd enjoy the sun. It's been a long winter up north. Hop in. You have an appointment to meet the President."

The convertible left the parking lot, merging smoothly with the traffic flow on the boulevard.

Morgan kept one eye on his outside rearview mirror, watching for anomalies in the traffic pattern along their backtrack, a vehicle hurrying to keep up, or running a yellow light to stay apace, the sort of thing that would indicate a tail. And he kept an eye on Garrett, who handled the big car like a seasoned wheelman, shifting lanes. Playing the traffic flow, they picked up speed.

Morgan said, "I was wondering who had the pull to yank me stateside so fast. Now that I know who, I guess all that's left is why."

Garrett was eyeing his rear view too. "In due time, Graveyard. I'm just the errand boy."

"You're a spook," said Morgan. "CIA, with access to the President. You're more than an errand boy. Where is he?"

"Right here in Palm Beach. The President and his family are spending the weekend at his father's place." Garrett shifted his attention to eye Morgan. "Did you read the file I left for you at the hotel?"

"I read it. This Cuban project is a big operation. No wonder it sprung a leak."

"Maybe a couple of leaks."

It appeared that they were not being followed. The remainder of the ten-minute cross-town drive passed in silence between them.

The convertible made good time. Traffic had thinned since Morgan was last in Miami, four months ago. This was the time of year when the population of seasonal residents, the "snowbirds," started returning to their homes in the north, abandoning Miami to the year-round inhabitants, resulting in a noticeable decrease in population density in everything from lines at the bank and the grocery store to traffic on the boulevards.

A Secret Service security detail at the gated entrance to the Joseph Kennedy estate stopped the car and checked their credentials carefully before waving them on.

After they'd passed the checkpoint, Garrett said, "Those Secret Service boys are the ones I'd like to trade places with."

"Why's that? Is that a cushier job than errand boy?"

"You could say so. The President likes to party. By that I mean lots of scotch and lots of broads. The boys on security detail, some of them get the leftovers and there's almost always enough to go around."

He was up shifting along a wide gravel driveway bordered with chestnut trees. Cypress and palm trees grew in abundance across the expansive grounds.

"I thought JFK was a family man."

"He is." Garrett chuckled. "That's why he has his security guys maintain constant radio contact with Jackie's bodyguards. He knows where the First Lady is every minute and when it's safe to let the presidential hair down. Hey, it's just the way the guy lets off steam. He's got the troubles of the world on his shoulders. Forget I said anything."

"Guess I always bought the image off the newspapers and TV. He comes across as a good man."

"He is a good man," said Garrett. "He loves his wife and kids. He just happens to be a very horny guy."

They drew to a stop before the main house, a three-story brick structure out of *Gone With the Wind*, complete with towering whitewashed pillars. A parking lot past the house was crowded with a couple of Buicks, three Chevies—one a convertible with the top down—and a black Cadillac with a liveried chauffeur relaxing against a front fender, taking in the sun, smoking a cigarette.

Morgan said, "We're not going to an orgy, are we?"

Garrett chuckled. "No such luck. The First Lady's off shopping but the kids are around. Anyway, our arrival is timed to catch the tail end of a breakfast the President is hosting for the leaders of the Cuban exile coalition. Size them up, okay?"

"Anything in particular I should watch for?"

"Let's hope you know it when you see it," said Garrett. "Chances are good that one of them is a Castro agent."

In the sun-lit dining room, the tables had been cleared of dishes. The aroma of cigar smoke drifted in through the open French doors that led to an Olympic-size swimming pool. Garrett effortlessly eased Morgan past the Secret Service team stationed outside the dining room. He was known here and obviously held a high security clearance. Morgan spotted half a dozen more dark-suited agents, positioned in pairs outside the French doors and at strategic points beyond rows of bougainvillea that surrounded the patio and pool. There was a tennis court where a trio of muscular men, dressed for tennis, stood waiting and he had no doubt that they too were Secret Service.

John F. Kennedy was holding court center stage amid a loose semi-circle of six Cuban men of varying ages, dressed in snappy business suits and Panama hats. There was the cordial murmur of polite conversation.

Morgan sensed that he was interrupting a round of pleasant good-byes, the polite wind-up to a working breakfast. They became aware of his and Garrett's presence.

Morgan came to attention and snapped a sharp salute. "Sergeant Michael Morgan reporting, sir."

The President returned a crisp salute. He wore a soft yellow polo shirt, white tennis shorts and sneakers.

"At ease, soldier." He looked older in person than he did on TV. His skin had the rich mahogany of a year-round tan. He stepped forward, extended a hand. "Welcome home, Graveyard." The handshake was firm, brief; a politician's handshake.

"Thank you, sir. It's good to be back."

"I wish I could say you're going to be around long enough to unpack your bags. Ah but first, these gentlemen were about to leave. Allow me to introduce my friends."

He proceeded to introduce, one by one, the leaders of the Democratic Revolutionary Front. They regarded Morgan with interest, English-speaking men of the professional class. Most of them had been educated in America, businessmen and representatives of the academic, medical and legal fields.

As they took their collective leave, one of them, a Doctor Rivas, said to the President, "Sir, you will be a hero to the Cuban people. The populace of every province will arise. Castro's own troops will defect. You will see."

"Yes, I'm sure success is within our grasp," said the President, and he saw them out. "Good day. Thank you for coming."

When they were gone, the Kennedy children, Caroline and little John-

John, appeared at the opposite side of the pool with their nurse, to begin frolicking in the shallow end.

The President indicated that Morgan and Garrett should stay with him in the dining room. He closed the French doors against the outside sounds.

"A cigar, gentlemen?"

"No thank you, sir," said Morgan.

Garrett accepted. Morgan knew the smell of good cigars. These were fat Cuban cigars.

"Sergeant," said the President, "you do know the background on the plan to invade Cuba." His slight but noticeable Boston-Harvard accented rendered the word *Cubar*.

"Yes, sir."

"Well, what you don't know is that the Cuban Brigade is within days of staging the invasion. Ships have already left the staging area carrying part of the invasion force."

Garrett said, "We've already had to cancel one strike date because word of it got to Castro. We think that leak came from inside the Brigade itself. Depending on the spy's placement in the chain of command, that could still mean serious damage if he got the right information to Havana at the wrong time for us."

Morgan had assumed the posture of parade rest, feet planted, hands clasped behind his back, eyes dead ahead.

"Pardon me for saying so, but if it could be anyone in the brigade, you've got fifteen hundred suspects. Your spy could have already left the staging area. He could be on one of those ships sailing to Cuba."

The President nodded for Garrett to respond.

Garrett said, "Word got to Havana this last time *after* the ships had set sail and before those aboard had received their final orders. That's how we know it was someone whose duty assignment is in Nicaragua. That's the only way it plays."

The President resumed. "One of Garrett's agents was sent to act as liaison with an anti-Castro faction inside Cuba. He never made it past the beach. He was killed. The significance of that, Sergeant, is that only the CIA control officer for this mission and the exile leadership, the men you just met, knew about his mission. Because of these breeches of security, I want a man, *my* man, down there with the Brigade. Call it damage control. Do what you can. That is your mission."

"The Agency is covering every tangible line of inquiry here in

Miami," added Garrett. "We're after Castro's man inside the Democratic Revolutionary Front, and there's a better chance we'll have that end tied up first with only one of six to choose from. That's how we'll identify the Castro spy in Nicaragua for you to deal with."

The President watched his children play in the pool but his features were somber.

"I don't want to use one of our people already in place down there for this job because, frankly, I don't know who to trust. Much as I hate to say it, Castro may have gotten to one of our own people. I want someone new to take this on. Someone from the outside, coming in fresh. Someone I know I can have complete faith in. Your cover will be that of general observer."

"Will I be going into Cuba with the Brigade?"

"Absolutely not. We have Special Forces involved in a strictly advisory capacity."

"Pardon me again, sir, but that's what they told me when they sent me to Vietnam last week. I shot my way out of a VC ambush. I was the only man to come back from that patrol. Some advising."

Garrett's complexion reddened.

The President dismissed the remark with a fleeting grin. "You'll do, Sergeant. I like your style. I flew down because I wanted this opportunity to size you up for myself. This is *that* important. And I'm not disappointed. That will be all, gentlemen. Good luck, Graveyard. And good hunting."

Without another glance in their direction, as if they were already gone, he opened the French door and returned to the patio. He clapped his hands twice and the children, who had been watching for just such a signal, came running as fast as they could with joyous smiles, excited and out of breath for his hugs, Caroline first, the little boy right behind her. As the President embraced his children, his expression remained somber and distracted.

CHAPTER 11

When Garrett returned to the office on Segovia Street, Resnick was yawning.

Garrett said, "You look like hell."

Resnick's thinning hair needed a combing. He wore the same linen slacks as yesterday, now in serious need of a press, and the same leather loafers. The shirt this time was a loud Hawaiian number with Hula girls and ukuleles.

"I feel like hell." He occupied his swivel chair, his feet propped up on the desk, legs crossed at the ankles, filling the office with cigarette smoke. "I wanted to make sure you got the report straight from me, since it was your bright idea that kept me up and out all night."

Garrett sat in one of the armchairs facing the desk, wishing that he hadn't decided to give up smoking. "What are you talking about?"

"Your hunch about the new man, Doctor Rivas' assistant, paid off. Either that or Rivas is dirty, and the doc has come up clean on every security check we've run."

"Let's hear what you've got."

"Armand Ortiz showed up last night at the church where Rivas was giving his speech."

Garrett frowned. "Why do I recognize that name?"

"From my reports to you up at Langley. Ortiz is a Castro agent. He runs a bar down in Little Havana. We've been using him to send Castro false information."

"Did he make contact with Rivas or Solas?"

"I don't think so." Resnick chain-lit a fresh cigarette and spoke through the smoke. "Dammit, I can't be sure. The place was packed. I kept losing sight of Ortiz in the crowd. After the reception, I followed Rivas and Solas out to Rivas' car and they drove to the Club Paradiso. That's the joint run by Ortiz. Rivas turned into an alley that runs behind the place. I was up the block. I parked my car and hoofed it across the street and eyeballed the alley but I couldn't see a thing, it was too dark."

Garrett tugged at an earlobe. "So we don't know if one or both of them went in to see Ortiz."

"After they left there I tailed them to Rivas' office. They were there for about five minutes, then the Doctor drove Solas home and went home to his own place."

"Current status? And goddamn it, Sam, I'm supposed to be your supervisor. Take your goddamn feet off the desk."

Resnick brought his feet down to the floor with a thump. "Grouchy grouchy."

"I need a cigarette."

Resnick nudged his pack across the desk with an index finger. "Take one of mine."

"Can't. I quit. Go ahead with your report."

"So I stayed outside Rivas' home after I called in for backup. Right now I've got a man watching the Rivas house and another keeping Solas under surveillance and so far today everyone's staying put."

"Okay then, Sam. What does your gut tell you? Is it Doctor Rivas or is his assistant the spy we're looking for?"

"My money is on the new man," said Resnick. "The Revolutionary Front guys get security reviews every sixty days and have since this operation began. If Rivas is embedded and spying for Castro, he's done one hell of a smooth job fabricating a background and connections to put him where he is today, which is enjoying cigars after breakfast with the President."

Garrett said, "So okay, we don't rule out Rivas altogether but, yeah, it looks like this boy, Solas, is the one we're looking for. Let's lean on Ortiz and get him to tell us who dropped in on him at his club last night."

Resnick squinted in the sunshine pouring through the windows. "His joint will be closed this time of day."

"All the better."

As they got to their feet to leave, Resnick patted his stomach. "But after lunch, okay?"

Garrett shrugged. "Okay."

"So how was your visit with the Man? I see the infamous Graveyard didn't eat you alive."

"I didn't give him the chance. He looks like one tough son of a bitch and he didn't seem to mind talking back to the President. I see where he got a rep for being his own man. But he's on our side."

"Glad to hear it. With a Castro spy moling away inside this op despite my best efforts, I guess at this point maybe I can use all the help they want to send me."

"Glad you feel that way, Sam, because you and Graveyard Morgan are partnering up for the rest of the day."

Resnick paused, eyes narrowed. "Say that again."

"Until he catches his night flight out of Opa-Locka tonight."

"What the hell for? Tal, I don't need a goddamn partner. I'm supposed to be running this operation."

"Cool down," said Garrett with a placating gesture. "Rivas and Solas, I didn't think it would break this fast. Whichever one is our spy, he's got information Morgan can use on his mission down south. The President wants Graveyard on top of this for today and that means you've got yourself a new partner."

Resnick's affable grin returned. "Ah, hell. As long as he doesn't eat me alive."

Garrett said, "I'll tell you where to find him."

Carmen Vasquez arrived to claim her brother's body at the rear entrance of the headquarters building of the militia post near Giron.

Cosme Gomez and three of the neighbor boy's friends accompanied her. Cosme pulled a plain flatbed cart to where a rough wood coffin had been left unattended next to a line of foul smelling garbage cans. The boys secured the coffin to the cart.

Medina observed this from the window of his second story office. Ramón stood at his side.

"Too bad," said Medina. "We have given them another martyr. You must be more careful in the future. You are my interrogator, not an executioner."

Ramón was sweating even this early in the day. His baldhead glistened like polished ebony. "I swear it won't happen again."

"I would be more harsh with you but for the fact that you have proven so effective in the past. In the year you have been with me, Vasquez is the first to die before he talked. And it is hardly pleasant work, what you do, torturing people."

"It's not so bad." Ramón's eyes followed the direction of Medina's gaze to the small group below with the coffin, watching them pass the checkpoint at the rear gate and leave the compound. "Those boys with her. I recognize them from the village. Do you suppose they are in the underground? And the sister, Carmen...Major, what about her?"

"She is not presently a member of the underground," said Medina. "That is why she will be of use to me, and why killing her brother before her eyes may yet have a beneficial effect."

"I don't understand."

"Carmen Vasquez has not belonged to any of the counter-revolutionary groups. But she will become one of them *now*. She *will* lead us to those we seek or they will come to her. And then we will have them. Felix Carriles and his group will be apprehended. I shall see to it. That young woman will be kept under close surveillance. It is only be a matter of time. They will all be put to death."

CHAPTER 12

Vera was returning from lunch with three of her women co-workers from the bank where she had worked for the past year, when she recognized the gait of the man striding across the parking lot toward them.

Mary Ann, who worked at the window next to hers and was a real card, was making some characteristically risqué observation about one of the busboys at Alberto's, where they'd had lunch, and everybody started laughing together like a bunch of cackling hens.

Vera's laughter froze in her throat. She drew back from the others, who continued on into the bank through the employee entrance, oblivious that she had detached herself from their small group.

Morgan wore a lightweight blue blazer, with matching slacks and a white shirt open at the collar.

She thought of the first time that she saw him. The day they met. The situation then and conditions had been drastically different than now in this sun-splashed Miami parking lot, but that way he had of walking...sort of a John Wayne stride but not so pronounced, subtle like the movement of a roving panther with his shoulders moving from side to side and his hands held at waist level as if ready to grapple with whatever came his way, friend or foe. Watching him draw closer, she felt herself becoming moist and tried to blink away the primal effect he still had on her.

That first day. Back in Milwaukee. The parking lot of the junior college. They were both freshmen. She was a chemistry major. Mike was enrolled in pre-law courses because he intended to become a policeman like his retired father. It had been snowing, to put it mildly. Sheer whiteout conditions. Classes had been let out early to allow students the opportunity to get home safely but she had stayed in the library, engrossed in cramming for a world history exam. She lost track of time and there she was in the dying light of a cruel, frigid day. The snow was howling, blowing vertically, and her battered little Ford coupe was not only half-buried in a drift, but one of the front tires was flat. She gave the tire an angry kick and some choice curse words. The wind was almost blowing her off her feet when *he* emerged from whipping, swirling snow, materializing at first like an apparition with the same confident stride that she was watching now. He had actually managed to get the tire changed but by that time, the storm had only intensified and travel home was out of the question, so they found sanctuary with a handful of other refugees from the storm in a cozy pub nearby where Vera thanked him by buying Mike Morgan the first round. They'd toasted to new friendships, and talked away the rest of the day and much of that night.

Two things happened that day.

They fell in love. She could see clearly now with more than twenty years hindsight. It was the sort of thing—a connection between two people—that you can't go looking for. She had always believed that love finds you, and love found them that day. At first, yes, the attraction for her was physical. Those shoulders. That gait. Those solid, square-jawed good looks. God, he was something. But as she they spent the day getting to know each other in a corner booth in that pub, with the city locked in the worst blizzard in thirty years and the wind howling outside, her response was strong to everything about him. The sound of his voice. The clarity and logic of his thought. She saw in him what she could only think of as a tender strength. He listened to her with genuine interest. Magic happened.

And they promised each other that day that someday they would live where it never snowed. Then and there they had decided on Miami, a place neither had ever been to but its year-round warm weather had sounded far more inviting than a Milwaukee winter.

From then on, life had moved slower and faster. Fast because they were married three months later. Their passion was a mutual, craving hunger that only grew hotter. Susan was born nine months later. But slow, yes. Godawful slow. It had taken longer than expected for their move to Florida because World War II intervened. Mike enlisted the day after Pearl Harbor, and had been a professional soldier from that day until this.

Working at the bank had given her life a center after Susan turned eighteen and raising their child was no longer a homebound responsibility. This daily interaction with the public, required by her job, the steady stream of faces past the window of her teller's cage, made the hours of her workday fly, and she got along well with her co-workers. She had taken to the freedom from a housewife's routine that employment brought her and could no longer imagine herself not being employed. She wouldn't change a thing about her life, certainly not the blessing of Susan, but in some ways she was at last getting a chance to live her life strictly on her own terms and no one else's.

If only that made life easier...

When he reached her and she was certain that they were out of earshot of anyone else, she said, "Mike, I don't want a scene."

"You know me better than that. I just want to apologize in person about last night, about some of the things I said. I know you wouldn't cheat on me, Vera. I shouldn't have said that. I shouldn't have thought it."

"You had a right to be angry," she said. "How long are you going to be in town?"

"I'm on assignment. I'm just passing through Miami for a briefing and to get my orders. I met the President this morning."

"If that was meant to impress me, consider it done. I wish we could talk but I can't. My lunch break is over."

"Give me one minute, hon. I've been thinking about the things you said last night, about what's happening between us."

She touched his arm. "I wish I hadn't said some of the things I said. You haven't been that bad a husband, Mike. The marriage hasn't been that bad."

"I'm glad to hear that."

"It's just that with Susan grown, I...I guess I don't want to live the rest of my life, waiting for the noble warrior to come home maybe. Maybe I'm just restless, but that's enough. Mike, I'm in the best years of my life."

"I could take an early out. My pension would be enough for us to live in."

She hadn't expected this.

Then he saw something over her shoulder and he said, "Uh-oh."

Her fingertips dropped from his arm. She turned to see a man of medium build, with thinning blond hair and a ruddy complexion, walking briskly across the parking lot in their direction.

When he reached them, the man gave Morgan a quick glimpse at credentials in a leather packet. "Sergeant, my name is Resnick, CIA. I've come to pick you up."

Morgan said, "I have my own car." Any trace of emotion was gone from his voice and demeanor. He reminded Vera of a panther, cornered and ready to spring.

Resnick said, "Sorry, Sarge. You've been assigned to accompany me.

I'm not crazy about the idea myself. Call Garrett for verification, why don't you?"

Morgan turned to Vera to say something.

Vera said, "This is the story of our lives, isn't it?"

She continued on into the bank without another glance in his direction.

CHAPTER 13

Flagler Street was Little Havana in microcosm, baking in the sun, overflowing with a steady stream of colorful vehicular and pedestrian traffic. Machinegun-rapid Spanish competed with blaring Latino music, spilling from nearly every doorway. The smell of frying empanadas seasoned the warm air. Shoppers brushed shoulders with refugees and well-to-do Cuban businessmen. An overweight nun tried to control a group of rambunctious ten-year-olds on a class outing. Gaudily dressed hookers stood in doorways.

Resnick wedged the convertible into a parking space across the street and a half-block away from the Club Paradiso, where a neon sign bearing the club's name was not blinking. The entrance doors were closed.

Resnick tossed away a smoked cigarette butt through the car's open window. "Looks quiet enough. Let's pay a call on *Señor* Ortiz."

Resnick seemed like an all right guy with his easygoing, affable manner despite his obvious lack of enthusiasm for having to work with Morgan. During the drive here, he'd clearly and concisely detailed the situation with Rivas and Hector Solas and what might be gleaned from leaning on a man they knew to be a Castro agent. Resnick had brought along a pistol for him, a snub-nosed .38 revolver, and a shoulder holster to be worn concealed.

The front doors of the club were locked, but not a back door they found when they went around to the alley.

Resnick said, "This is the door Solas or Rivas would have used last night to visit Ortiz."

They stepped into a narrow corridor. It took only a short time for their eyes to adjust after the sunlight.

Conversational voices speaking in Spanish carried from the front of the club, around a corner at the far end of the corridor.

Morgan said, "I speak Spanish but I can't make out what they're saying."

"Let's check it out."

A couple of janitors were working in the empty club. Chairs were stacked on the tables. One man worked a wet mop across the floor with desultory swipes while another polished a bar top that ran the length of the place. They were chatting about a professional fight televised the night before. They saw Morgan and Resnick and stopped what they were doing.

Resnick held up his badge. "We're looking for Armand Ortiz," he said in Spanish.

Both janitors' immediate reaction was to make a simultaneous beeline out of there, running down a hallway in the opposite direction.

Morgan started after them.

Resnick said, "Hold it, Graveyard. Let 'em go. They won't know anything. It's Ortiz we want. Let's go find him. If we don't find him, we'll give his office a frisk." He unholstered his revolver.

That was good enough for Morgan, who brought out the .38 from its shoulder harness. They advanced cautiously down the corridor. The first door on the right was a broom closet. The door on the left was full of stacked cases of beer and liquor.

They found the dead man behind the third door.

Rigor mortis had set in. The over-ripe stench of death was just starting to rise from the remains of Armand Ortiz. His eyes and mouth were open in a rictus of death, the tongue protruding from his mouth like a rotting sausage.

Resnick holstered his pistol. "Now that's damn inconsiderate. He could have talked to us before getting himself bumped off."

Morgan holstered the .38. He indicated the drawn drapes, the switched-on desk lamp. "It happened last night, maybe while you were sitting in your car watching the alley."

Resnick studied the body at their feet with visible distaste. "Rivas or Solas. Who did this?"

Morgan said, "Solas." He was reading from a desktop appointment calendar.

He slid the calendar across the desk, which allowed Resnick to read what had been written there: the name, and a telephone number.

"Oh hell," said Resnick with feeling. "I'd better call this in."

CHAPTER 14

One of the principal centers of anti-Communist activity in Miami was a two-level house of sand-colored brick on a residential street just off Calle Ocho, Miami's Southwest Eighth Street in the heart of Little Havana.

Middle-aged men, many of them carrying briefcases, congregated there daily. There were no chairs or benches, so they stood in the bare living room or on the front porch, near the Coke machine, or leaned on the porch railing to exchange and discuss their political opinions, often heatedly. A receptionist was kept busy at her switchboard inside the front door and, near her alcove, carpeted stairs let to the offices above.

Doctor Rivas had his own office. His desk faced a Democratic Revolutionary Front wall poster which read: *The Communists neither sleep nor rest. Can we who fight against them say the same?*

He passed Maria Quintana's desk.

"Will you be gone for the day, Doctor?"

"No, Maria, I'll be right back. My stomach has just reminded me how long it's been since my last meal."

"You had better start watching your health more closely, Doctor. You do the work of ten men. You must take care of yourself."

He smiled. "Yes, Doctor."

Her gold-toothed smile seemed to brighten the room, and she returned to her switchboard duties.

Rivas walked to a restaurant on Eighth but he did not enter. He stepped into a phone booth adjacent to the front entrance and dialed a number from memory.

Hector Solas answered midway through the first ring.

"Yes?"

"Hector, you must get out of your apartment at once." Rivas pitched his voice to an urgent whisper.

There came a gasp across the line. "Doctor!" Solas paused, uncertain. "But...why?"

"I can't tell you that now. There isn't time. Do as I say, Hector. An attempt has just been made on my life. They're coming for you next."

"I should not have stayed home today," said Solas. A rising anxiety was clear in his voice across the line. "My place is at your side, Doctor. I should be protecting you."

"Protect yourself, Hector. I have learned only minutes ago that they are coming to kill you."

"But what should I do? Where should I go?"

"Hide. That is all you can do for now. Castro's people in Miami are striking at us. Get out of your apartment at once, at *once*...and beware. Ortiz has gone to his Mafia friends for help."

"Mafia? What do you mean?"

"The men coming to kill you are not Cubans. They are Mafia assassins. They may already be at your doorstep. Flee for your life, Hector."

"They had better not get in my way," said Solas, and he broke the connection.

He had been staying in a shabby one-bedroom apartment, three blocks away from the brick house off Calle Ocho. His furnished room was littered with political pamphlets, the walls decorated with flyers and posters, one of which depicted Fidel Castro with a noose around his neck and a hammer and sickle on his sleeve. He had been feeling like a caged animal, pacing the small apartment all day, the pressure of inactivity building within him since the Doctor's call that morning, advising him not to come in.

He made certain that his revolver rode loosely in its belt holster. He went to a scarred wood dresser and, from the top drawer, removed a handful of loose cartridges, which he dropped into his pocket.

Hector kissed the crucifix worn on a gold chain around his neck and hurried out of the apartment, down the steps, toward the street.

CHAPTER 15

An agent named Masden was pulling stakeout duty on the apartment house where Hector Solas lived. Masden was a short, stocky man, affecting the disheveled, seedy appearance of a transient down on his luck. He had positioned himself in an armchair in the lobby of a hotel for transients across the street, providing him with a good view of the apartment house through a smeary plate glass window. A half-dozen men, of similar demeanor and attire, lounged about the dim lobby.

When Morgan and Resnick walked up to him, Masden rose and said, "He's home if you want him. There's a back entrance but if he tries to use it, he still has to come out from that alley over there."

"We want him," said Resnick. There was nothing of the affable sportsman about Resnick at this moment. His eyes were cold, his jaw was set.

Morgan said, "Is that him?"

A man came hurrying down the front steps of the building across the street, slim and well-groomed in brown slacks, a pale yellow shirt and a brown jacket.

"That's him," said Resnick. "Look sharp."

Solas saw the three men advancing toward him, crossing the street from the direction of the hotel. He unholstered a revolver and fired. The gunshot was a flat, dull *pop!* in the open air.

Masden emitted a gasp of pain and surprise as the bullet struck him in the abdomen. His body jack-knifed violently, his feet lifted from the ground. He dropped to the pavement and a pool of blood, sparkling brilliant red in the sunlight, began spreading rapidly beneath him.

People were shouting, scrambling frantically for cover. A driver tromped his brakes, there was the squeal of tires on pavement.

Morgan and Resnick automatically split away from each other, unholstering their weapons amid the frightened screams and general chaos. Bystanders, scattering for cover, obstructed Morgan's line of vision and when he again got a clear view of Solas, the Cuban had almost regained the front door on his way back into the building. Solas spun, tracking his weapon around. Morgan had the .38 out. He squeezed off a shot, a near miss that ricocheted off the brick near Solas, who forgot about returning fire and dashed into the building. Morgan took off running after him and gained the front steps, then the entranceway. He pressed his back to the wall alongside the front door.

Resnick assumed a similar position, opposite him. He nodded in the direction of the fallen body.

"He's dead. That little son of a bitch took out one of my men. Masden has a wife and two kids."

Morgan said, "I'm going in. Stay here in case I miss him and he comes out."

"Take him, soldier. Just remember, we want him alive."

"I'll do my best."

Morgan stormed in, half expecting to be fired on once he was inside. But no one shot at him. He ran down a hallway of doors opening just enough for curious, cautious eyes to stare out. He took the inside stairs to the second level four at a time.

Along the second floor hallway, an open doorway loomed.

He reached it just in time to see Solas straighten on to the fire escape, having climbed through an open window on the other side of a shabby, furnished room. Morgan jerked back a heartbeat before Solas fired three rounds that dotted the faded wallpaper across the hall from the apartment door. Then he heard the clatter of Solas, scampering up the fire escape. He rushed in and raced across the tiny apartment. He risked a glance out the window.

Looking up, he saw Solas take aim at him over the edge of the roof. He opened fire first, pulling off three fast rounds that drove the Cuban out of his line of vision. After several seconds of nothing, Morgan climbed onto the fire escape, grabbed hold of an iron ladder that led to the roof and went up, the .38 held up and ready. He paused at the top of the ladder and chanced a look over the ledge.

No one was on the roof but on the roof of an adjacent, identical building, Solas was hunched over a door that would lead down into that building, struggling futilely to wrench it open.Morgan climbed onto the roof, took a running start and leaped across to the next rooftop. Solas gave up struggling with the door handle and tracked his pistol around and fired. Morgan dropped to the tarred roof and the bullet punched empty space inches above him. He used his elbows to steady his aim and drew a bead on Solas but held his fire.

"No, Graveyard," he muttered to himself. "Take him alive."

Solas must have thought he was hit. The Cuban fired a shot at the lock mechanism on the door, then yanked the door open and dived inside, out of sight.

Morgan hurried after him. He paused at the doorway. He could hear panicky footfalls pounding down the stairs below. He made much less noise hurtling down those stairs in hot pursuit. He gained the ground floor landing, only vaguely aware of more opening doors and inquiring faces whizzing past as he ran. The sunlit front entrance of this building yawned open ahead. Solas was racing back out into the street.

As Morgan reached the front door, he heard Resnick shout at Solas from across the street.

"Halt! *Freeze!*"

Morgan reached the front step and saw Resnick, in the center of the street near Masden's crumpled body, assume a shooter's crouch, his revolver tracking on Solas, giving the running man a chance to respond to his command.

Solas darted away from him and kept on running, throwing panicky, fearful looks over his shoulder, barely watching where he was going.

Morgan raised his .38 to try for a leg shot.

A city bus, traveling faster than it should have, wheeled around a corner, onto the street. The driver saw Solas, who turned his head and saw the bus, but by then it was too late. Morgan heard plainly the *thud!* The impact threw Solas back in the direction he'd come from. He went down and stayed down, adding his own spreading pool of blood on the hot pavement.

CHAPTER 16

Felix Carriles never slept more than two nights in a row under the same roof.

A single lighted, curtained window could be seen in the Vasquez house.

Mosquitoes buzzed around his head. He had spent the preceding hour crouched in the close darkness of the canebrake, exactly where he had concealed himself on his previous visit to Carmen, when Major Medina had come. He had arrived tonight at dusk and watched to try and ascertain whether or not the house was under surveillance.

A network of people throughout Oriente Province, sympathetic to the anti-Communist cause, had provided him shelter in the months following his training at the CIA "farm" outside Miami and his subsequent return to Cuba. He was nineteen years old, intense and muscular, and not a few of those providing him with shelter were girlfriends. He had grown up in Oriente Province.

His family were poor farmers. They had started with nothing, but had worked hard. His mother helped his father in the fields while raising a family. At last, after years of barely eking out a living, Felix's parents had earned a farm of their own. Not much of a farm, true, but it was theirs. Theirs, until three months earlier when the farm had been taken from his family as part of Fidel Castro's so-called Agrarian Reform. Everything had been nationalized, no matter how small; every farm, every business. His parents had sweat and slaved their lives away, only to have what little they owned stolen from them by the so-called "glorious revolution."

His family escaped to Florida and in less than a week he was recruited by a CIA agent in Little Havana.

Within a month the black man, Riley, who did contract work for the CIA, was returning Felix to Cuba so that he could meet Diego Vasquez and Diego's sister, Carmen. His mission was to organize, train, and set up the lines of supply and communication between cells of the anti-Castro underground inside Cuba, a prelude to the imminent invasion. There were others like him with the same mission, operating in the other provinces across the width and breadth of the island. At least, that's what he had been told. And why would the Americans lie?

Since his return, he had accomplished much. Communication between the cells in his sector was fully coordinated. Caches of weapons were hidden. From the ranks of everyday people, he had trained team leaders who were to train others. At his command was a well- equipped army of one hundred saboteurs.

Before he was able to approach the house, a neighbor woman, *Señora* Gomez, and her son, Cosme, arrived. He knew the *Señora* and her son helped Carmen with errands and the responsibility of caring for Carmen's sick mother. They remained inside. Felix was debating with himself the advisability of withdrawing and returning tomorrow night.

As he was preparing to withdraw, the neighbors took their leave. There were muted goodbyes, and they walked off, disappearing into the gloom.

Felix went to the house and, without knocking, let himself in through the front door, which was unlocked. The house was silent, the front room cloaked in semi-darkness. He could barely discern the shapes of its furnishings. A rectangle of illumination emanated from the open doorway of a bedroom. He went to that doorway and peered in.

A figure on the bed was completely covered beneath a drawn-up sheet.

Carmen sat in a chair beside the bed, her hands clasped in her lap. She saw Felix, but registered no reaction.

She said, "My mother has just died. *Señora* Gomez has gone to inform the authorities."

Felix wished that he were somewhere else. Anywhere but here. He hadn't expected this. Discomfort curdled through him. "My condolences, Carmen. Your mother was a fine woman."

"Her spirit is free of her pain. She is in a better place. But already I miss her so." A single tear formed in the corner of one of Carmen's eyes and rolled down her cheek.

Felix thought again about leaving and returning tomorrow night, but he swallowed hard and plunged ahead. "Carmen, forgive me, but they will be here soon. I must be brief."

"My father. My brother. My mother. A year ago we were a family. Now I'm an orphan. Now only I am left. I feel so alone."

"You're not alone, Carmen. Don't think that way. You are a sister to all of us who fight for a free Cuba."

"Felix, what are you doing here?"

"Forgive me, Carmen, but we can wait no longer. We have to be careful, but you must show me where Diego hid the transmitter and codebook. We have already missed contact with the Americans offshore. We must get through to them."

"All of this secrecy," she said in the same quiet voice, void of emotion, "and I'm in the middle."

"Diego never told me where he hid it. A standard security measure. If someone is made to talk, they cannot tell what they don't know. But they caught Diego, not me. And now that he is gone, I must act in his place. For that, Carmen, I need your help. I'm sorry."

She touched her fingertips to the shrouded form on the bed. She remained like that with her eyes closed for more than a minute. He saw her lips moving but he could not hear her soundless words of prayer.

Then she stood, her back held straight. Her eyes glowed with a new and dark intensity.

"There is nothing more I can do here." She spoke briskly, in a cool voice. "Come. I will show where Diego hid the transmitter. And you're right. We must be *very* careful."

She led him through the network of paths that crisscrossed the cane fields, the way Diego had shown her, to the spot where the cane gave way to sand dunes.

They paused at the edge of the canebrake. A half moon cast silvery illumination over the ocean and curving shoreline. Foaming water hissed across the sand. She pointed at an old palm tree curving up toward the night sky, not far from where they stood.

"There, beneath that tree," she whispered.

"Wait," said Felix. "I want to see if we're being followed."

She gazed along the beach toward the lights of Giron, twinkling in the near distance. "Diego was killed not far from here. Why was he not more careful?"

"Perhaps he was. Perhaps he was being watched, as you are."

"Me?"

"But of course."

"But I know everyone in my neighborhood. I would have noticed anyone watching me."

"Not if it was someone you trusted. Someone you see every day."

Her eyes and mouth tightened. Her fists clenched. "Look what they've done to our country. They make us distrust our friends and neighbors."

"And not without cause. All right, I don't think there's anyone behind us. It's a chance we have to take."

He moved the rock back from the indentations carved into soft soil at the base of the tree trunk, revealing the compact radio and codebook contained in a waterproof black box. He switched on the transmitter.

"Tonight is designated for transmission," he told her. "They'll be wondering why we've been missing contact."

After contact was established, there was a flurry of exchange. Felix jotted rapidly and after he signed off, Carmen resealed the radio in the box while he referred to the codebook. He snapped shut the codebook.

He picked up the box. "We're taking the radio with us."

"Can you tell me what they said?"

"I will tell you when I tell the others."

"Others?"

"I told you, Carmen, that you are not alone. It is time for you to meet the other members of our group. Come, this time I will show you the way."

He led her further away from the lights, to a spot where the beach gave way to rocky, craggy coastline, and they continued on. She encountered some difficulty in keeping up with his sure-footed gait, but she managed with the help of the moonlight. He led her to where thick foliage overgrew a narrow gash, a fault in the stony surface at a low jut of rock completely camouflaged by dense thickets growing around it. What appeared at first to be no more than a pitted, ancient configuration of rock was in fact the entrance to a cave.

She followed him into the cave, which was no more than ten feet high and perhaps thirty feet deep. Battery-operated lamps lighted the interior, and the light had been undetectable from outside.

A half dozen people rose to greet them. Four young men and two women instinctively reached for their rifles. Bandoleers of ammunition were in evidence, and sleeping bags and knapsacks. The group relaxed and lowered their weapons when they saw Felix. They gathered around.

"I bring important news," he announced. "But first, I want you to welcome a new member to our ranks. This is Carmen Vasquez, Diego's sister.

He introduced her to them, one by one. She knew the young women and one of the men from having seen them about the village. The others were from neighboring communities. There was a warm, communal feeling to this place, these people. They had accepted her without question, with friendly nods and smiles.

A good natured, blustery bear of a man named Santos asked, "And what is this important news you bring us, amigo? Medina and his men are scouring the provinces for us. We can't hide out here forever."

"We won't have to. The invasion is about to happen."

Santos snorted derisively. "We've heard that before."

"This time they're serious, I tell you." Felix set down the radio. "We need to establish contact with the other cells. It will happen for certain sometime within the next five days. We must be prepared to supply full tactical support."

"Serious, eh? Well, then, I say we have a drink!"

When the others had drifted away, she realized that Felix was staring at her.

"Yes, Felix?"

"Carmen, I must ask you to be sure. You must be certain. Your commitment to our cause must be one hundred per cent. You can leave now and no one will stop you or think any less of you. But you must decide if you are ready to commit. Are you one of us?"

"Yes. Yes, I am, Felix. I would die fighting for a free Cuba."

He reached behind him, picked up an assault rifle and extended it to her.

"Here then, take this. It's yours. In the morning, I'll teach you how to use it."

CHAPTER 17

Beachcomber Bob's had always been the Morgan family's favorite seafood restaurant, and so when her Dad finally reached her by phone that afternoon at her desk at the newspaper, Susan suggested there for dinner. Bob's was softly lighted, with the standard seafood restaurant accouterments of fishnet suspended from the ceiling and a motif that included everything from starfish placed everywhere to a truly impressive marlin mounted behind the bar. The murmur of conversation, the clink of silverware from nearby tables and the soft strains of piped-in Caribbean music made for a perfect, comfortable backdrop. It was a family place, quiet on weekday nights.

Bob himself showed Susan to a corner table. She wore a blue dress with a white belt and white pumps. Her father arrived five minutes later and she did everything but run over to greet him, she was that happy to see him. Their affectionate hug was warm and extended.

Dad ordered the surf and turf. She ordered fried sole with potatoes and Brussels sprouts, and they proceeded with small talk about the weather, how glad they were to see each other and so on, until about halfway through the meal.

Then her father observed, "You keep looking around as if you're expecting someone to show up."

She was a little stunned because that's exactly what she had been doing, though she'd thought she was being subtle about it. She managed a grin.

"I never could get much past you, could I?"

"Who are we expecting?"

She sighed. "No one, I guess. I told Mom that you and I were getting together here for dinner. I told her that I thought she should come join us. I hope that's okay."

His shrug was too casual. "It's okay with me. Doesn't look like it was okay with your mother."

She decided to go ahead and just speak her mind. "I wish you two would straighten this thing out between you, whatever it is. Everything else is going so good in my life, except for...except for our family falling apart. I'm finally getting an opportunity at the paper to write the kind of in-depth story that I can really sink my teeth into, and I've met a nice guy through some friends and we've been dating."

The way her dad's expression became suddenly grave was almost comical. "Now that's something I'd like to hear about."

She couldn't help her small, good-natured laugh. "I'll bet it is. But it's nothing serious...yet. We've just gone out a few times. But I don't want to talk about Chuck."

"Chuck? No, tell me about Chuck." And he wasn't kidding.

"You sound like you're ready to sit on the front porch with a shotgun to make sure he brings me home on time."

"Well—"

"Daddy, You and mom raised me to be a good girl, and Chuck and I aren't even close to, uh, anything like what you're worried about, so," she gave a shrug, sugarcoated with a smile, "don't worry. Let's talk about what *I* want to talk about, okay?"

He blinked, slightly taken aback. "You're bossy just like your mother."

"I'm her daughter, too. And I'm not going to give up on this family so damn easy."

He took his time chewing and swallowing his next forkful. "Nothing's easy about this, angel, believe me. Your mother has her point of view of things and I have mine. I'm glad you're not taking sides."

"You're a soldier," she said. "I don't see that changing anytime soon."

"Oh, you might be surprised."

She paused in her eating and set down her silverware. "What do you mean?"

"I'm just saying."

"Well you're right, I would be surprised. I can't imagine Graveyard Morgan *not* being a soldier."

He winced. "Susan, you know I don't like it when you use that name."

"I've grown up, Dad. I'm going to be one hell of a reporter and I'm just saying that I'm grown up enough to know what you do for a living is hell on earth. I'll bet there aren't many men who can do what you do. I think I understand that about you. But I understand what Mom's going through, too."

"Well, could you tell me about it?"

"I'm not the one you should ask. Mom is."

"You're right. You are grown up. You've turned into a wise soul while I've been out busting my ass to save the world."

"Oh, Dad, why can't you see? That's right. You're gone all of the time. And now that I've gotten my own place, Mom has...nothing but her freedom. I don't know, maybe I'm not so damn wise. I just want to see the two of you work things out."

"You see both sides better than I do."

She laughed. "It's my Libra sun, remember? The sign of the scales. The ability to see conflicting issues clearly."

He groaned. "Don't do that to me. Not the astrology stuff, please."

"Of course you're not into astrology." She grinned. "You're a Taurus."

"Now you're just trying to get my goat, aren't you?"

"Goat. That would be Capricorn."

"Susan."

"Sorry."

"I am smart enough to figure out that your mother has just about had it with me being a soldier."

She resumed finishing her dinner. "Well there you are."

"Tell me the truth, Susan. There's something I'd really like to know. Was I a good dad? I mean when you were growing up, those were good times, right?"

"Of course they were." She chuckled with fondness. "I was the envy of every kid I knew because my dad could build a better tree house than any of their dads could. Sure, you were gone most of the time, but you know what?"

"What?"

"Now that I look back on it, I think you were the perfect dad exactly because of the life you lived. It took me awhile to figure that out for myself, but there was a precious gift in the way I was brought up. I grew up spending half my life *anticipating*. Anticipating your return from whatever other worlds you visited outside of my own little universe. I remember the anticipating as a sweet thing. And when you did stride in through our front door, when you'd sweep Mom and me off our feet together with one giant bear hug...you always lived up to that anticipation. I valued you more than most kids do their fathers because our time together was so precious."

"Right," he said with a bleak smile. "Because there was so damn little of it."

She looked him squarely in the eyes. "Dad, you're the best dad a girl could have because you gave me a damn high standard to measure the Chucks of the world up against."

He blinked, and the bleakness evaporated. "Well, I'll be damned. Thanks, honey."

There was a pause in the conversation as a busboy cleared the table and their waiter took orders for coffee, cheesecake for her dad while she passed in the interest of maintaining her figure.

When the waiter was gone, Morgan said, "So if I can't talk about the boyfriend—"

"He's not my boyfriend. We're...just dating."

"Okay, so what can we talk about? How about that interesting assignment at the paper? Your mom told me you took my advice and leaned on them about going to work for a TV station."

She nodded. "I was sure they were going to tell me to take a walk, but guess what? My editor is a gruff old bird but he finally admitted that he liked the way I wrote. He said I have style."

Morgan grinned. "You've got loads of that, kiddo. You get that from your mother, too."

"I know. But I'm not talking about what you're talking about. I'm talking about the way I write. Mister McCray said I was even able to make a fashion show sound interesting. Turns out they've been looking for a new slant on the Cuban refugee situation and everything going on down in Little Havana, so I convinced that good old boy that what he needed was the woman's perspective. And guess what? That's what they gave me? I've been interviewing people in Little Havana for the past week for a series of articles I'll be writing about everything from the boat people who are living in squalor to the profiteers to the anti-Castro movement. I'm scheduled to interview Doctor Rivas tomorrow."

His eyes narrowed. "Really?"

She took a few heartbeats and studied him, and it was like seeing him through a new set of eyes.

"That's why you're here, isn't it? Cuba's the biggest hotspot that our hemisphere has seen in this century...and they need Graveyard Morgan over here more than they do halfway around the world in Southeast Asia. I should have connected the dots when Mom first told me you were coming home."

He didn't respond as their coffee and his dessert was served.

When the waiter was gone, she said, "You're trying to make up your mind about something."

"Stop reading me, dammit. Mmm, great cheesecake. Want some?"

"You're trying to decide whether or not to take advantage of my position at the newspaper."

He set his fork down and pushed away the unfinished cheesecake. "I don't know about the astrology, but you may be psychic."

"All women are, Daddy, didn't you know that? At your age, too."

"Don't be smart."

"Okay, I'll be serious. If there's anything I can do to help, I will. You're giving me an inside track to the biggest story of the century, America's invasion of Cuba."

"America is not going to invade Cuba."

"Of course not. The invasion will be by Cuban anti-Castro "liberators" who will just happen to have been supplied, trained and transported by the U.S."

"How do you know so much?"

"I told you. I've been spending time in Little Havana. The word is on the street. Maybe not the exact time and place for the invasion, but everyone knows it's coming and soon. They know that as a fact. If I can land an inside scoop on that, we'd be talking Pulitzer Prize."

He drew the cheesecake to him and resumed eating as a way of not looking her in the eye.

"Your mother would skin me alive if I was responsible for anything happening to you. Honey, you've got to promise me that you will absolutely *not* put yourself in any sort of personal danger."

"Dad, it's a dangerous world."

He repeated, "Dad, it's a dangerous world," and chuckled. "Damn. Seems like just yesterday I was bringing home your new tricycle from the PX."

He finished the cheesecake, set down his fork, sipped his coffee and looked at her across the rim of the cup.

"If there is a story in it for you, you're going to have to wait until after it's finished before I give the say-so. Susan, you've got to give me your word on that and that you'll be careful and not put yourself in any kind of personal danger. Promise me."

"You're just afraid of Mom."

"Promise me."

"Okay. I promise, I promise, I promise."

He growled like a bear. "That was too damn easy. But a promise *is* a promise, and I want you to keep yours. I don't like bringing you anywhere near this, but I find myself in a mess of spies and hoods and political fanatics and I don't know who to trust. You're right. As a reporter, you could learn things that I could use."

She said, "You can trust me not to write a word until you me give the go ahead."

He thought about it some more. "No, I don't think so," he decided aloud. "This is classified information we're talking about. And I'd be putting you in harm's way."

"You're talking about the spies and the hoods and the political fanatics."

"You're damn right I am."

"You're talking about needing information and not knowing who to trust. Trust? Daddy, I'm your daughter. Your daughter. I have your blood in my veins. I'll keep my promise to you about sitting on whatever I dig up. You can trust me."

He studied her long and hard. Then he sighed the same way and changed his decision. "Damn me, you are good, Susan." Another sigh and he made the leap. "Okay, here it is. It has to do with a street shooting this afternoon in Little Havana. A Cuban from the Democratic Revolutionary Front named Hector Solas and a CIA agent named Masden were both killed. I was there"

"Hector Solas? He works for Doctor Rivas. I just saw him at a refugee fundraiser. I have an appointment to interview him tomorrow."

"At that fundraiser, you might also have seen a hotshot named Armand Ortiz."

She nodded. "He was murdered at his nightclub. The crime desk drew that one, but I know those guys. We kibitz all the time.

"Tell me what people are saying on the street about an invasion."

Her brow furrowed. "Ortiz was tied up in that?"

"Strictly low echelon. Someone wants it to look like Solas killed Ortiz."

"But...why?"

"Solas is supposed to be a Castro spy. Ortiz was a Castro spy. The killing is supposed to read like a falling out among spies."

Susan pursed her lips and softly said, "Whew. That's hot stuff. But you sound like you don't think Solas did kill Ortiz."

"It fits too well. Too tidy. In my business, tidy never happens. It gives us our Castro spy inside the coalition, so we can stop looking for anyone else. The main thing I don't like is how Rivas is key in the case against Solas. He claims Hector asked him for a lift to the Paradiso and that he waited outside in his car while Solas went in around the time Ortiz was murdered."

Susan was frowning. "But Doctor Rivas has done time in a Castro prison. He has a record here in Miami of loyal service in the anti-Communist movement. He's raised more than half a million dollars for the refugees."

Morgan's frown matched hers. "And Hector Solas was a new man in the organization with no traceable personal history. The CIA has told the cops to lay off the case, that they'll keep an eye on Rivas, and maybe they do have an airtight case against a dead man who can't defend himself. I just want to be sure."

CHAPTER 18

Seven years earlier, the U.S. Naval air base at Opa-Locka, in suburban Miami, had provided air support for the CIA's secret involvement in the Guatemala coup. These days, the airfield was largely abandoned. Rows of two-story barracks buildings were unlighted, murky hulks set well inside the chain-link fence. Even the runway was blacked out.

Morgan arrived with Resnick, clad again in the jungle camouflage fatigues he'd worn in Nam, cleaned and pressed and fitting him like a second skin. He had eased thoughts of everything else from his mind, including—especially—any thoughts about Susan or Vera, and was focused on nothing but the mission, thankful for the training and discipline that allowed him to do this.

A group of men was gathered in front of a dark hangar, standing near an unmarked C-54 transport plane. The C-54 had been used to transport recruits to the training camps early on in the operation. Its windows were painted black. As he and Resnick drew closer to the group, Morgan identified Garrett and the leaders of the Democratic Revolutionary Front.

While still beyond their earshot, he said, "What's Rivas doing here?"

Resnick sent him a sideways glance. "What do you mean? I'd say he was cleared of suspicion when that bus ran down Hector Solas."

"But what if we're wrong about Hector and he wasn't a spy?"

"Then why the hell did he open fire on us? Why did he shoot down Masden like a dog in the street?"

"I'm just thinking."

"Don't worry, Graveyard. Garrett had to give a briefing that he'd scheduled with the coalition here tonight or it would have looked fishy if he'd cancelled. That's why they're here. They've been given your cover story that you're flying down as an observer, nothing more. They don't even know that we suspect that one of them is a spy."

"What about Ortiz? You and Garrett aren't writing that off as a closed case, are you?"

"Don't worry," said Resnick. "I don't like the smell of that one, either. I'll follow through on Rivas personally and Ortiz, and I'll let you know what I come up with."

There followed a brief exchange with Garrett and the others. Garrett was cordial but cool. Rivas flashed a toothy smile when he and Morgan shook hands for a second time that day.

Then Morgan was making himself as comfortable as possible amid the bulky shapes of secured parcels and supplies in the cargo bay of the C-54. Within minutes, the plane was accelerating down the runway into the take-off.

And not long into the flight, with the steady thrumming of the engines and the smoothness of flight lulling him, unbidden thoughts of daughter and wife managed their way through the training and discipline, to pester him with concern and second thoughts.

He shouldn't have asked Susan to help. She had jumped at his offer, of course, visions of a Pulitzer Prize dancing in her head, and he'd been so frustrated by his uncertainty about Rivas and not knowing who to trust that it had blinded him when he first realized that his daughter could be a source of critical information. And so he had put her in harm's way. He had drawn her into a shadow-world where a man had been strangled last night and a CIA agent gunned down today, a world of treacherous, amoral, deadly people. He had allowed her to willingly become a part of it. He shouldn't have. He was watching his marriage, his world of normalcy that nurtured and sustained between missions, slip through his fingers. Was he losing his professional grip, too? Graveyard Morgan, the screw-the-book maverick, had really screwed up this time, compromising his integrity by discussing classified information with his reporter daughter just because a spy from Havana was supposed to be so damned important. That's what Vera was talking about, wasn't it? Always the mission came first, even before their own daughter and his integrity. Yeah, a *big* screw-up. He saw that clearly now. And yes, Vera would skin him alive just hearing about it and he wouldn't blame her. There was a communications blackout, with the invasion already set in motion, and so there was no way for him now to contact Susan and instruct her not to get involved.

And if he could reach her, would she listen? No, she would not. It was too late to stop what he'd started by drawing her in.

Eels of apprehension slithered across the lining of his stomach. If anything happened to Susan, he would not be able to live with himself.

What the hell was happening with his family? Susan and Vera. The two most important people in his life. Their photos in his wallet accompanied him on missions. Yet with every passing minute, aboard this plane, everything that meant anything to him was slipping away behind him. Or maybe they were leaving him behind, the two most important people in his life moving into the future, changing and growing like people were supposed to as they moved through life, while he remained as he had always been, as if nothing could ever change.

But he was a soldier, dammit. What was his life about if not duty?

But what was his *first* duty? A man's first duty was to his family. His father had taught him that. Pop had never *not* been there for his family. He and mother were gone now, but the image of watching his father strap on a policeman's badge and gun before he left for work every morning to earn a wage to support his family, was something Morgan would carry to his grave. The old man gave everything he had, every day of his life, for the ones he loved the most.

But then, Pop never gave up being a cop...

Morgan thought maybe the best thing he could do for everyone involved was to let Vera go. Let her have the divorce if that's what she wanted. He was growing uneasy about this life he led, so why shouldn't she? But he was a soldier and a soldier couldn't just walk away.

Stated simply, it came down to which was more important: saving the world, or saving his family?

He had to stop thinking like that.

He had a job to do.

CHAPTER 19

Maria Quintana awoke with torturous images wracking her mind, the remnants of a nightmare. Gradually she realized that it had been a nightmare. She was in her bed, warm and safe in her husband's arms.

Morning sunlight tinted the drawn shade a reddish gold that warmed their bedroom. She became aware of the world beyond the open window, the scents and sounds of Little Havana. A samba played from someone's transistor radio nearby.

"Wake up, Maria." Rosario's embrace hugged her. His whisper in her ear was gentle and soothing. "It's only a dream, my darling, only a dream."

Her Rosario was a good man, a strong man. A laborer. His meager wages, combined with her income as Doctor Rivas' secretary, allowed them to afford their small apartment, which was the only place in the world where she felt truly comfortable and secure. Only this month they had begun a joint savings account.

She was three months pregnant, which is why Rosario was so gentle. Soon her belly would swell. She hoped that he would still find her attractive...

As always, images from her nightmare faded slowly, but not the depression of her spirit that they always left in their wake.

She said, "I was in prison again."

He kissed the back of her neck, sending sweet shivers down her spine, as always. She loved his kisses.

"You have not had the dream in a long time. The memory fades. It *is* fading, Maria. Release it. Let it go."

"But...there was more this time."

"More?"

"A face. I remembered...a face." A tremor coursed through her and she drew deeper into his embrace. "It was...terrible."

"But it was a dream, my love. You have been through so much."

"And I can't stop thinking about Hector. I can't believe he was a Castro spy. Only two nights ago he was with me, assisting Doctor Rivas in raising funds to fight the Communists. I can't believe it, Rosario. I just can't."

Rosario whispered in her ear. "I so hate to see you like this. Let me make the memories go away. It is a husband's duty, is it not?"

They had been married for a month. A good man, yes. They'd met at a church dance. Like her, Rosario was forty-five years old and, like her, he had been in America for little more than a year. In Cuba he had driven a truck for one of the oil companies and after the revolution no one would hire him. They had taken a liking to each other from the moment they met. She had previously noticed him at Mass. Soon he was courting her and three months later they were married.

Rosario made her feel beautiful, as no man ever had. When she looked into a mirror, she saw the lines at the corners of her brown eyes and mouth, she saw the extra weight she'd put on and the streaks of silver in her jet-black hair. But Rosario made her feel as if he had never held a woman as beautiful as she, and he proved his words most passionately in their marriage bed. It was wonderful to be in love and feel *alive* again.

She had not had the dream since their wedding day.

Until now.

It hadn't been easy for her after the revolution, before her escape from the island prison that was Castro's Cuba. She had been an office clerk, had never been a political person, but members of the staff at the company where she worked, including her best friend, were very political anti-Communists. Castro's government had made it extremely difficult for her until they were convinced beyond a doubt that she knew nothing of her friends' counter-revolutionary activities. Once this was established, the government had no use for her and completely lost interest in her. She'd had some money saved, hidden away. Her mother and father were with God. She had never re-married in Cuba after she lost her first husband to cancer seven years earlier. She left aboard one of the fishing boats that carried refugees for a price. After arriving in America, things had been difficult at first too, as they were for most refugees. But she had employable skills and these had led to her position with Doctor Rivas.

Her life—a loving husband, a grueling work schedule—had seemed to hold at bay those terrible, vivid memories that had lived in the nightmares that had tormented her for months after *it* happened.

The dream.

That dream.

She was back in the cell at the militia post at Giron, where they were being held for interrogation...

But this time, she had seen a face in her dream.

A face she somehow knew from somewhere. A face she had seen recently and yet a face from the past. A face she had blocked from her tormented memories.

Rosario nibbled her left ear lobe. The nibble made her sigh. Arousal stirred within her and when she moved against him, within his embrace, it was playful and sensual. The images of her dream were receding beneath her growing desire.

She whispered, "You're right, darling. I need you. But is there time?"

Without looking at the bedside clock, Rosario reached over and turned the clock so it faced the wall.

"For us, Maria, there will always be time."

They often made love in the morning, despite the early hour each was due at work, and usually a pleasant, relaxed-yet-vibrant feeling stayed with her out in the world, once she left the secure sanctuary of their home, often well into the afternoon, to be renewed when she and Rosario would speak briefly on the telephone during his lunch break.

Today was different.

The brisk pace of her schedule at the two-level, sand-colored brick house just off Calle Ocho, which was only two blocks from her home, did not erase the wispy tendrils of her nightmare. She arrived an hour before Doctor Rivas, as was her custom, and had been kept busy ever since fielding the barrage of phone calls and people coming and going, not to mention trying to catch up with correspondence.

Most days, her job required her complete concentration. But this morning, she couldn't shake the idea that *something* from her subconscious needed no more than the slightest nudge to force it through to the surface and be recognized for what it was, and then she would know the face in her dream.

Or maybe she was just upset by what had happened to Hector. She had so liked the earnest young man fresh from the island, so impassioned about his work for *La Causa*. For Hector to shoot a Federal agent to death, and to then die so horribly, chased into the path of a bus before it could truly be determined whether or not he was a Castro spy was so shocking, so terrible, so sad.

Doctor Rivas told her about it when he arrived for work, and he told her that the incident involving Hector was not being made public. When anyone asked why Hector was not about, queries were to be shrugged off as if Hector had merely left town unexpectedly without telling anyone. Doctor Rivas seemed to accept at face value the allegations against Hector.

She could not, and she had said so. She felt sorry for Doctor Rivas. She'd been his secretary long enough to read his moods. An attractive man for his age with classic Castilian good looks, he was withdrawn today. He must have felt a terrible inner disappointment and sense of betrayal.

Or was it something else?

Maria wondered, And why should I think such a thing?

A man named Resnick had come upstairs to visit with the Doctor shortly after eleven.

Resnick had been with Doctor Rivas behind the closed door of the Doctor's office for more than thirty minutes when Susan Morgan arrived for her appointment.

The young woman from the Herald wore a summer print dress, white shoes with sensible low heels and a matching handbag. *"Buenos dias,* Maria."

Maria brightened at the friendly, forthright manner of the young woman that had caught her attention at the church fundraiser. It wasn't often that the Americanos who came to the house, like Resnick, ever bothered to speak Spanish.

"Buena dias, Miss Morgan. Habla espanol?"

"No, I'm afraid that's about the extent of my vocabulary for now, but I hope to learn. And please, Maria, call me Susan."

The office door behind Maria's desk opened. Doctor Rivas and Resnick emerged, cordially shaking hands. Agent Resnick wore a straw hat and lurid print Hawaiian shirt.

The Doctor was saying, "Mister Resnick, if at any time you wish to discuss this matter further, by all means expect my full cooperation. I apologize again for being so lax in my judgment as to have not realized what Hector was up to."

"I appreciate that, Doctor, and thanks." Resnick gave a nod that took in Maria and Susan. "Well, you folks take care." He departed, not waiting to be introduced to Susan.

As Resnick's footsteps grew fainter down the stairs, Maria said, "Doctor Rivas, may I introduce—"

The Doctor's features brightened and his smile flashed almost as brightly as the sunshine streaming in through the windows.

"But of course, the lovely lady reporter from the Herald." He extended a hand. "Miss Morgan, was it not?"

They shook hands.

"I'm flattered, Doctor. Thank you for seeing me. I hope this is a good time for a short interview."

"But of course. And how short the interview is will be determined by how far back you want me to go, miss. What has happened to me in the year-and-a-half since the bastard Castro imprisoned me at Giron would fill a book."

He motioned her through the doorway, into his office, and Maria caught a gleam in the *gringa's* eye. The lady reporter was young enough to be her daughter.

Doctor Rivas added, "Please hold my calls, Maria."

And his office door closed after them.

She remained at her desk and for several seconds could not move, so much was happening at once within her stunned mind. She felt as if her brain wanted to explode from the pressure of everything racing through it. The *something* in her subconscious had suddenly nudged through to conscious awareness. She realized that she'd raised the back of a clenched fist to her mouth. She was gnawing on a knuckle. She stared at the door to the inner office. The Doctor speaking to the gringa reporter, an offhand remark...and the demons of Maria's past had prompted the nudge.

Anxious fear crept through her like cold blood. She should never have left the safety and security of Rosario's strong arms, the intimate warmth of their bed. She could not take her eyes away from the closed office door.

Could she be wrong?

She sat there like that for a long while, not knowing what to do.

CHAPTER 20

"Garrett."

"It's me," said Resnick. He stood in a phone booth on noisy Calle Ocho, one block away from the sand-colored brick house. "Have you got the scrambler on?"

"Always. So how's the good doctor?"

"On his guard but I guess that's only natural with the invasion set to start."

"How did you play it?"

"Rivas has got no reason to think my visit was anything but routine follow-up."

"What did he say about Ortiz?"

"Claims he's never been to the Paradiso except for the other night when Hector asked him for a lift after the fund raiser. Claims he knows about Ortiz by reputation only."

"You told him Ortiz was a Castro spy?"

"I did. Didn't seem to faze him. He was friendly as hell, as if he expected me and wanted me to know that it was okay, he didn't hold it against me personally for asking him questions."

"In other words, zip."

"Not in other words," said Resnick. "That is the word. If Doctor Rivas is dirty, we're no closer to getting any proof of it than we were before."

Maria had decided what to do by the time Susan stepped from Rivas' office, following their interview. She could have been gone for lunch, but often stayed at her desk during the noon hour, wanting to be here if Rosario called but also because there was always a backlog of work.

Rivas said, "Maria, how nice that you are here. Miss Morgan was hoping to interview you next."

Maria hadn't expected this. "Of course, Doctor."

"Well then, I'll leave you two," said Rivas. "Good day, Miss Morgan."

"Good day, Doctor, and thank you again." She waited until Rivas had returned to his office, closing the door after him. Then she said, "And thank you, Maria. I needed to interview Doctor Rivas, but I feel it's equally important that our readers get the woman's perspective of what's happening here."

When Maria saw up close the unwavering directness and intelligence in the eyes of this young woman, she knew that she was right in taking the chance, the big risk, that she was about to take.

She rose from her desk. "I was wondering, Susan." She spoke with a cautious glance in the direction of the Doctor's office door. "Could we have lunch together?"

The Blue Palm was a friendly neighborhood bar and grill that did a brisk lunch hour business. Recorded Latin jazz created a pleasant musical underpinning to the chatter of conversation from surrounding tables. A waitress appeared. Maria ordered a salad. Susan ordered the same.

When the waitress was out of earshot, Maria plunged ahead without further considering the matter. "I want you to know, Susan that I appreciate very much your agreeing to have lunch with me so that we may talk."

"It's my pleasure." Susan made an exaggerated display of sniffing at the aromatic scents from the direction of the kitchen. "This place smells delicious."

"Before we begin," said Maria, "I must ask you to promise me that what I am about to tell you will remain confidential, between the two of us only."

Susan's eyes grew serious. "I hope it's something that leads to something that I *can* use."

"Please understand. I wish to protect innocent people from harm."

Susan nodded. "I understand. You'd like me to hear what you have to tell me, then forget that it was you who told me. But I am free to write about anything I learn after you've pointed me in the right direction."

"*Si*. Is that too great a favor to ask?"

"Well, you have me interested. Okay, Maria, our conversation is confidential. Does this concern Doctor Rivas?"

"*Si*, it does. But first, Susan, I must beg your indulgence. I must tell you about a dream, a nightmare that I have had many times. It haunts me."

The young woman across the table was eyeing her intently now. "Tell me whatever you wish, Maria."

And so she told Susan about her arrest after the revolution, of her imprisonment at Giron, of her interrogation about the political activities of her friends. She paused only when the waitress brought their food.

Susan listened without comment.

Maria said, "They never physically tortured me at Giron. They tortured others, and they tried to frighten me. It is of one such incident that I dream. It is my nightmare." Her voice tapered off.

"Maria, you can finish this after we eat, if you'd rather."

"No. The nightmare...it really happened. It was the second week of my confinement. At night, from the dirt floor of my cell where I tried to sleep, I could hear the screams of men and sometimes women being tortured." A shudder coursed through her. "I will hear the screams until my dying day. Then one morning, the man in charge, a major named Medina, came into my cell with another man, to try again to make me tell him what he wanted to know. I have lived what happened next over and over in my nightmare.

"Major Medina is shouting questions at me. Then the other man holds out his hand for me to see what he is holding." Maria closed her eyes. "*He was holding...a bleeding eyeball in his hand!* He—*Madre de Dios!*—this man said to me, '*This eye belonged to Camilla.*'" Maria's eyes opened. They were glazed with moisture. "He did not need to tell me that. I recognized the... the thing he was tormenting me with. Camilla was my best friend. She had beautiful eyes, gray shot with a brilliant emerald green and a golden sliver in the iris. Yes, she was a beautiful woman, my friend, and we had been sent there together, then separated. And now her bloody eye, once so lovely, was a disgusting thing that stared up at me from the palm of the man's hand. The beast, Medina, gloated at my horror and put his face close to mine. '*She will not talk and so we did this to her,*' Medina told me. '*If you will not testify against them, we will tear out her other eye...and then we will do the same to you.*' That is my nightmare, Susan. That is what happened. A living nightmare. In truth I knew nothing about my friends' politics, and eventually I was released."

Susan had stopped eating. Her complexion was pale. "And your friend, Camilla?"

"I never saw her or the others again. When it comes to that part of the dream where the man shows me...what he showed me, I wake up. I wake up screaming. I have forgotten the face of the second man who was holding...*it*. I remember Major Medina, I remember everything else, and then...the shock of the moment erases the face of the man from my mind." Maria smiled self-consciously. "I have a friend who was a psychologist in Havana before the Revolution. She waits tables now. She is our waitress here today. She has told me that it is not unusual for a person to block out parts of a bad memory. She helped me to understand. Then, not long ago I got married."

"Well, congratulations."

"*Gracias.* After Rosario and I married, the nightmares went away."

"Yes, love will do that, I'm told."

Maria said, "Until this morning. I awoke from the nightmare today."

"Something triggered the nightmare," said Susan.

Maria nodded. "Then at the office, when Doctor Rivas invited you into his office, he spoke of having been imprisoned at Giron after the revolution. I knew he had been detained there. He and I were held there at different times, I several months after him." She interrupted herself, asking, "Do you know about Hector Solas?"

"I know what happened to him, and that some people think he was a spy for Castro."

Maria hesitated. "I was told that information would not be released."

"Please, Maria. I'm on your side. Go on with your story."

"Very well. I believe you, Susan. You have honest eyes. The night I met you, when Hector and I were with Doctor Rivas at his speaking engagement at that church to raise funds, we were very successful. You see why it is so difficult for me to believe my intuition. The Doctor has done so much for *La Causa*."

Susan leaned forward, and seemed to be holding her breath. "What happened at the church?"

"There was the crowd to hear him speak, of course. I knew some of the people in the audience. Others were new to me. But there was one man...I had the sensation that I *knew* him from somewhere else. I asked Doctor Rivas who he was and the Doctor told me the man's name was Armand Ortiz."

"He ran the Club Paradiso until he was murdered that night after the fundraiser."

Maria returned to pecking at her salad idly with her fork. "It bothered me. Where would I know such a man? Did you ever have the feeling of knowing that you knew someone from somewhere, but you cannot remember where?"

Susan exhaled her held breath slowly. "Ortiz is the face in your nightmare."

"*Si*. His was the face that I had blocked from my memory for so long. He was the one who did that to Camilla...and showed *it* to me. He tortured and killed the others. There were screams every night from the cell where he worked. It was Ortiz. Then today, when I overheard the Doctor speak to you of being held at Giron, everything came together in my mind. At that instant it came to me that Armand Ortiz was the man with Medina."

Susan's face grew serious creases. "Are you sure?"

"*Si*. There is no doubt in my mind."

Susan leaned back, her frown only deepening. "If Doctor Rivas was imprisoned at Giron, he would have been interrogated by Ortiz. And when he saw Ortiz at the church fundraiser, he would have then known at once that Ortiz was a Castro agent."

Maria nodded. She clasped the crucifix at her throat. "I cannot tell you how good it feels to share this with someone. I do want to think the best of Doctor Rivas."

Susan said, "Maybe Ortiz was not the man Medina charged with interrogating Doctor Rivas, and so their paths never crossed at the prison."

Maria closed her eyes. "Ortiz was the man in my nightmare. The man who tortured my friends. I'm glad he's dead, whoever killed him. But if Doctor Rivas did recognize Ortiz and said nothing, does that not mean that Doctor Rivas is a Castro agent, not Hector Solas?"

Susan paused until after the waitress came to refill their drinks and leave a check.

"My God, Maria. This could be dynamite."

"Dynamite, *Si*. It is why no one must know that I've told you these things. And I feel guilty, suspecting Doctor Rivas. I have the highest regard for him. He works tirelessly for *La Causa*. What right have I to suspect him of anything? Dreams. Intuition. Uncertainty. Coincidence."

"Yes, Maria. I'm a woman. I understand these things. But what made you so suspicious in your heart that you'd risk contacting a reporter?"

"They think Hector Solas was a spy." A trace of anger and indignation tinged Maria's words. "Hector attended Mass with Rosario and me. He was a guest in our home. I cannot believe he was dishonest. The man he killed... yes, he was hot-tempered. He was *Cubano*. If he had been lied to, driven to desperation...I believe our friend Hector was a victim, not a spy. Susan, what should I do? If Doctor Rivas is a Castro agent, if he was responsible for what happened to Hector, then I must be a part of doing something about it."

Susan smiled a humorless smile. "I don't think Rosario would approve. You've done more than your part, Maria. Let me take it from here. I'll look for proof. You go on about your job. Don't get into this any deeper."

Maria reached across the table and clasped Susan's hands in both of her own. "*Gracias, mi amiga.* I know I have done the right thing."

Rivas sat behind the steering wheel, alone in his Buick, parked a half-block away on the opposite side of busy Calle Ocho. He watched through the Buick's windshield as the two women said goodbye and parted company in front of the Blue Palm.

Susan Morgan walked to a Ford Fairlane.

Maria Quintana walked away, down the sidewalk in the direction of their offices, not looking to her left or right.

The Ford Fairlane drove off.

Rivas did not follow it. His eyes remained on Maria.

CHAPTER 21

Gulls swooped. Their cawing mingled with the sibilant surf. Huge combers, long, white, regular, rolled onto the beach at Giron, within view of the entrance to the Bay of Pigs. The sun was a yellow ball in a clear white sky.

Fidel Castro stood on a sandy knoll with Major Medina and Colonel Parnov, the chief Russian liaison officer. As always, he wore green field fatigues with a holstered sidearm.

Behind them was a column of armored military vehicles that had brought Castro and Parnov here from Havana. A security detail had established a defense perimeter, blocking off this part of beach. Nearby, laborers worked industriously on the final stages of construction of a line of stucco bungalows.

Castro observed this, his boots firmly planted, his hands on his hips, a cigar protruding from the corner of his mouth.

"Did you know, *amigos*, that one of my passions is undersea fishing?" He spoke in English, their mutual language. "I like to weigh down my belt with two pounds of lead. I can stay underwater for two minutes. That is a long time without oxygen tanks. Hunting *pargo* fish and lobster with a spear gun here around Giron, the memories this place holds for me...it's good to visit here again.

Parnov was a squat man with jowly, flushed features. He wore a straw fedora and a shapeless suit of dull gray. He squinted in the harsh sunlight.

"Three days since their invasion force set sail from Puerto Cabezas. The invasion is inevitable. Señor Premier, we should be in Havana, monitoring developments."

Castro said, "I know, but sometimes those damn walls close in. I was raised in the country, you see. It's where my soul lives." He surveyed the bungalows under construction. "When this tourist village is completed, it will be a boon to the local economy." He directed a meaningful glance at Medina. "I only wish, Major, that you were making better progress at rounding up Felix Carriles and his band of dissidents."

Medina's uniform was crisply pressed. His spit-polished boots reflected the sun. "I have mobilized every resource, *Commandante*."

Parnov said, "You must do better. We have traced radio signals to this vicinity."

Medina directed his response to Castro. "I have a network of informants. Surveillance of suspected dissidents has been intensified. We will crush them, *Commandante*."

Castro blew smoke in his face.

"See that you do, Major, or you will no longer be a Major. You are dismissed." Castro eyed Parnov. "That is unless you have anything further you wish to discuss, Colonel."

Parnov said, "That will be all," and when they were alone, he said to Castro, "We've supplied your armed forces with the best training and equipment available. They're about to have their mettle tested."

Castro's gaze was fixed over the roofs of the bungalows, out across the blue-green expanse of ocean.

"You don't care about my men, *comrade*." He emphasized the word with subtle scorn. "You care about how their performance in the coming battle will reflect on your standing in the halls of the Kremlin."

Parnov irritably wiped sweat from his eyes. "And what's wrong with that? I miss Moscow, and my family."

"You will see both soon enough and with much to your credit. Do not worry, my Russian friend. The Soviet Union buys the sugar and the oil we'd been selling to the *Americanos* before their embargo, and you supply us with the means to protect ourselves. We have an interest in common. But make no mistake. My people fight and die for Mother Cuba. They will not fail her. They will not fail *me*. Let the invasion come. We are ready."

"What news from Miami?"

"Doctor Rivas appears to have been successful in diverting suspicion from himself, but he has nothing new to report."

"And your man in Nicaragua with the brigade?"

"Still no final word on precisely when and where the strike will come."

"And the American soldier sent by the President to Puerto Cabezas, Morgan? The man is in our KGB files, did you know that? They call him Graveyard because he is so dangerous."

Castro glowered at the glowing tip of his cigar. "No one is more dangerous than Fidel."

Parnov swallowed hard, then said, "There is concern that you are most dangerous to yourself."

Castro's bushy eyebrows drew together. "What do you mean by that?"

"I mean," said Parnov rapidly, "that it may have been injudicious of you to kill the American agent, Lehman, when he landed here to assist the underground. He could have been made to tell us things."

Castro studied his cigar, then returned it to his mouth and returned his eyes to the sea. "When this is past, I will reward myself with a visit back here for sport. But as you say, Colonel, we should be in Havana. Let us return to Point One. This resort has been a pet project of mine. It's done my spirit good to see my dream become a reality."

He stalked back toward the column of vehicles. Parnov hurried to keep apace.

Castro halted abruptly. He turned and studied the beach.

Parnov said, "What is it?"

Castro's eyes were narrow. He was scrutinizing the bungalows and the beach beyond.

"You know, this would make a great place for a landing." He pointed to a one-story concrete house near the bungalows, which commanded a full view of the beach. "We should place a .50-caliber machine gun there, just in case."

From several hundred yards beyond the defense perimeter, Felix Carriles centered the crosshairs of his rifle's scope on Castro's forehead.

He whispered, "I could take him out so easily right now. We would be gone before they knew where the shot came from."

He and Santos and Carmen were stretched flat, side-by-side, on an outcrop of ground that overlooked the beach and the vehicles and the figures below.

Santos' face gleamed with sweat beneath his shaggy hair and beard. He rested his hand on the barrel of Felix's rifle and lowered it.

"We would only give our enemies a martyr. If Fidel was dead, there are others—Che and Fidel's brother, Raul. They would step in to take command."

Felix removed his eye from the scope. "It is as you say." He sighed. "But what a pity to pass such a golden opportunity."

Carmen watched him with uncertainty. "I joined this group to become a freedom fighter, not an assassin."

Santos chuckled and arched a bushy eyebrow at Felix. "The little one is troubled by ideals, I see."

She lifted her chin. "I have as much reason as anyone to seek vengeance. Fidel must pay for his crimes, but not with an assassin's bullet. He must be tried in a Cuban court of law."

Santos tugged at his beard. "I hate to say it, Felix, but she does make sense. Give Fidel a fair trial, *then* execute him."

As they watched, the figures below boarded the armored vehicles and the convoy drove off, leaving the beach to the workmen at the bungalows, to the gulls, the sun and the eternal lapping of the combers upon the beach.

Felix got to his feet. "We should not be out like this in the daylight, not with the invasion so close."

They withdrew.

Santos' bear-like frame jiggled with mirth. "At least I can look forward to telling the others how close Fidel came to catching a bullet!"

CHAPTER 22

The staging area's airstrip, at Puerto Cabezas on the northern coast of Nicaragua, was code named Happy Valley.

It reminded Morgan of Vietnam.

A ten-foot-high bamboo fence, topped with concertina wire, enclosed the motley collection of Quonset huts clustered at one end of the runway under a low, black cloud cover. It had rained during the night, making the jungle around this makeshift staging area nothing but a steam bath, mist rising from the ground, the dripping sounds of water falling from everything.

He arrived in time for morning chow, and so he was wide-awake by time he was shown into the operations shack, which was in its own specially secured area behind a bamboo fence manned by rifle-toting sentries.

Three men wearing casual civilian attire were waiting for him, seated at one end of a twenty-five-foot long table. A huge map of Cuba pinned across an entire wall dominated the interior of the shack. The ceiling was decorated with unfolded orange-and-white parachutes. The constant rumble of cargo runs from Opa-Locka, touching down on the newly constructed landing strip, spilled through the open windows.

The man at the head of the table, a dark complexioned man in his early thirties, stood and extended a hand with a lack of enthusiasm bordering on indifference. "Sergeant, I'm Ben Conklin. I'm the Air Operations Director here. With most of the Brigade having set sail, I guess that also makes me the ranking Agency officer-in-charge here."

Morgan nodded. "Conklin."

Conklin nodded to the men with him. "This is General Hudson," he indicated a gruff-featured six-footer who gave Morgan a curt nod of welcome. "The General is honchoing the air force the Agency put together for us. And this is Todd Medlow, Assistant to the First Secretary of the Nicaraguan American Embassy. That means he's the Agency's Regional Chief of Station."

Medlow was blond-haired, in his late twenties, with a trimmed moustache and horn-rimmed glasses. An Agency COS post was a one-year tour of duty and was generally considered a stepping-stone for assignment up and out of the field. An international incident during a station chief's watch would be catastrophic to his career. Medlow wore the look of a man wholly aware of this.

Medlow ignored Morgan. He glared at Conklin.

"Why don't you just hand out cards with my address and phone number while you're at it? Just what we need, one more goddamn Green Beret G.I. Joe."

Morgan said, "Shut up, squirt."

Hudson grinned. "Welcome to the nut house, Graveyard. Yeah, they told me your handle. Don't let Medlow get on your nerves. Everyone here would like to be somewhere else. Hell, I'm supposed to be CO of an Air National Guard unit back home and here I am swatting mosquitoes big as birds and nurse-maiding a pack of hotshot Cuban pilots."

Medlow shifted his angry eyes to Morgan. "Conklin tells me that you've got top security clearance and that you've been briefed. But no one's gotten around to briefing me on what the hell you're doing here."

Conklin sighed as if he thought this subject had been laid to rest. "Let's just say Morgan is here to assist me in whatever capacity I deem appropriate."

Morgan said, "So that's why they call this place Happy Valley. You guys are just one big happy family."

Hudson harrumphed. "Anything but. This is the most fucked up, asinine operation I ever saw and believe it, I've seen my share. A few days ago we sent off a navy made up of six rusted out hulks that stand a good chance of sinking before they reach Cuba. They're small and they're not even military vessels. Those ships are old tubs and we're sending them into combat. And I can't say much better about this air force I've been handed."

"We've done our job," said Conklin. "You've seen to it that your pilots, maintenance and armament specialists have had the best training." He added for Morgan's benefit, "Washington sent us old B-26 bombers left over from the last war, but they've been mothballed outside Tucson where the dry air kept them from deteriorating."

Hudson harrumphed again as if this too had been haggled over. "We'll see."

Medlow was shaking his head. "So the bulk of the Brigade set sail two days ago and most of the instructors have rotated back to the states and only the paratroopers are left, waiting for their orders. That's great. We should be closing up shop here. I don't like it."

Conklin said, "Relax. Hey, the spics get on my nerves too with all their political squabbling. Cubans. What a bunch. In tears one minute, cracking up laughing the next." He said to Morgan, "Most of the guys in this Brigade fancy themselves lovers, not fighters, and they're right about that. But they're what we had to work with."

Morgan said, "They're also the guys who are going to do the fighting."

Hudson nodded. "And the dying. An operation like this should be in military hands, not CIA. The Pentagon should be handling the training and support, not a supposedly covert spy organization, for crying out loud."

Conklin said, "Enough. The only thing that matters right now is getting this mission done. Morgan is here on observer status. That's all anyone needs to know. Now let's get to work."

Medlow and Hudson rose from the table at the implied dismissal. Hudson nodded to Morgan and left. Medlow stayed behind.

"I'll want hourly reports radioed in code to your contact in Managua," he told Conklin. "I don't want anything to go wrong here, do you understand me? This whole thing could blow up in our face at the last minute."

Conklin gave him a nasty grin. "Shut up, squirt."

Medlow's pale face flushed a sudden and brilliant red, but he said nothing. He stormed out.

Conklin's grin grew less nasty once he and Morgan were alone. He said, "That little butt-hole has been getting on my nerves since I got here."

"Let me get this straight," said Morgan. "You're the only one who knows the real reason I'm here?"

"Yeah, but I didn't want you to be a complete mystery man. Those two had to meet you or they'd have made a point of finding out why you're here on their own, or they'd have raised hell when they couldn't find out."

"Up North, they think you've been infiltrated by a Castro spy. Anything to it?"

"The Harvard boys at Langley have more information to work with than I do. They could be right."

"Then we'd better tag him. Those ships of yours won't be floating around the Caribbean forever."

"My orders are to cooperate with you in dealing with the spy when he's tagged. So what do I do, Graveyard? Hold him down while you slit his throat?"

"No need for that," said Morgan. "I do my own dirty work."

Conklin's tour of the base took more than an hour because Morgan insisted on a pace that allowed him to absorb the staging area's layout. He was showed the Quonset huts and hangars where the supplies were stored, the Air Operations shack where they spent time chatting with General Hudson, and he saw the lines of tents where the Brigade lived, surrounded by barbed wire and Americans in civvies, armed with automatic weapons. Morgan picked up on a collective mood of anticipation mixed with impatience. Beyond the living area were the bulky C-46's that would carry the paratroopers into combat, parked near the B-26 bombers. This "air force" had been sanitized. There were no numbers or insignia on the aircraft.

Morgan and Conklin encountered a cluster of Cuban paratroopers, busy cleaning their rifles in the shade of a tent.

The platoon leader who stepped forward to greet them was in his early twenties, sporting a pencil-thin moustache, a toothy smile and an energetic, earnest manner. A crucifix was visible at the 'V' of his sharply pressed fatigues. His boots were spit-polished.

Conklin introduced them. "Sergeant Morgan, Antonio Perez."

They shook hands. Perez had a firm handshake.

Morgan asked, "How's morale, Top?"

Perez's chest almost puffed out visibly. "Morale is very high. We are freedom fighters." He threw back his shoulders. "We will accomplish not only our combat mission but also the ultimate objective, the overthrow of Castro."

"You've memorized that speech pretty well." Morgan softened the barb with a smile.

Perez took no offense. "I speak the truth, *señor.*"

"But not the whole truth. Right, Top?"

Perez glanced at Conklin, who nodded.

Perez grinned and shrugged expressively, a purely Latin gesture. "If you insist. Like any Cuban, I enjoy a good debate. It is widely felt within the ranks that control of the Brigade should not be in the hands of foreigners, no matter how friendly you are. It is felt by many that command should rest with the Cuban leadership exiled in Florida."

"Problem is," said Conklin, "none of this would be happening if it wasn't for us friendly foreigners. We've trained you, supplied you and we're transporting you."

Perez nodded. "Exactly. You are transporting us into combat. The concern is that you will desert us when we need you most, when the fighting begins."

Conklin said, "Dammit, Antonio, we've been over this. There will be U.S. ships along the route, watching. They're supposed to be weather ships but they're more than that. And you'll have air cover when you get there. U.S. marines will be offshore in case they're needed. And there are other landing forces that have trained just like yours in other places, and they're poised to strike."

Several of the men had set down their rifles and stepped forward to listen in.

One, a huge man with a brutish face, stepped closer. He smelled of rum. "You get us to Havana, gringos, and we won't need your help. The Castro scum will be lined up against the wall and shot, and those will be the lucky ones. There will be no mercy."

Perez turned to face the man. "I would expect you to say that, Garcia," and he returned to Morgan and Conklin. "That's another reason why our Cuban leaders, not you Americans, should have been approved appointment to this Brigade. They would not have condoned the recruitment of Batista gunmen like Garcia here. There are more than two hundred of his ilk serving with us. Some are convicted felons."

The report Morgan had read in Miami had pointed out that the Brigade represented every walk of life in Cuba. There were the sons of families dispossessed by the Revolution, both of rich families but mostly what in America was called middle class, and there were the Batistanos like Garcia who had until not so long ago enforced the will of the brutal military government that had been overthrown.

Garcia's features darkened. "And why shouldn't those of us who served under Batista also serve in this Brigade?"

Perez said, "Batista was as merciless to my family as he was to the peasants from the hills who overthrew him. We only want what is ours— our homeland, no more. We want justice, not vengeance."

Morgan said, "Knock it off, both of you. Settle your internal differences after the mission is accomplished."

Garcia growled like a bull. He said, "Fucking gringos," and his right hand snaked around behind his back and reappeared with a wide-bladed combat knife that gleamed in the sunlight. He lunged, slashing out at Morgan.

CHAPTER 23

The blade swiped air where Morgan's throat had been seconds earlier. Garcia drew back for another lunge while Morgan was already moving in. Conklin pawed for his pistol. Then Garcia was brought down from an angle that took everyone by surprise.

Perez took Garcia by the arm and used the large man's weight to topple him to the ground. Perez remained standing and when Garcia started to draw himself up again, Perez kicked the knife from his hand.

Morgan laughed. "Girls, girls. Don't fight over me." He watched Garcia's every move, angry with himself at having been taken so unexpectedly.

"That's enough," said Conklin. His sidearm remained holstered but with his hand on the grip. "Break it up, both of you."

Perez's fists were drawn up. He shifted his weight from side to side, wordlessly challenging the other man.

Garcia ignored him. He brought himself to his feet. His brutish features were emotionless. "What about my knife? I need my knife."

Morgan said, "Take it. You guys are in this together whether you like it or not. The odds against you are high. Don't waste your time and energy fighting each other."

Garcia said nothing. He picked up his knife, returned it to its sheath at the small of his back and walked away, disappearing into the group of onlookers.

Conklin's hand remained on his holstered pistol as he watched Garcia walk away. "You'd better watch that one, stud."

Perez had stopped shifting his weight and clenching his fists. He said, "Garcia and I have been at odds since we met, but it should not have come to this."

"I owe you," said Morgan. "He could have gutted me like a fish." Perez smiled. "Oh, I think you would have handled him on your own, *señor*. I intervened only because I was standing closer to him than you. And these men are my responsibility, whether they like me or not."

Conklin spoke as if Perez was not present. "This is the kind of bullshit I was talking about. And they call themselves soldiers. No military discipline."

Perez drew himself erect. "We stand ready to fight. My men are restless, waiting for their orders. I'll determine how Garcia acquired the alcohol to get drunk, but I can sympathize. It's the waiting that gets to a man."

Conklin said, "Restless, hell. Your clique and that Batista bunch just flat hate each other's guts." He spat upon the ground. "Well, get over it. There's a practice jump this afternoon. That ought to keep you out of trouble."

Perez smiled his toothy smile at Morgan. "*Señor,* you're a paratrooper, is that not so? Would you care to join us on today's jump?"

Conklin scowled. "Hold on. That's a no go. It's not regulation."

Morgan said, "What about this operation is regulation? Sure, Antonio, I'll join you men for a jump. Thanks for the invitation. I'd be honored."

Conklin said, "Now wait a minute."

Perez's grin grew wider. "Meet us at the plane at 1300 hours. We will not leave without you."

And he left them to rejoin his men.

Morgan said to Conklin, "That part about giving them air cover, about other landing forces training for the invasion, about U.S. marines standing by. I, uh, hadn't heard about that."

Conklin grinned unpleasantly. "That's funny, neither have I."

"It's not true, then?"

"What the hell do you think? You want to know what I think?"

"Tell me."

"I think you're overstepping your orders, mister, going skydiving with those unruly sons-of-bitches."

"Don't worry about it. This won't slow me down. It could help."

"Help how? You think Perez is your man?"

Morgan shrugged. "I'm just wondering how he knew that I qualified to make a jump."

At 1300 hours, Conklin halted the Jeep next to the C-46 troop transport. Perez's platoon was unloading from the tarp-covered bed of a truck parked next to the plane. The airstrip sweltered in muggy, tropical jungle heat. Perez was just stepping down from the truck.

Conklin said, "There's your spy. What are you going to do, see that he has an accident during the jump?"

"I didn't say he's our man."

"Then how did he know your background?"

"Most of these guys aren't professional soldiers and they're sure as hell not professional spies, either. He let something slip that he shouldn't have known about. That doesn't make him a Castro spy. I'm not that easy to convince."

Conklin bristled visibly. "No one's trying to convince you of anything. I get the notion you're half soldier and half spy yourself. So how else would our friend, Antonio, know that you were a paratrooper?"

Perez saw them. He set his chute down on the truck bed and came toward the Jeep while his men continued from the truck, up a ramp and into a huge, black yawning mouth that was the tail end of the plane, each man carrying his parachute.

Morgan said, "I spent enough time in Miami to see that this operation has more leaks than a sieve. Who knows what information about any of us is floating through the rank and file? Perez could have picked it up like that and mentioned it because it's common knowledge. The guy's either a real amateur spy to slip up that easy, or he's no spy at all. If he's our man and he knows I'm down here to nail him, why didn't he let Garcia take care of me?"

"The spic's playing a ballsy game, I'll give him that," said Conklin in the final seconds before the subject of their conversation advanced to within earshot.

Morgan said, "I want to keep Perez alive. Maybe he's the key to another door."

Perez reached them, his toothy smile drawn wide for Morgan. "Amigo, you were not kidding! It is good to see you."

"Good to see you, Antonio."

The Cuban drew a deep breath, as if the air was not heavy with humidity. "I feel invigorated. This jump is no more than a training exercise, it's true, but it gets the heart working, no?" His grin faded and his glance took in Conklin. "A hell of a lot more fun that sitting about waiting for orders, that's for damn sure."

They watched Garcia, the last of the men to leave the truck and board the big transport plane. Garcia avoided looking in their direction.

Morgan said, "Any more trouble between you two?"

"No, I am happy to say. He avoids me, and that is acceptable."

"Yeah, I know what you mean. Don't know if I'd feel that comfortable with him along on the jump, if I were you."

Perez gave his Latin shrug. "I must trust him, whether I care to or not. Now, come. After the jump, let us go to the cantina in the village for *cerveza*."

"Sounds good," said Morgan with complete honesty. He alighted from the Jeep, toting his parachute.

"Remember," said Conklin, "you're only going up with these crazy Cubans for one jump, no more. Goddammit, Graveyard, I don't like this."

The plane's props thundered to life.

"Can't hear a thing you said," said Morgan.

He jogged with Perez to the back of the truck. Perez retrieved his parachute from the truck bed.

"I like your style, *amigo*."

"*Gracias*. Good luck, Antonio."

"As you Americas say," said Perez, "luck has nothing to do with it."

They double-timed up the ramp and boarded the plane. The hammering drone of the propellers made further conversation impractical.

The idea of going aloft and making a jump helped ease his irritation at not being able to get a better reading of Perez.

The C-46 taxied along the bumpy runway and felt to Morgan as if it were struggling to lift off into the cloudless, pale blue sky. He glanced around the interior of the plane. Perez was seated to his left, Garcia across from them. Garcia continued to avoid making eye contact with them. Shortly after they were airborne, the transport banked into a hard turn and the red light beside the open rear of the plane went on.

The crew chief braced himself against the powerful slipstream that pasted his flight suit over the contours of his body. He shouted in Spanish. "All right, everybody on your feet. Hook up! Check your equipment!"

Morgan stood with everyone else and cinched his harness straps tighter. He checked the quick release mechanism at his chest and adjusted the chinstrap of his helmet. There was something about leaping from an airplane at five hundred feet that was like nothing else. It was frightening to some, but the prospect did not frighten him. Like Perez, he found it exhilarating.

A buzzer sounded.

He hooked the snap fastener on his static line to the anchor cable that ran overhead and gave the line a testing tug, then began a hurried shuffle forward with the others, belly to backpack, toward the rear of the plane. Perez now stood behind him, the next one after him. Garcia was to Morgan's left. The wind howled through the gaping maw of the plane's tail end. The world five hundred feet below was a blur of green.

The crew chief was yelling, "*Go go go go go!*" as he tapped each man out in rapid succession.

Morgan's turn came. He went tumbling out on the heels of the man before him, diving into the plane's roaring prop-blast with Perez right behind him. Opened chutes dotted the sky below, the good-natured hoots and shouts from those men drifting up through the fading drone of the plane as it lumbered on. A series of gentle tugs at his back, a swinging lurch, and Morgan's rate of descent was checked. His parachute blossomed overhead.

A surprised scream pierced the air. A dark form went plummeting past Morgan after caroming off the side of his chute. Morgan quickly worked the risers, stabilizing his descent. He spent several moments searching before he spotted the figure below in a hurtling free fall, a six-foot length of static line whipping behind the man plunging toward earth. He had made eye contact with the man as he'd hurtled past. It was Antonio Perez.

Morgan wrenched his eyes away an instant before Perez impacted with the drop zone far below.

In the Operations Shack an hour later, Morgan inspected the static line clip in his hand. He and Conklin were alone, seated at the long conference table. Several inches of line dangled from the clip. After a careful study of the end of the length of line, Morgan returned the clip to Conklin.

"The cut is too clean. Those lines just don't break. There's maybe one chance in a million of that happening."

"Garcia did it. He had the opportunity. It would only take half a second when no one was looking."

Morgan nodded. He'd been thinking the same thing.

"He did it after Perez set his parachute down in the truck bed and came over to talk to us before the jump. Garcia was the last man out of that truck. He used the knife Perez gave back to him this morning. Garcia slipped the blade inside the loop and cut it three-fourths of the way through. That would be enough to withstand a safety check when we were aloft, but not enough to snap open the chute like it was supposed to."

Conklin tossed the static line clip onto the table. "I'm just glad Perez is out of the picture. He's the one they flew you down here to take out. Garcia just saved you the trouble."

Morgan's eyes lingered on the clip. "I wonder."

"About what?"

"I'm not sure. It's that something I told you about that keeps bugging me. I was impressed by Antonio's platoon on that jump. They've been made into ready-to-go airborne. A platoon leader has to take a lot of credit for that."

Conklin made a rude sound like he was coughing up phlegm. "They were trained by Green Berets before they got sent here, that's why they're good."

"Perez lived with those men. They were his brothers-in-arms. I'd be curious to know why and how he could talk himself into betraying them by becoming a spy for Castro."

"One of those noble brothers-in-arms sliced his static line."

Morgan said, "Garcia. I want him pulled from that platoon before the invasion."

Conklin laughed. "Now who would give a damn what you want, soldier boy? This is a CIA operation you've been assigned to, and your mission was to identify and nullify a spy. That was Perez and he's been nullified. Your work is done."

"I'll decide when my job is done. You've got no business sending Garcia into combat with those men."

Conklin's laugh became a sneer. "You're just pissed at Garcia because he killed that spy before you could. He did us all a favor. Garcia stays. I need every man I've got."

"You're going to get good men killed. The men in that platoon have trained long and hard to become as good as they are. They'll have enough to deal with when they hit the ground without having to look over their shoulders to make sure Garcia isn't coming at them with a knife."

Conklin's eyes were like flint. "Maybe you'd better read your orders again, Sarge." There was a knock at the door and he called, "Come in."

The communications officer appeared, an earnest, freckle-faced young man sporting a crew cut. "There's an Eyes Only for you at the radio shack, sir."

In the Comm shack, a Xerox Cryptomatic sat in the corner with its red light flashing. Conklin produced a set of keys. He unlocked and opened the classified drawer and withdrew the envelope, containing the transmission that had been automatically sealed. The envelope was labeled *Eyes Only—Station Commander.* They stepped out of the shack and found a spot where there was no foot traffic.

Conklin said, "Let's see what the eggheads at Langley have to say this time," and he opened the envelope. He started reading, then briskly folded the sheets without finishing them and slipped them back into the envelope.

He said to Morgan, "Well, that didn't take long. I've got to round up my platoon leaders and pilots. We're having us a briefing. Graveyard, your mission has just become irrelevant." He tapped the envelope with his fingertips. "This is it. The invasion is a *go.*"

CHAPTER 24

Maria Quintana looked at her wristwatch for the seventh time in ten minutes. She was alone in the upstairs of the house, at her desk. Late afternoon sunlight through the office windows did nothing to warm a chill of foreboding that she was unable to fight off. Traffic sounds from nearby Eighth Avenue carried through the open windows, but that was all. The dinner hour had emptied the lower level of the house as well. It was unusual for the house to be this quiet.

She wished Rosario would arrive.

Doctor Rivas had left for the day, ten minutes earlier.

"Offer you a ride, Maria?"

"No thank you, Doctor. My husband is meeting me here and we're going out for dinner."

"How nice. Well, good evening."

"Good evening, Doctor."

She did not regret going to meet the reporter, Susan, for lunch. There was no way Doctor Rivas could have learned about it. He'd acted no different toward her this afternoon; courtly, yet formal in an Old World manner, as was his style. At first after returning to the office following her lunch break, she had experienced some mild pangs of guilt. Then she told herself that she had done the right thing. Doctor Rivas had nothing to fear if there was a reasonable explanation for her suspicions.

She eyed again the closed door to his office. Only she and the Doctor had a key for it. And the Doctor never returned once he left for the day. Should she step into his office and make a hurried search for anything that might refute or confirm her suspicions?

No. She told herself, *I cannot do that.* She glanced at her watch again and thought, *Rosario, please hurry.* Another minute passed. She had not told him anything about any of this but decided that she would tell him everything tonight, over dinner.

She rose and crossed to the top of the stairs, listening. She heard nothing from inside the house. The sun dipped behind the line of trees across the street and the warm sunshine gave way to darkening, lengthening shadows in the office that only intensified the sense of foreboding within her. She returned to her desk and plucked the keys from her purse. She unlocked the door to Doctor Rivas' office, leaving the door slightly ajar so she would hear if anyone approached.

Dusk shrouded his office in semi-gloom.

She felt furtive, guilty. Her pulse raced. She went through the things on his desktop first, then the drawers, without finding anything the least bit suspicious. She did not know what she was looking for. She opened a narrow drawer and felt around inside, feeling nothing at first except for the usual personal odds and ends and some office supplies. She was withdrawing her hand when the edge of her thumb brushed across something that felt out of place.

A matchbook.

Doctor Rivas did not smoke. She withdrew the matchbook and looked at it. Across the outside were printed the words, *Club Paradiso*. Doctor Rivas had told her and Hector, that night at the church, that he had never been to that club.

She thumbed open the matchbook. A telephone number had been jotted across the inside.

Doctor Rivas spoke quietly from the doorway. "Looking for something, Maria?"

She could not stem her yelp of surprise. She had not heard him coming! She turned to face him, palming the book of matches. She plucked an eraser from the middle drawer and closed the drawer.

"Oh hello, Doctor. I didn't hear you."

"I see that," he said with a small smile.

"I, uh, I needed an eraser. I meant to buy one on my lunch break today but I forgot and I needed it for some late work I was doing. I thought you might have one."

"You were doing no work when I left. You had finished for the day. There is no work on your desk now."

She felt as though she could not breathe. She could think of nothing to say. He didn't believe her.

A voice called from below.

"Maria? Maria, are you up there?"

Relief swept through her. *Rosario!*

She called to him, "I'm up here, my darling, with Doctor Rivas. Wait for me...here I come." She hurried to the door. "Excuse me, Doctor. I must be leaving."

"Of course, Maria. Good night. Give your husband my regards."

After she was gone, Rivas went to the window of his office. He watched them leave the house and walk away, down the street.

That's when he remembered the matchbook Ortiz had handed him at the Club Paradiso, with the telephone number of a man named Morales, who was to be Rivas' new contact with Havana.

He sat down and went through the narrow desk drawer. He searched for the matchbook, knowing that he would not find it.

CHAPTER 25

Susan went out for dinner with her mother.

It went well enough, quite a bit different than her dinner with Dad the night before. Different restaurant—*Mama Louisa's*, another family favorite; soft lighting, quiet music in the background, polite and efficient waiters—and table conversation about everything except the things that mattered. They spoke of the weather and about Susan's job and about a new department store in town. Later, when Mom steered her Ford into the driveway of Susan's home, a modest wooden frame duplex on a street of similar homes, Susan found herself feeling relieved that the evening was over. She knew her mother had wanted to discuss more important things. So had she. Yet they'd been unable to establish that deeper level of communication.

"Goodnight, Mom. I'll call you tomorrow."

"Okay."

Her mother gave no indication of backing the car out of the driveway. Susan leaned in through the open passenger window.

"Mom? What's wrong?"

After a long pause, Vera said, "I was just wondering...how dinner went with your father."

"It went good." Susan bit her tongue, thinking, *Dammit, girl, you're a reporter. A writer. Talk like one!* "It went well," she said. "I wish you'd been there."

This was not exactly true. She loved both of her parents equally and had always thought of their relationship as solid. She'd never imagined a day when they would be considering divorce. She wanted her parents to reconcile more than anything. Or...almost anything, as it turned out. If Mom had joined them for dinner, her father would never in a million years have thought of inviting her to assist him by gathering information.

She had spent most of the day in the newspaper morgue in the basement of the *Herald*, reviewing the complete file on Doctor Ernesto Rivas, which she'd previously perused in preparation for her interview with him. The portrait that again emerged was of a committed, tireless anti-Communist. Rivas had been a rural general practitioner in a remote Cuban province. There was mention in several articles of his imprisonment at Giron by the Castro government before his release. Like Maria Quintana and thousands of other refugees, he had reached Florida by paying off a fisherman to smuggle him across.

Vera said, "I thought about joining you and your father but that wouldn't have been a good idea. When I'm with him, I...I have trouble saying what I think. I don't think clearly."

"Are you sure?" Susan asked, gently. "Maybe you see things the clearest when you are with him, and *that's* what's confusing you."

Vera studied her. "What do you mean?"

"Mom, I do wish that you and Dad would patch things up so our lives could get back to normal."

"It's not that easy, honey. Someday you'll understand."

"I do understand that being married to a man like Daddy can't have always been easy."

Vera sighed and stared ahead across the steering wheel as if she were driving. "I was always strong enough because I always thought our family was worth it. Your father's a good man. But, honey, I just don't think we're...right for each other anymore. Or maybe I'm too strong to let things stay the way they always have been. You've left home. I'm working. Change is a part of life."

"Mom, I'm not giving up on our family and I don't think you should, either."

A longer pause than before.

"Did you and your father talk about us?"

"Of course we did. You and Dad are both asking serious questions, reassessing yourselves and your life together and you both happen to be doing it at the same time in your lives. Why can't that be a good thing? Why not let it strengthen you and draw you together instead of letting it become a wedge that drives you apart?"

"I've thought of that. I told you this isn't easy." Vera's eyes shifted to meet Susan's. "You can't help taking his side, can you?"

A telephone began ringing inside Susan's apartment.

"Mom, let's talk about this tomorrow, okay?

"Okay, honey. Tomorrow."

There was a resignation in her mother's voice that stayed with her as Susan hurried to the front door and let herself in. The Ford's headlights withdrew from her driveway and arced around to drive off. She caught the phone on what must have been the ninth or tenth ring, certain that the caller would be hanging up just as she brought the receiver to her ear.

"Yes, hello?"

"Susan, this is Maria Quintana. I'm sorry to call you at home, but I have something that I feel is most urgent."

"That's okay, Maria. What is it?"

"I think it is best that I show you. I want to give you something. I don't want to keep it."

"I can meet you now. Where do you want to meet?"

"A public place, where we will be safe because there will be people around. Where we met before," said Maria. "The Blue Palm. Is that all right?"

Susan said, "I'll be there in twenty minutes."

You didn't have to be a reporter to see that something was wrong.

The street around The Blue Palm was congested. Susan had to park nearly a block away. She hurried to the periphery of a dense crowd of onlookers where officers deployed for crowd control manned strips of yellow police scene tape. Beyond them were official vehicles, including an ambulance, blinking multi-colored lights, the crackle of police band radios and earnest, professional personnel hurrying purposefully here and there.

Her press credentials passed her through to the officer in charge, a detective named Vickers. "You're the first reporter down here," he told her. "Why should a random hit-and-run rate a reporter on the scene? Don't they usually wait for the routine morning report on something like this?"

A cold fist tightened her throat. She nodded toward The Blue Palm. "I was - I was just stopping by for a nightcap on my way home."

"Looks as if the victim was heading there too," said Vickers. "She was crossing the street."

"She?" "Her name was Maria Quintana. It may have been deliberate. The car stopped. Witnesses thought the driver was getting out to help. He knelt down beside her and then he stepped away, then he drove away real fast."

"Maybe he went to check on her, and when he saw that she was dead, he panicked and fled."

Vickers eyed her closer than before. "Or maybe he was searching her purse and pockets for something and he did or did not find it. Any idea what he might have been looking for, Miss Morgan, was it?"

"Yes. And uh, no," she heard herself say. The coldness was spreading throughout her body. "I told you—"

"Right. You were just stopping by for a drink. Did you know the victim?"

"No. No, I didn't. Do you have a description of the driver, or a license number on the car?"

"Not yet, it just happened," said Vickers with some show of impatience. "Give us time. Right now, you'll have to excuse me." He strode away to where a crime scene technician was beckoning him.

The ambulance pulled away from the scene and proceeded down the street at a moderate pace with no sense of urgency, its rooftop lights no longer blinking.

CHAPTER 26

The President rarely deviated from his set routine of reading the morning newspapers with breakfast in his bedroom. As soon as his order was placed with the cook, strict instructions were left that he not be disturbed until he had finished both of the papers and his breakfast.

But at 6:00 AM on the morning of Friday, April 14, John Kennedy broke that routine for a meeting in the tiny, drab conference room behind the office of Dean Rusk, his Secretary of State. Present at the round table were the Secretary of State, a balding man with an earnest, professorial air about him, and half a dozen others. On the table in front of each man was a reddish-brown manila file with a string tied around it.

The President reached across and poured himself a cup of coffee from the oversized pot that adorned the center of the table. There were discolored pouches beneath his tired eyes. He sipped the coffee and winced.

"Too damn strong." He set the cup down and said, "There's been a casualty at the Brigade staging area. A paratrooper named Perez."

Robert Kennedy was seated directly across from his brother. "Is that the spy Morgan was sent down there to terminate?"

"I'm not sure, Bobby. I have my doubts. It's too simple." Frown lines deepened in the President's mahogany-brown face. "There's more than one Castro spy in this and the one that concerns me most is a lot closer than Puerto Cabezas."

Robert frowned, emphasizing the family resemblance to his brother. "You're talking about that CIA agent, Lehman, buying it on that Cuban beach."

The President nodded. "They were waiting for him, remember? That means they were supplied with information that could only have come through the Cuban exile leadership…or someone on our payroll."

Atwater's eyes narrowed thoughtfully. "There could be someone in the CIA's chain of command."

The President said, "I've been worrying about a third world war. I remember a First World War starting over some obscure archduke getting himself assassinated, and millions died. Japan attacks Pearl Harbor and millions die in a Second World War. Anything, small or large, can trigger such a catastrophe. Who's to say what horrors beyond our comprehension could be unleashed if this thing goes sour? And it will go sour for sure unless Castro's inside man is tagged and nullified before the invasion commences."

General Atwater finished his cup of coffee and poured another. "Mister President, the invasion, for all intents and purposes, commenced when those ships left the staging area." He spoke with unconcealed disapproval.

Secretary of State Rusk was in shirtsleeves. He had an exhausted, rumpled appearance as if he had been up all night. He ignored the coffeepot and sipped from a glass of orange juice. "And what about Miami?" he asked without enthusiasm. "The Cuban exile leadership is in complete disarray. The Democratic Revolutionary Front is threatening to go public with the entire operation to gain popular support. That's how unhappy they are with us."

Atwater nodded. "They've got good reason to be pissed off. The CIA has bypassed them at every point. Action was taken in their name without their knowledge. Castro's got Soviet tanks and advisors. The Front wants us to commit Marines and planes."

"It was our understanding," said Robert sharply, "that the leaders and the Brigade were willing to risk this effort without our military participation. It was to have been made clear to them that we would not intervene if their invasion failed. "

The President poured himself a glass of orange juice and winced again, this time as he often did when a jolt of pain stabbed at his back. He tapped the file before him. "This is a precise hour-by-hour plan of the operation. D-Day is this coming Monday, April 17th." As the men opened their folders and began to read, he said, "General?"

Atwater cleared his throat. "The invasion area is a place on the southern coast of Cuba called the Bay of Pigs. The site has been deemed most feasible because there's an airstrip there that will accommodate our B-26's. Most of the ships will unload at Blue Beach, at the village of Giron, and at Red Beach, at Playa Larga. It's a remote area and the two main roads into Giron will be easily cut off. Castro has sixteen operational aircraft. The operation's most critical element therefore is air power. We have to neutralize their air force and whatever naval vessels are capable of opposing the landing. We're flying a bombing run over Castro's airfields tomorrow morning."

Robert looked up from his briefing documents with a sudden scowl. "Tomorrow? Tomorrow is Saturday. You said D-Day was Monday. We'll be sending Castro an advance warning. All-out surprise air strikes on D-Day are the only way to go"

Atwater met the scowl with one of his own. "The D-minus 2 strikes are desirable if we want this to look Cuban."

The Secretary of State eased the reddish brown folder away from him with his fingertips, as if he had seen and heard quite enough.

"Gentlemen, I cannot stress enough the words, *plausible deniability*. We *must* maintain our distance from the invasion itself. There is our international standing, world opinion, to consider. There is the Pandora's Box of Latin politics. America cannot be seen as launching an unprovoked attack on a neighboring country."

Robert said, "Our position will be that the air strikes originated inside Cuba, flown by defecting pilots from their Air Force."

The President sipped his orange juice and set the glass down with a clunk. "Too damn sweet," he growled. "We're going to need one hell of a lot of luck on our side with this, aren't we, General?"

"Yes sir," said Atwater. "Everything rides on the air strikes against Castro...*tomorrow*." He looked pointedly at Robert.

An aide entered and placed a typed report before the Attorney General. Robert scanned the report and when he looked up, some of his boyish eagerness had faded.

"Trouble in Miami," he told the others.

CHAPTER 27

After the warmth of humid April sunshine, the Dade County Morgue had a clammy chill that penetrated Tal Garrett to the marrow. High intensity fluorescent lighting illuminated a tile floor and facing walls that were lined with two levels of metal drawers.

Garrett and Resnick stepped aside when swing doors opened to admit an attendant showing in a pair of men, a Miami homicide cop named Vickers and the man he was escorting, Rosario Quintana. Vickers was slim-shouldered with cop eyes that had seen everything. He saw the CIA men, frowned and continued with Quintana to where the attendant stopped midway down the opposite row of drawers.

Rosario was nearing fifty, his features softened with age but of classic Latin good looks. Heavyset, he carried a slight paunch. He wore a wrinkled brown shirt and matching, unpressed slacks, as if he had dressed hurriedly. The attendant slid open the lower drawer and drew a sheet back from a face. Rosario howled an almost inhuman wail of anguish and collapsed across the body, hugging it, sobbing uncontrollably.

The attendant stood there, a disinterested man who witnessed this often.

Vickers stepped over to Garrett and Resnick. "Might've known you birds would show up. Maria Quintana worked for Doctor Rivas, one of the Cuban exile guys, and you Feds have those guys wired, right?"

Garrett had once been a city cop himself, in a city far away, before being drafted by the Agency. He sympathized with Vickers. He said, "Sorry, Lieutenant. You know we can't talk about that."

Resnick said, "Like Garrett said, Vic, we're sorry." He wore a straw hat and a loud Hawaiian shirt that shone like neon in these surroundings. As the CIA's Officer in Charge in Miami, he had worked with Vickers before.

Vickers said, "Sure you are. Well, goddamn."

The sobbing of the man over the woman's body intensified, magnified by the tiled floor, by the metal walls, by the room's very coldness, thought Garrett.

He asked Vickers, "Any chance the husband did it?"

The cop's slim shoulders shrugged. "He's Cuban, ain't he? That hot Latin blood. Man, there's so many hubby-wife kills down at that end of town, most of them don't even make the news anymore. But I've got to say that most of those are knife jobs, sometimes a gun maybe, but I can't recall anyone down there using a car as a lethal weapon."

Garrett sympathized with city cops, but he had never cared for racial stereotypes. He let it slide, though. Vickers had enough aggravation.

Resnick said, "Have you brought Rivas in for questioning?"

"There's not a trace of the Doctor to be found. There's an APB out for him now."

Garrett, who already knew this, said, "What have you got on the victim?"

"The husband says she had some kind of suspicions about Doctor Rivas. She'd already talked to a *Miami Herald* reporter about it. They argued about him not wanting her to be involved. She stormed out and walked to the restaurant to meet the reporter, but she never made it. He says that's all he knows."

Garrett said, "What's the reporter's name?"

Vickers made a face. "I get it. The yokels share everything they've got just before you slam the door."

Resnick sighed. "Something like that. Come on, Vic. What's his name?"

"Her name," said Vickers, "is Susan Morgan. She showed up right after the accident and I let her slip through my fingers and now we can't find a trace of her, either. She's a feature writer for the *Herald*." He nodded toward Rosario. "What about him?"

"We won't interfere if it's a domestic killing."

"It's not and you know it. "

Garrett said, "That will be all, Lieutenant."

Vickers' glared. "You still want that APB out on Rivas, I take it."

Resnick said, "Yeah, Vic. Thanks. Let us know what comes in."

Vickers said, "The hell with both of you," and returned to Rosario Quintana, whose sobbing had become more subdued, though he still knelt and did not want to release his wife.

Garrett and Resnick left the building.

Garrett said, "So she suspected Doctor Rivas of something."

Resnick paused on the top wide stone step of the building to light a cigarette. His loud shirt and high-life sportsman appearance appeared more natural in the sunshine, but he wore a sour expression. He exhaled a stream of smoke with a heavy sigh.

"She suspected that Rivas was the Castro spy that everyone's looking for."

Garrett caught the scent of tobacco smoke and wished like hell that he wasn't trying to kick that damn habit. "Sam, I thought you personally gave Rivas a clean bill of health. I told you that poor damn assistant of his was being framed. I'm a goddamn out of towner, for chrissake, but you're the OIC of the Miami station. What the hell?"

Resnick pitched his cigarette away angrily. "Dammit, Tal, there isn't any *evidence* against Rivas. There isn't any *proof,* all right? What are we back to, McCarthyism? But we need proof, and you should get off my goddamn back."

"Maybe so," said Garrett. They started down the steps toward Resnick's convertible, which was parked at the curb. "With the local cops combing the streets for Rivas, we've got to concentrate on this reporter the Quintana woman was in touch with."

"You think Rivas could be planning to kill her next?"

"He's a spy and he's covering his tracks," said Garrett. "We've been screwing up, Sam, and that poor bastard's wailing over his wife's body is still ringing in my ears. We're going to get us a spy before he does any more damage, before anyone else dies. We're done screwing up. Let's find Susan Morgan in time."

CHAPTER 28

Morning was Vera's favorite time of the day, when the chirping of birds, the warmth of the sun and the very newness of the day itself bespoke the unlimited potential of life. She always rose early enough on workdays to linger over a cup of tea with grapefruit and jellied toast on the patio or at the breakfast table if the new day decided to be rainy. At this stage in her life, she saw every morning as a daily affirmation from nature that her life was of unlimited potential, on the cusp of blossoming into something new and alive.

On this sunny Saturday, she had finished breakfast, gone for a walk and was seated in her work nook, where the octagonal window looked out on the driveway, putting the finishing touches on a Gauguin print she was framing, when Susan's white Ford Fairlane turned into the driveway. The Morgans lived in a ranch-style house, white with brown trim, on a winding suburban street. She rose from her task and hurried out with a smiled greeting that caught in her throat when she saw her daughter up close.

"Honey, what's wrong?"

Susan's eyes were wide, glazed orbs of fear. Her complexion was pasty white. Deep, unattractive worry lines creased her pinched expression. Casting frightened glances in every direction, she hurried past Vera, bolting into the house. Vera followed and found Susan pressed to the living room wall, next to the front picture window. She continued scanning the street that ran past the house.

"Mom, I'm in big trouble. I think I'm in danger."

Vera had never seen Susan like this before. Usually when she looked at her grown daughter, she still saw without half-trying the freckled, happy-faced, braces-wearing twelve-year-old that Susan had once been. But this harried, haunted creature bore little resemblance even to the grown woman Vera had shared a dinner with last night.

"Honey, what in the world—?"

"Someone's been murdered. At least I, I think it was murder. It was a hit and run but I think the police know it was premeditated...and I think the killer may be after me too."

Vera heard all of this but for some reason the words were so outrageous, Susan's appearance so startling, that at first what she heard did not register.

"Susan...is this a joke?"

Susan wore the same sky-blue blouse and white slacks as she had last night at *Mama Louisa's*, but they badly needed a washing and ironing. She gestured to her unkempt appearance. "Does *this* look like a prank? Do I sound like I'm joking?"

Vera flinched. "Of course you don't." The harsh tone was exactly what was needed to make her accept the naked fear she saw and heard. "I'm sorry. Honey, use the bathroom to freshen up. I'll make coffee and we can—"

Susan's eyes darted back to the street. "There isn't time. I've come to get you. You may be in danger too. We need to get out of here. I thought maybe we could go to the cabin. I stopped off for some things at my place. You've got time to pack one suitcase, Mom, if you move fast. I came for Daddy's gun."

Vera took Susan by each arm and turned her daughter so she could peer directly into Susan's eyes. What could only have been maternal instinct settled an objective calm over her.

"Honey, you could be hysterical. Please tell me what's going on."

"I'm not hysterical." Susan's voice was brittle, like thin glass ready to snap. "I am scared out of my wits."

"Tell me."

"I've been working on a series for the paper."

"I know. The Cuban refugees."

"Well, I stumbled onto something. The refugee leadership that opposes Castro and has gotten our government to back them...one of those men is a spy for Castro. I was supposed to meet a woman last night, the man's secretary. She told me she had proof that he was a spy. But Maria was...she was dead when I arrived for our meeting."

"You said it happened last night. Didn't you tell the police what you know?"

"Mom, I'm a reporter and I haven't reported anything, not to my paper, not to the police. All I did was talk to a police detective on the scene who let me know without intending to that I'd be detained if I did tell what I know. I won't divulge that information. Not yet. I can't. So I drove around, then I drove down to the beach. I sat in my car and listened to the ocean and tried to think."

"What have you been thinking about? I don't understand why you haven't reported this."

A tremor shivered visibly through Susan. She avoided Vera's direct gaze. "I, well, because...Mom, this is *big* and I don't know who to trust. That's what Dad told me before he left and that's the way I feel."

The chill within Vera dropped several more degrees. "What does your father have to do with this?"

Susan abruptly strode down the hallway in the direction of the bedrooms. "Mother, if you ever only trust me once in your life—"

"Of course I trust you," said Vera. "I raised you to be sensible and resourceful. It's just that—"

"I mean if you *really* trust me unconditionally, then do so now. Please! Pack a suitcase fast as you can, enough for a few days."

Susan went into her parents' bedroom and slid open the mirrored door of the closet. She pushed aside shoeboxes and hatboxes on the overhead shelf. She well knew that a .45 automatic resided with a box of extra shells in a hatbox to the rear of the overhead shelf.

Morgan had insisted that a gun always be kept hidden in their house and Vera had long suspected that this was not only for defense against prowlers but also in case his violent "other world," where he worked, somehow managed to follow him home. This had never happened, thank God, but she'd spent nights worrying and for years had recurring nightmares of violence, even when Mike was home; of people breaking into their home, of violent, bloody death. She had never liked the idea of having a gun in their home and had made no secret of her feelings, but her husband made it clear that the subject was not open to conversation and that was that. As a member of the National Rifle Association, Morgan had seen to it that she received advanced training in the use of a handgun. Susan too, when their daughter was old enough. Vera hated the damn thing. The awful noise of the gunfire at the range could nearly deafen you even with earplugs. The presence of the gun in her home had come to represent those poisonous aspects of her husband's world that were toxic in her life. She had begun thinking more and more about getting rid of the gun, selling it while Morgan was gone. And if he didn't like it, that would be too bad.

Vera withdrew a suitcase from the hallway closet and brought it into the bedroom. She began hurriedly packing, as instructed. But not liking it.

"Susan, I want some answers. I won't be thrown off the track. What does your father have to do with this?"

Susan retrieved the hatbox from the closet. She set it on the bed beside the suitcase and withdrew the pistol. "Before he left, he asked me to help him."

"Help him?" Vera froze in the act of reaching into a drawer for underwear. "Help him what?"

Susan held her white purse upside down and shook its contents onto the bedspread. She placed the gun inside her purse. "Mom, please. Keep packing. We may not have much time."

There was no doubting the anxious sincerity in her manner and words, and so Vera resumed packing as fast as she could. "This is crazy! How dare he draw you into his contemptible...how *dare* he? And that's what you were meeting this woman about?"

Susan replaced only her wallet in the purse with the gun. "Dad needed to know about a man named Rivas, the anti-Castro Cuban I told you about. Whatever proof the secretary was bringing to show me, Doctor Rivas retrieved after he killed her. He's that desperate."

Vera snapped her suitcase shut, knowing that she was forgetting about half a dozen things due to haste and distraction but not giving a damn. "And why is it that we're running away and hiding and not doing the responsible thing by going to the police?"

Susan returned to the living room picture window. Vera again hurried to keep up, to find Susan staring up and down the sun-splashed street before the house. A mail truck rattled by, the only traffic in sight.

She said, ""Daddy must have had a reason for not knowing who to trust. Doctor Rivas knows about me, too. I've interviewed him. The job Dad is on has to do with Cuba. It won't take long for Rivas to make the connection between Susan Morgan and Graveyard Morgan, if he hasn't already. I'm afraid he'll come here."

"In broad daylight?" asked Vera. For the first time everything was sinking in and fear was pushing aside everything else in her mind, cramping the muscles in her abdomen.

Susan said, "Daylight is the only thing holding him back. If he's desperate enough, and I think he is, he may think that if he can just silence me, he can still get away with it. And he has gotten away with it so far, as far as I know. The thing is, Mom, we need to make ourselves scarce."

"But what about your job? Won't the people you work for wonder where you are?"

Susan cracked the smallest and briefest of smiles. "I've been known to sweet talk my editor when I have to. Right now all I care about is getting us away from here to someplace safe."

Vera said, "I wish there was some way we could reach your father."

"There isn't." Susan moved from the window, toward the door, keeping one hand inside her purse.

"Honey," said Vera, "you're so like him. This is the way he'd take charge if he was here."

Susan opened the front door less than an inch and peered out. "Rivas may know what I'm driving so we'll take your car. We should hole up and follow the news for a day or so. The word everywhere in Little Havana is that something big is about to happen in Cuba."

Vera said, "Your father would be part of something like that. I can't believe he did this to you, putting us at risk like this. My God."

Susan said, "The only ones putting us at risk right now are you and me. Let's go. I'll feel a whole lot better when we're on the move."

She left the house.

Vera followed, toting her purse and suitcase. She paused to lock the front door, and wondered when she would see her home again.

How quickly her normal life had fallen apart.

What would happen next?

CHAPTER 29

Punto Uno was the national military headquarters, occupying a roomy two-story villa on 47th Street in Nuevo Vedado, Havana's residential district. Point One also served as a communications center with the rest of the country.

There had been so many indications in recent days that something was about to happen that Fidel Castro had decided to make Point One his temporary home. His office overlooked the Zoological Gardens and, beyond rows of tree-lined streets and houses, the vast open expanse of Campo Libertad Airport. He was reviewing budget estimates for a paved road in the Camaguey Province, filling the air with cigar smoke, when Che Guevara and General Almeida were shown in.

Che said, "You look tired. You should get more sleep."

Castro frowned and set aside the budget report. "I cannot sleep. I only nap. I cannot relax."

Almeida nodded in sympathy. "Something is about to happen. I feel it, *Commandante*."

Che said, "The calm before the storm."

Castro's cigar had gone out. He reached for an ornate gold lighter on his desk, clicked it a few times but there was no flame. Almeida leaned forward and re-lighted the cigar using his personal Zippo. Castro puffed on his cigar and exhaled blue-gray smoke that eddied in the shafts of Caribbean sunshine pouring in from the veranda. He started to say something.

The morning quiet was suddenly split asunder by the whistling drone of a plane, flying over at extremely low altitude, rattling windows and filling the office with thunder. They rushed to the veranda. The first plane had passed and was already swooping in toward the airfield. Another, identical plane flew in from behind, thundering over Point One as if racing to catch up with the first.

Squinting after the planes in the sunlight, Almeida said, "B-26's."

Che added, "With Cuban markings."

The planes began diving at Camp Libertad. The hollow thumping sound of bombs exploding in the distance was punctuated by the steady, rapid-fire *boom!-boom!-boom!* of hammering anti-aircraft guns. The anti-aircraft guns hammered but the fighter planes continued to bank, dive and climb like playful birds avoiding a net, then the thumping of more bombs exploding, more rockets fired from the planes and the chatter of machinegun fire.

Almeida's clean-shaven features were flushed. "But this is madness!"

Castro snarled an obscenity. He whirled and stormed toward the door. "I must get over there. I will take command!"

Che rushed to intercept him, positioning himself between Castro and the door. "Fidel, no! Your place is here."

Castro's fury was towering. His features were flushed. "My place is in battle with my men. Step aside. I must be gone."

Che did not step aside. "To lead Cuba, you must remain alive. Your courage is so great that it borders on the insane."

The words, spoken coolly, momentarily took Castro aback. He removed the cigar from his mouth and his eyes narrowed. "Only you and my brother could ever speak to me so, and live."

Che did not flinch. "Fidel, do you remember that time in the Sierra Mestra when we were but a ragtag rebel army fighting to even survive, when every one of your officers signed a petition imploring you to stop exposing yourself to hostile fire?"

"Yes, Che. I remember. But what makes you think that I have changed? I was at the front line in every skirmish and every battle. I led every march, every attack. And now, *now* you would ask me to sit here and do nothing while they kill my people?"

"Only until the attack is over, Fidel. Your place now is as a leader, as a rallying point for your countrymen, not as a common soldier risking your life in combat."

"What makes you think I can be one without the other?" Castro demanded. "I am their leader because I *am* a common soldier."

From the veranda, General Almeida cleared his throat. "*Commandante,* it appears that the attack is over."

Air raid sirens began braying from the airfield.

Castro returned to the veranda. Every outer vestige of his rage had vanished.

The fighter planes were gone. Pillars of oily smoke snaked up into the sky above Campo Libertad.

He again started toward the door. "Come, *mis amigos*. Let us witness the damage. Hurry if you wish to keep up with me."

The body was that of a very young man, no more than seventeen or eighteen years of age, clad in mechanic's coveralls, sprawled face down upon the tarmac where he had fallen, one arm outstretched; the back of his coveralls pulverized by bloody exit wounds. A pool of spilt blood was a burnt brown on the sunny asphalt around him. At the end of the extended arm, an extended index finger pointed to a word written in blood: Fidel. The fingertip touched the bottom of the l, which was shaky.

Castro looked up from the body. He stood with Che and Almeida and the commander of the airfield, a stocky, grim man wearing sweat-stained fatigues, who had brought them here to show them this.

Castro said, "A young man who is dying. His protest against his dying is to write a name with his blood." Smoldering eyes snapped at the Commander. "How bad is the situation? How many dead? How many injured?"

"Seven dead, *Commandante*. Fifty-two wounded."

"Assemble the men. I would speak to the pilots, the mechanics and the anti-aircraft artillerymen. See to it."

"At once, *Commandante*." The man hurried away.

The runways were pockmarked with ugly craters that rendered them unusable for takeoffs and landings. Nearby a crew was hosing down one of several still-smoldering piles of burnt, misshapen rubble that had been airplanes. Soldiers fought to contain a blaze where one of the bombed-out hangars had caught fire.

Castro said, "This attack is a prelude."

"Correct, *Commandante,*" said Almeida. "An invasion would begin by destroying what few planes we have. Cuban planes with Cuban markings... could some of our own pilots be turning against us?"

Che had not taken his eyes from the sprawled body at their feet. "This is the work of the Americans. Our air force is small enough for us to have monitored a mutiny if one had been brewing. This trick will not work."

Almeida was watching the horizon to the north, the direction taken by the bombers. "There could be more air strikes."

"I will order the pilots to spend today and tonight under the wings of the remaining planes," said Castro. "At the first sighting of the enemy, our pilots will be airborne to engage them. Our air force may be depleted, but we will not be caught on the ground again as we were this morning."

Almeida said, "They flew in low enough to avoid our radar. I will order all military installations and militia to full combat alert."

"I also want pressure put on our men who are charged with rounding up dissidents and counter-revolutionaries," said Castro. "The Americans will activate and use those groups when they strike. The time to crush them is *now*. Those are my orders. See that they are carried out implicitly."

"Si, Commandante."

Almeida rushed off, leaving Castro and Che standing alone over the body.

Che said, "We are about to be tested by the fire, Fidel. It will be the supreme test."

Castro nodded. "And we will prevail."

CHAPTER 30

Carmen Vasquez had just completed reassembling her rifle after having given it a thorough cleaning, when the barrel-chested, bear-like figure of Santos filled the cave entrance. He was carrying a heavily loaded sack over his shoulder. The others in the cave rose to greet him. Like everyone, she was fond of this boisterous bear of a man. Carmen smiled. As he tossed the sack onto the cave of the floor in the glow of the battery operated lamps, Santos reminded her of a youthful Santa Claus.

"My friends, I have been to Giron!" He was out of breath, as if he had hurried across a considerable distance. "Here is food and supplies, and I have glorious news." He took inventory of the faces before him. "But where is Felix?"

Carmen said, "He is making radio contact with the Americans offshore. What is this wonderful news?"

"It's war!" Santos crowed. "Havana has been attacked! I heard it on the radio in town. Rebel Cuban fighter pilots attacked Camp Libertad and two other airports. Castro's own pilots are defecting!"

There were excited mutterings among their group.

Someone asked, "Any word of the damage?"

"It only happened an hour ago. I ran all the way from the village." He managed to catch his breath. He reached for his knapsack. "This calls for a drink!"

At that moment, Felix stepped into the cave, carrying the group's compact transistor radio. Santos started to repeat his information, but Felix held up a hand. His youthful, intense features were aglow with a patina of excitement. He gestured with the radio. "I've heard the news. It has begun."

They left the cave, stepping into the warmth of the sunshine. The salty tang of the sea drifted in on a warm breeze.

Carmen detected in the others the same quivering interest and excitement that was racing through her. She asked Felix, "What do the Americans say?"

"Early tomorrow morning there will be landings at Giron and Playa Larga." He seemed to be containing his own enthusiasm only with considerable effort.

It was as if an electrical jolt coursed through those present, thought Carmen. She herself felt a tingling sensation of excitement.

"Giron!" Santos exclaimed. "Good! We will be in the thick of it!"

"When we are sure the invasion is on schedule," said Felix, "we are to proceed to San Blas and continue north under cover of darkness."

Carmen felt some of the euphoria dissipate. "If there is heavy fighting," she said, "that may not be as easy as it sounds. The San Blas road north cuts right through Zapata Swamp."

Santos laughed. "That doesn't matter." He took a hearty swig from his bottle of rum. "I've been waiting too long to kill some Castro soldiers for me to worry about a swamp."

"When a beachhead at Giron has been established," said Felix, "the invasion force will push north to Covadonga. Transport planes will be flying in to drop paratroopers who will join in the assault. They expect heavy resistance. We have been instructed to position ourselves so as to offer full tactical support. I made phone calls in Giron. The other cells of our network have received their missions as well."

Santos passed his bottle around and got a few takers. He emitted a deep-chested laugh. "It comes at last. The invasion we have been waiting for to overthrow that son of a bitch, Fidel!"

"Let us pray," said Carmen said, "that nothing goes wrong."

The Jeep braked to a sharp, rocking halt in the shade of a tree where the teenage boy and girl sat near their bicycles, their arms around each other's waist, overlooking the ocean from where the road crested a bluff. They leapt to their feet, startled and fearful, seeming to shrink in size when the hulking, baldheaded, scar-faced black giant stepped from the Jeep. Ramon raised his left hand and made a curt "come here" gesture to the boy.

Cosme Gomez looked for some way to escape, but there was none. The Bay of Pigs was sparkling blue behind and below them under a clear sky, and there was the Jeep. The thin, stern, erect figure of Major Medina occupied the passenger seat.

The girl remained where she was.

Cosme approached Medina.

Medina's fatigues were smartly starched and pressed, as always. The expression on his emaciated face was severe. "I am displeased, Cosme."

"Major, I—"

"Silence. Your orders were to keep Carmen Vasquez under close surveillance at all times. Your family lives on the next property to hers. It should have been easy."

Cosme stared at the ground. He held a straw hat in his hands, turning the brim in small circles. "I did my best, Major. I went with Carmen to reclaim the body of her brother."

"Yes, I saw you. And you were there when her mother died. But you were decidedly *not* there when she disappeared. She hasn't been seen for days, not since her mother's death."

Cosme lifted imploring eyes. His lips trembled. "But, Major, I could not stay with her every minute!"

Medina regarded him coolly. "*Señora* Vasquez was held in high regard in Giron. Her friends saw to a proper burial. It is rumored in the village that Carmen has joined the counter-revolutionaries led by Felix Carriles. He is the one I want."

"Major, I've done the best I could." Cosme's fear made the words gush from him. "Remember, it was I who provided you with the information that led to the arrest of Carmen's brother. I was the one who told you that Diego Vasquez was bringing an American agent ashore, the night when our Fidel came to personally execute the American."

Medina's cool eyes shifted to the girl. Lupita sat beneath the tree, out of earshot, her arms around her knees, which were drawn up to her as if for protection. She was watching them with apprehensive eyes.

"Tell me, Cosme. How is your lovely bride-to-be?"

After hesitating, the teenager gulped and said, "She is fine, Major. We are to be married next month."

"Splendid. And her, shall we say, delicate condition?"

"She will have our baby in October."

"The money I pay you should come in handy, then."

"It already has, Major. You are most generous."

"But it would not be so good for you, my young friend, would it, if word were to begin circulating in these parts that you have cooperated with me, that you have spied on their beloved Carmen for money? That you were responsible for Diego's death? He too had many friends around here."

The boy's eyes grew wide with new fear. "You would...do that? You would tell them?"

"Many of the people in Giron love Fidel. He has built roads, a school, a hospital. But Carriles and his scum have their supporters, too. You would be sought out, Cosme. They would kill you. Your child would be born without a father. "

Beads of perspiration pearled along Cosme's upper lip. "Major, please, there is no need to talk like that."

"If you do not soon produce satisfactory results," said Medina, "I could do things to express my displeasure that you might find equally objectionable." He nodded to the black giant who had again sat beside him at the steering wheel. "Ramon, what do you think of this young man's betrothed?"

Ramon had been staring at Lupita. He ran the back of one broad hand across his moist lips. "She's a pretty one. There are things I would do to her, yes. I hate women. I would kill her slowly."

Cosme gulped, slack-jawed.

Medina said, "And so you see, Cosme, that you had better find out where Carmen Vasquez is. Do this for me, and you will be handsomely paid. Fail, and..." He let the words taper off.

"Please, Major, don't hurt Lupita."

"You have lived in this area all your life," said Medina. "That, and the fact that you lived next door to Carmen, is why I approached you. I too would like our association to continue as it has. You will find out for me where Carmen Vasquez is, and that will lead me to Felix Carriles and his gang. Do you understand, Cosme?"

"Yes, Major."

"Very good. Contact me in the usual manner as soon as you have something to report."

"Yes, Major."

"And I leave you with one parting thought. Do not fail me, my young friend, or you see the suffering will not be solely endured by your lovely fiancée. Ramon hates women. But he loves boys."

CHAPTER 31

He approached Morgan outside the Operations Shack at Puerto Cabezas. Morgan guessed his age at around twenty, which seemed the average age of those in the Brigade. He was clad in fatigues and carried a rifle by its strap behind one shoulder, his parachute slung over the other shoulder.

"Excuse me, *señor.* Might I have a moment of your time?"

Around them, the base crackled with activity, with the almost palpable anticipation of imminent action. The planes were lined up and ready for takeoff and had been so for hours. Platoons were assembled around their leaders for their final briefings. Everywhere there was movement and sound.

It took Morgan a moment, then he placed this one. He said, "You were in Antonio Perez's platoon. You stood across from me in the plane when we made that jump."

"I am José Cardena. I have been appointed platoon leader after," a slight groping for the proper phrase, "after what happened to Sergeant Perez."

"What can I do for you?"

"I am not sure how I should phrase this, *señor.* The men of our platoon have gotten together," he faltered a moment more, "and...we had an idea based on our impression of you. You are not like the other gringos here, like Conklin, so ready to exert their arrogance as they send others to do the fighting."

"Well put. I think you've got that pegged about right."

"Then perhaps we have you pegged also, señor. You are no stranger to war, that is apparent to even the untrained eye. The way you carry yourself. The way you took charge on the ground after what happened to Perez. You have been in combat, no?"

"A few times. So far, so good on the analysis. What is this leading to?"

José glanced around to make sure they were not within earshot of anyone before he said, "You would be right to laugh outright at our idea."

"I'd have to hear it first."

"The men of the platoon have asked me to inquire if you would care to accompany us when we make our jump into Cuba. You have *machismo*, *señor*. You did not have to accompany us on that practice jump when we lost Antonio. But you did, and we recognize you as one of us."

"I'm honored. You're brave men."

"My platoon is eager to get to Cuba, to do what we have been trained for and victory. But Sergeant Perez was more highly trained than the rest of us."

"So you're not just short a man. You lost a valuable man."

"And so we took a vote among ourselves, and I have come to you."

"What about Garcia? I don't know about your platoon, but around the head shed he's considered responsible for what happened to Perez. We think he cut Antonio's static line. He murdered him because of the political quarrel they had."

"*Si*, that is our suspicion as well. But as you know, there is no proof. And what if there was? There is gossip that Antonio Perez was a spy for Castro."

"Either way, Garcia is a loose cannon. I can still feel a cool wind from that blade he tried to cut me with. He's trouble."

"Does that mean you will not join us?"

"José, there is one way that I am like the gringos running this operation. I *am* a gringo. Tell you what. I'll put in a request. But don't hold your breath."

Inside the Operations Shack, Conklin was waiting for him at the head of the conference table. Medlow, the young CIA agent from the embassy, and Hudson, the gruff General who commanded the Brigade's air force, were seated to Conklin's either side.

"Okay, here's the update." Conklin spoke without preamble. His features expressed nothing, like a man playing poker. "Washington's propaganda campaign, that yesterday's bombing raids in Cuba were carried out by defecting Cuban pilots, well, it didn't wash. The press started punching holes in it almost before those B-26's landed in Florida."

Medlow removed his horn-rimmed glasses and massaged his eyes, as if suddenly very tired. "I knew it wouldn't take long for this to turn to shit."

Morgan sat in the chair at the opposite end of the table from Conklin.

"That's just starting, and it's not about to get better."

Conklin said, "There's more. No one in Washington anticipated the reaction such attacks would have on the Cuban population."

Medlow sat up straight and replaced his glasses. "What are you talking about?"

Morgan said, "He means that an act of war was committed without warning. That will unite the people behind Castro, even a lot of those who didn't like him before. People don't like having their country attacked. Or maybe you're too young to remember Pearl Harbor."

Hudson was glaring at Medlow. "Hey, whiz kid. I thought your intelligence reports said there would be mass uprisings in Cuba once the people became aware that they were being liberated."

"Stop it," said Conklin. "Relax, General. You too, Graveyard. The Brigade hasn't even landed yet. The fleet steams into the Bay of Pigs at midnight tonight, per schedule. But we've got a more immediate concern. The second air strike at Castro has been scrubbed."

Hudson registered instant disbelief. "But aerial recon showed those air strikes yesterday took out only five aircraft. This entire operation was constructed on the premise that no Castro planes would get off the ground."

Morgan said, "The pols back home are getting cold feet."

Hudson thumped the table with a fist. "Damn politicians. They're pulling the rug right out from under us."

"No, they're not," said Conklin. "The Brigade is so eager they don't give a damn about the odds. They came into it knowing that the chances of this operation's success were estimated at thirty-five percent. That didn't cool anyone's enthusiasm, so why should this?"

"Those men," said Morgan, "are under the impression that U.S. military forces will openly and directly assist them. I heard you tell them that."

Conklin bristled, but only in the eyes. The rest of him remained poker-faced. "My orders come from up above, just like yours, soldier. But get this, mister. We're Americans. We go where we want to go," said Conklin, his eyes bright, "and when we get there, we do what we feel like doing. And if there's anyone who doesn't like it, they'll find out what it feels like to have a world power stomp their asses to hell and gone."

"Yeah," said Morgan. "I was just telling someone that. Gringos." He rose from his chair. "The men in Perez's platoon have asked me to make the jump with them."

Medlow snorted. "That's ridiculous."

General Hudson could not raise his eyes from the table. "I'm afraid you're on the bench, son. You know the President's order. No American will participate in Cuban military operations. We don't have to like it, but orders are orders. Especially from the Man."

Conklin said, "Get it, Graveyard? Your request is emphatically denied."

The seven iron connected with the golf ball. The crisp report traveled to echo back from the stand of blossoming dogwood trees on the far boundary of Glen Ora, the President's weekend home in Middleburg, Virginia. John F. Kennedy straightened from the swing, his eyes following the arc of the ball. Like his brother Robert, he wore casual sports clothes. It was a clear day with the temperature in the high fifties. They stood alone, out of earshot of the Secret Service detail that lounged conspicuously about.

Considerable effort had been expended to make yesterday and today appear to be very much just another placid weekend in the life of the President, a carefully orchestrated, determined show of business as usual. Saturday morning was mostly taken up with keeping routine appointments with his staff people and a walk to the eighth-floor reception lounge of the State Department to deliver a brief address to a group assembled in honor of African Freedom Day. He had left Washington at 12:40, Saturday, by helicopter, to join his wife and children at Glen Ora. Sunday morning saw the Kennedy clan attending Mass at St. John's Parish in Middleburg.

After returning home from church and changing clothes, the President stepped out onto the lawn and spent time with his brother, practicing his golf swing. Robert's family had come over for dinner.

The President sent another ball arcing cleanly into the trees.

They had not spoken for more than five minutes when Robert said, "I guess you'd have to be family to see how gloomy you look up close, Mister President."

"Bobby, I appointed you to the Cabinet because I needed someone who would give me absolute loyalty. If I need a diagnosis, I have a personal physician."

"The pressure's on," said Robert. "Your first major presidential decision. You're still worried about the advisability of going ahead with the invasion."

"That, and the irksome feeling that keeps eating away at me whenever I give it the chance. A CIA agent dead on a Cuban beach. A Castro spy among us. Who, dammit? Who could it be?"

"And what about the invasion brigade?" asked Robert.

The President reached for another golf ball but did not stoop to place it on the tee. "It's too late to head them off. The deadline to recall the fleet carrying the Brigade has passed." He stared into the distance and tossed the golf ball up and down in his palm. "No one thinks yesterday's air strikes were by Cuban rebels. A second wave of air strikes will raise the international noise level to an intolerable degree."

"The stakes are higher than we've ever dealt with. The invasion of a neighboring country. That's big time, big brother. So what have you decided?"

The President thwacked another ball.

"We'll airdrop the Brigade paratroopers. A quick fly-over and they'll merge with the force coming in by sea. But there can be no more air strikes until the bombers can logically appear to be launched from the beach head."

Robert whistled under his breath. "That's going to make it a tall order for the invasion force. We're canceling the air cover they'll need to survive on the beach and in those swamps. Without air cover, with Castro's military supremacy on the ground...it'll be a massacre."

"I know. And now you know why I'm so gloomy, little brother."

CHAPTER 32

Late Sunday night, under low, sparse, cloud cover, the invasion fleet steamed single file into the silent, inky blackness of the Bay of Pigs. The small ships moved almost without sound, dark except for a lone light on each stern mast, visible only from the rear.

At about midnight on Sunday, Cosme and Lupita strolled to the bluff overlooking the bay where, the day before, Major Medina had accosted Cosme. It would have been a difficult walk had they not known the winding, deeply rutted road almost as intimately as they knew each other's bodies. The road twisted and turned as it climbed from the village of Giron. There was a moon but mostly it stayed behind the clouds. Beneath a palm tree on the bluff was "their spot," where they had first made love on a night much like this one. The lights of the village were a half-mile below and behind them. Between their spot and the village was a gaping maw of blackness that was the beach. The sound of the surf carried clearly up to their spot. They sat beneath the tree.

Lupita wore a plain white cotton summer dress, the same one she'd worn here on that first night. In the moonlight, clad in white that left revealed tawny shoulders, arms and legs, she looked like an angel, thought Cosme; an earthly angel of firm, young curves and hair that was darker than the night and brown eyes that danced with reflected moonbeams. An ache of need for her began in his groin and he wondered if he would feel this way when she was big and fat with their child. He told himself that a romantic night like tonight was no time or place for such ideas, and he wanted her here now, under the stars.

But first, he must deal with what he had been sensing since they slipped away.

"My darling, you have been so quiet. Tell me, what is it?"

"I'm afraid." She spoke in a small voice that he barely heard.

Lupita lived with her mother and father, her five siblings, of whom she was the oldest, and an uncle and her mother's parents. Cosme and Lupita alternated Sundays with each of the families and this was their weekend at her home. As a group they had watched Fidel Castro's televised funeral oration that afternoon from Colon Cemetery.

Fidel, wearing fatigues, had roared defiance and outrage from the podium, fueling the emotions of the crowd assembled for the burial of those who had died in the bombing raid on Campo Libertad. *"The attacks against us yesterday were no different than the raid on Pearl Harbor, except that it was twice as treacherous and a thousand times more cowardly!"*

Cosme remembered those around him nodding in agreement with Fidel's flickering image on the television screen. He doubted if anyone who viewed the broadcast, and that certainly included nearly the full population of Cuba, would soon forget the dramatic image of their leader strutting behind the microphone as waves of angry response from the crowds washed down over him.

"The attack yesterday was the prelude to the aggression of the mercenaries paid by the United States. Compare the admirable achievement of the Soviet Union in putting man into space with the American achievement of bombing the installations of a country that has no Air Force!" Fidel was pounding the podium with both fists, leaning closer to the bank of microphones. "What the imperialists cannot forgive us is that we have made a Socialist revolution under the nose of the United States. Are these the men who will come to overthrow the armed people? Don't make us laugh!" The voice rose to a thunderous climax. "We shall defend with these rifles this Socialist revolution of the humble, by the humble, and for the humble!"

The TV screen had next shown a sea of people raising their rifles in the sunlight, many hundreds of rifles, to the chants of *Fidel! Fidel!*

The telecast had been followed by a Sunday dinner enlivened by Lupita's father, who was a tailor, expounding at considerable length on the merits of Fidel and the Revolution. It had been a relief to get away.

Lupita gazed off across the waters of the bay, which were dappled with the moon's silver. "I'm worried about the world we're bringing our child into. How can our lives not be affected by what is happening? By this war Fidel says we will fight with the Americans? We want to raise a family. We have our whole lives ahead of us. But the future is so uncertain. What will happen?

"I don't know, Lupita." He reached for her. "Come into my arms. Let us forget these things."

She drew back. "Not tonight, Cosme."

"But, darling—"

"Cosme, when we were here yesterday, when those soldiers drove up and spoke with you–"

His throat grew dry. "Did you tell anybody about that?"

"No. You told me not to and I haven't. But, Cosme, *I* want to know."

He looked away. "I don't want to talk about it."

"But I do," she said. "If we are going to be husband and wife, we should have no secrets from each another?"

"It's best not to talk of some things."

"Please. You asked me to tell you what was troubling me and so I have."

He considered this. She waited for him to speak. He said, "The man I spoke with is Major Medina from the militia post, and his assistant. They are cruel, evil men."

"I could see that. I could not hear what you and he were saying, but I was frightened, Cosme. The driver, the black man with the bald head and the scarred face...it was like he was raping me with his eyes."

"Ramon. Yes, they frighten me also."

She touched his chin with fingertips and drew his face to hers. "How did you come to be involved with such men? Are you involved with them?"

The natural, musky scent of her tantalized his nostrils. His hands itched to touch her, to caress and stroke her body. He wanted her, and he well knew her stubborn streak. "What I tell you must stay between us alone."

"I promise."

A breeze off the ocean whispered through the pine needles overhead and stirred strands of her fragrant hair across brown eyes and tawny flesh that he so longed to kiss. She brushed the strands of hair back into place and this too excited him. He had to have her.

He said, "Well, as you know, my father belongs to the Revolution Defense Party in Giron."

"I know, and so does mine. They watch for anyone who does not love their Revolution. They spy on their neighbors. I do not care for politics, Cosme. I care only for our baby."

"It was through the Defense Party, I think, that Major Medina learned that I sometimes ran errands for our neighbors, the Vasquez family. My mother cared for *Señora* Vasquez and, since I was around, I came to know Carmen and her brother Diego."

"But what is Medina's interest in them?"

"It doesn't matter. He had me spy on them. I was made to feel that I had no choice. The Major threatened me without seeming to, you understand?"

"I do. I told you how they frightened me yesterday. Yes, I can understand how they could intimidate you."

Cosme thought he saw something in the near distance from the corner of his eye. The bay shimmered in the moonlight. Curiosity made him draw away from her, distracted from desire, and he stretched forward to get a better look from their grassy spot. Then he was certain of what he saw.

He pointed. "Lupita, look."

It took a moment before she too saw the shape that was an inky blur in the darkness, which had somehow positioned itself below their spot while they had been so caught up in their own world, in their conversation.

She gasped. "A ship!"

"I think I see another one."

They crouched side-by-side, leaning forward, squinting into the night.

Lupita said, "But what in the world are they doing out there?" She was mentally grappling with this startling discovery, just as he was.

Before he could think of something to say, a vehicle could be heard coming down the road where it snaked below their vantage point, along the beach, approaching from the direction of the militia post. Headlights probed ahead across the beach, then a Jeep drove into view, a heavy searchlight mounted on the back of the Jeep throwing a swath of light across the beach and surf.

Cosme flattened himself to the grassy ground, pressing Lupita to the earth beside him, the palm of his hand to the small of her back. "Down!" They hugged the ground together, peering at the activity below.

The arc of the searchlight brushed across something moving. Sound carried clearly on the night breeze. A Cuban soldier in the Jeep shouted something and the vehicle skidded to a stop, a loud squeaking of brakes and the searchlight was trained on at least a dozen men, waist deep in the water, coming ashore. Men in combat fatigues, carrying field packs on their backs and holding rifles. Behind them small, scattered black shapes bobbed in the surf.

"Rafts," said Cosme. "A landing party from the ships! But they hit the coral reefs."

The bark of weapons fire, sounding strangely flat in the wide-open spaces, and lances of saffron flame, crackled from the figures wading ashore.

Lupita gasped louder than before. "Oh, my God!"

There was sparse return fire from the Jeep. It had been a routine patrol. The soldiers were outnumbered. The landing party continued to advance and gained the beach. The exchange of gunfire ceased. Cosme was unable to tell whether the militiamen in the Jeep had been killed or had fled. There were shouts from the bodegas along the beach and from some of the other structures. Moonlight provided a view of the handful of invaders running up and down the beach, firing their rifles into the air and into the bodegas and running toward the village. One of them shouted, "*We've come to free Cuba from Communism!*" Within minutes, multicolored blinkers were winking.

"Landing lights," whispered Cosme.

Motorized sounds could be heard. Engines gunning to life. Splashing noises from the bulky shapes of the ships.

Cosme said, "This is it. The landing is *here*, at Giron!"

Lupita leapt to her feet, drawing him with her despite his reluctance. His heart was pounding against his ribcage.

She said, "We must go to our families."

"But we're safe here."

"Our place is with our families, Cosme. They may need our help. If you're not coming, I'm going by myself."

"I'm coming."

They ran hand-in-hand down the hill, toward the village.

CHAPTER 33

Carmen crouched with Felix, Santos and the others at a break in the trees up range from the beach at Giron. Felix was observing the landing through a pair of U.S.-issue field glasses. It was difficult to discern much of anything in the darkness except for the blinking lights the invaders had placed along the beach and, of course, the stabbing saffron flashes of gunfire that carried across the distance sounding like ignited strings of children's firecrackers.

When the gunfire eventually tapered off, Santos sighed. "I wish I could be down there with them."

Carmen said, "Be patient, big bear. Our turn will come soon enough." Like the others, she held her carbine with a round chambered, her finger on the trigger. An ammo pouch at each hip carried spare clips of ammunition.

Santos grumbled. "Patience is not my nature. At least I should be able to drink to the landing of our liberators."

Carmen chuckled. "You would drink to the sunrise and the sunset and everything that happens in between."

"And what would be wrong with that?"

Felix lowered the binoculars. "Nothing, if we weren't about to go into battle." His features were more intense than ever, but Carmen thought again that Felix seemed to have aged ten years during the past few hours. Felix placed an arm across Santos' broad shoulders. "When this day is done, we will drink a toast together to having survived it."

The bear's bluster melted into amiable warmth. "I don't believe I've ever seen you take a drink, amigo. That will be worth staying alive to see."

"Let us be gone, then. We're on to San Blas to take up our support position."

They group moved out at combat intervals, as they'd been taught. Felix and Carmen hadn't gone five paces, though, before Santos checked them with a meaty hand gripping each by an arm.

"Hold on, you two."

Felix glared down at the sausage-like fingers wrapped around his arm, then up into Santos's bearded face. "What foolishness is this?"

"Won't take but a second," said the bear. "Sometimes people don't know what's best for them. But in this case, I, Santos, know what's best. I know how you feel about Carmen, you see."

Felix's voice dropped dangerously. "Santos, be quiet."

Carmen found herself smiling in the darkness despite the meaty paw that pinned her arm. "Santos, please."

Santos' wide grin was resolute. "This may be the last chance you two will have to speak alone before we go into battle. Tell her what is in your heart, Felix, or I will." Santos released them and ambled off after the others.

Felix was more embarrassed than angry. "I could strangle that big oaf."

Carmen touched his arm. "Don't be harsh with him, Felix. I did not need our big bear to tell me how you feel."

The confusion that touched him then softened his hard features into the boyish demeanor she knew. "Carmen, I don't know what you mean. I...I have always been fond of you, it's true, since your brother Diego first introduced us—"

"Then I'm wrong," she said, knowing that she wasn't. "I must have misunderstood the affection I see in your eyes whenever we're together, even if there are others about."

He looked away. "I don't know what to say."

"Would it surprise you very much to know that I have a similar attraction to you?"

"I confess that it would."

"Felix, you are one of the bravest men I have ever known. Even when I worried about my brother being part of your group—of *this* group—and even when I resented you for placing him at risk, I always respected your bravery and integrity and your patriotism. Losing Diego and my mother so close together...you provided me with inspiration in my darkest hour, the way you persevere, risking your life every day for a goal, for our freedom from a dictator."

Felix let his breath out slowly. He clasped her hand. "Carmen, you fill my heart with joy. But if you've known how I felt, why have you not given me some sign or spoken to me of *your* feelings?"

"For the same reason that you withheld yours from me, or tried to. For now we must think only of victory against the enemy and concern ourselves with the task at hand. And we had better get started or we'll never catch up with Santos and the others."

"Perhaps I won't strangle him after all."

She delivered him a quick, chaste kiss to the cheek. "That would be ungrateful, wouldn't it? Come, now. Let us talk of these things when this day is over."

Castro was exhausted when his bodyguards escorted him from Colon Cemetery following his funeral oration Sunday afternoon. He had been working without rest for more than thirty hours. He retired early that evening.

An excited Che Guevara awakened him at 1:15 AM.

"The microwave radio stations at Giron and Playa Larga have reported military landings!"

Castro swung his feet to the floor, snatched a fresh cigar from his nightstand and stuck it in the corner of his mouth. "The Bay of Pigs. Of course. Remember, I said as much when we were there on Friday."

"The microwave stations have gone off the air."

Castro began dressing rapidly. "Naturally. The invaders must set up their provisional government as quickly as possible, to legitimize this attack. They will try for one major beachhead and Giron is it. And if they control Playa Larga, they can cut off our advance."

Che was frowning. "But can we be sure? Could it be that the Giron and Playa Larga landings are not really the main ones? General Almeida suggests these attacks may be a diversionary tactic designed to trick us into committing our forces in a side show."

They strode to Castro's office shoulder-to-shoulder with Castro setting a brisk pace, almost running.

"Remind the General of my intimate knowledge of that area. I know every path. The area is isolated, much of it is swamp. Very few roads lead in or out. There's an airstrip. For setting up a government under arms, it is perfect. This is the real enemy effort."

"Then the beachhead must be wiped out."

They stepped into Castro's office. He switched on the lights. "Their ships must be sunk, then the beachhead will have to collapse."

"We won't give them a chance to settle in and fortify," said Che.

Castro nodded. "And we must get what planes we have into the air at once. I'll be leaving here with the first column to the front."

"It will be daylight before our full force can reach the area."

Castro reached for the telephone on his desk. He remained standing. "There's a cadet school at Matanzas. I'll call the principal. Issue orders for troop mobilization directed immediately into the Bay of Pigs region."

"*Si*, Fidel."

Che hurried from the office.

Castro dialed the telephone.

A sleepy voice answered, "Captain Fernandez. Who is calling me at this ungodly hour?"

"This is Fidel."

"*Commandante*, my apologies!"

"The invasion has come, Captain. They're landing at different points near the Zapata Swamps. I want you to take your student battalion to the beaches to assist the militia in confronting the enemy without delay."

"But, *Commandante*, there is the matter of transportation."

"Your instructors will seize every truck in the area. See to it without delay."

"But this school is not organized as a combat unit."

"You will take the road through Covadonga to San Blas."

"But, Commandante–"

"Silence. Coward! See to it. I will be there as soon as possible with reinforcements to take full command."

CHAPTER 34

Five hours after the C-46's and their escort fighter planes had taken off from Puerto Cabezas, the Happy Valley staging area was ghostly quiet in the half-light of dawn.

Conklin walked into the Air Operations tent, where General Hudson sat sipping coffee.

"Have some," Hudson offered. "You look like you need it."

Conklin poured himself a cup. "Goddamn politicians, canceling those air strikes." He kicked a folding chair with enough force to clatter it into a corner. He threw the full coffee cup onto the ground after it. "Goddamn, how could they do this? An invasion without air cover? They're crazy!"

"Cool off. We all feel that way."

"I just left Medlow at the Op Shack, drunk on his ass. Maybe that is the best way to deal with a disaster in the making."

"So what's the latest? Or did you just walk over to get away from your friend, Medlow?"

Conklin took a deep breath, and drew another cup of coffee. "Assholes like me don't have friends, General, or haven't you noticed? What's the latest? Well, there's heavy fighting on the beaches. Seems our intel that the landing zones were without communications was dead wrong. They must have gone up recently. At Playa Larga there was a microwave radio station only a hundred meters from the beach and they had to have transmitted warnings to Havana before we took them out. The Second Battalion at Giron is taking heavy losses. It doesn't look good."

"Maybe they can still pull it off," said Hudson. "Our Cubans are well trained. The weather is favorable. Our fighter planes and the C-46's should be entering Cuban air space right about now to drop in the paratroopers."

Conklin sat opposite Hudson, ignoring his cup of coffee. "You haven't seen Morgan around, have you?"

"I thought you said he went into Puerto Cabezas on a drunk after you turned down his request to fly with the Brigade."

"Yeah, that's what he said he was going to do. Only he'd be back by now."

"So he bought himself a whore and went on a binge."

"Not that guy. Graveyard is meaner than hell but word is that he never fools around. Has himself a wife and supposedly loves her."

"So where do you think he is, Ben?"

Conklin's eyes narrowed. "I've just put it together. That mother humping son of a bitch is about to parachute into Cuba with those Cuban paratroopers."

Hudson chuckled wryly and refilled his coffee cup. "I'm glad that grunt isn't my headache. You should have expected it. I've heard the scuttlebutt. This isn't the first time he's played by his own rules."

"Yeah, not the first time," groused Conklin, "but this stunt is goddamn well going to be the last. Graveyard's going to find nothing but his own grave inside Cuba. He stowed away on a suicide mission."

The bulky C-46's approached the Cuban coast, each with an American fighter plane, flown by a CIA contract man, holding a defensible position right off the right wing. They passed over the Brigade ships that dotted the bay. Then they were flying over the village of Giron at no more than fifty feet to escape detection by radar, then into abrupt climbs as they approached the drop zone.

When the warning lights flashed, Morgan glanced at his Rolex. 0600 hours. Ten miles further and they'd be eight hundred feet over the DZ, over the road north from San Blas. He stood with the thirty paratroopers and went about checking his gear. He was fully rigged for a combat jump, the Randall knife on his hip, and assault rifle slung over his back. There was no escaping the sense of déjà vu that came with preparing to jump with these same men he had accompanied on a practice jump in Nicaragua. Minus, of course, Antonio Perez, the man who had leaped to his death on that flight.

Morgan hooked his static line to the anchor cable and took his place in one of the twin lines facing the rear of the plane. He caught the eye of the young platoon leader, José Cardena. They nodded briefly to each other. Then José went back to keeping his eye on the hulking, brutish Garcia who stood opposite him.

There had been some last minute confusion at the staging area as the airplanes had loaded, making it easy for Morgan to board with José's unit. The men had seemed pleased but not surprised when Morgan merged with them as they boarded. Garcia had looked right through him and when Morgan saw the big ex-Batista soldier up close, he knew why. Garcia looked like he'd already gulped down handfuls of the little yellow bennies every combatant had been issued to keep them going.

Morgan dozed during much of the five-hour flight. He never used bennies in combat or anywhere else. He wanted to keep his mind clear, his reflexes sharp. Adrenaline would keep him awake. And there was the loose end left behind to nag at his mind. He had been sent to identify and take out a spy within the Brigade ranks. But that mission was being overtaken by greater events. Had Antonio Perez been the mole he'd been sent to find? The nature of Morgan's work was leaving loose ends behind, but this one irked him. He had liked Perez. In all likelihood, he would never learn if the guy had been a spy or not. This irked him. He had long ago learned to accept loose ends, but never to like them.

And like most of the men on the plane, he suspected, his thoughts touched on home and family during the five-hour flight to Cuba. He thought about Vera, and about his daughter. He hoped like hell that Susan had learned nothing, had uncovered no information about Doctor Rivas or his activities that would put her at risk. About to enter a war zone, he should be dropping into the fire with these men, doing so with the knowledge that his family was safe back in "the world." He was doing this for his family. This was his job, his duty, yes, and he would have it no other way. A Soviet foothold in the Western Hemisphere, ninety miles from the American mainland? No, that could not stand. Before long the Soviets would be shipping more than food and military advisors to Cuba. Soon there would be missile silos all over that island, with nuclear warheads targeting American cities. Averting something like that, and the inevitable destruction of those cities when Soviet missiles were launched from Cuba, was a duty he welcomed. But Susan and Vera...this should not involve them. He regretted more than ever getting his daughter involved. What a fool he had been. He thought, *God, let them be safe...*

The buzzer sounded. The rear exit door yawned open to expose the sky above and the road, bordered by swampland, blurring by below. Positioned as he was near the front of the line of men, Morgan got a clear view of fires billowing along the road. He saw a Jeep full of soldiers. As the plane flew over the Jeep, the soldiers in it opened fire with rifles and pistols. He flattened himself against the bulkhead, as did the others near the exit. The C-46 flew on several more minutes, following the road north. When the red light went on again, Morgan, José, Garcia and the rest went running and tumbling out into space, a planeload of men jumping in less than fifteen seconds.

Their C-46 banked around to join the others in withdrawal.

Morgan rode his risers, aiming for the road, with men floating down all around him. The smell of the swamp, the stink of decay—animal, vegetation and human—rose up to draw him into a tangible embrace.

He was several hundred feet from the ground when an anti-aircraft gun, sounding like a big bass drum from three quarters of a mile to the south, opened fire on the formation of planes. A mobile job, thought Morgan, concealed under camouflage netting. There was a fiery flash from the same C-46 they'd been aboard and a few seconds later the *ka-whump!* of the explosion carried to him, muffled by the distance. Then a high keening whine as the big plane went into a slow, almost graceful nose-diving tailspin, trailing black smoke like a grim streamer from its tail. The big plane disappeared into the dense green of the swampland and seconds later a red fireball rose into the sky, bright as the sun. A thick black pillar of smoke snaked into the air, marking where the C-46 had gone down.

The accompanying fighter planes banked around and dived into a strafing run at treetop level. The anti-aircraft gun fell silent. The fighters flew off to rejoin the remaining cargo planes, which by now were receding black specks in the pale blue sky.

Morgan landed with bone-jarring impact. He rolled once and came up running onto the wide shoulder of the dirt road. Like those landing around him, he hurriedly circled the canopy and collapsed it, popping the quick release box to shrug off the harness. He snatched up the kitbag and stuffed his chute and helmet into it. He sprinted over to join the platoon, who were gathering nearby, their rifles ready, and every man eyeing the dense, green wall of swamp.

The hot sunshine was oppressive even at this early hour. The swamp should have been alive with the prattle of crickets and the croaking of bullfrogs. There was excruciating stillness to the surrounding spongy morass of decay and waterlogged muck that permeated the senses. The swamp made Morgan think of a monstrous living organism only pretending to be dead, waiting patiently to devour them.

Further up the road, it sounded like no more than half a mile, an exchange of weapons fire could be heard.

José completed a fast headcount. "It looks like we're all accounted for. We made it!"

"Good for you," said Morgan. "Welcome to hell."

CHAPTER 35

The convoy was a mile long and roared past the ragged line of civilian vehicles, which had been forced to pull off the road to allow the column from Havana to thunder past, stirring up thick clouds of suffocating dust. There was singing from the military convoy hurtling by. Bearded, rifle-bearing soldiers were shouting: *Viva La Revolucion!* The trucks and trailers, filled with troops, were followed by Howitzers and anti-aircraft artillery, then a dozen or more tanks poured by on their way to Giron.

Medina sat in the tonneau of a ten-year-old Peugeot at the head of a line of civilian cars. Captain Fernandez, Commander of the Matanzas cadet school, chauffeured the Peugeot. Ramon sat next to Fernandez in the front passenger seat. The car's interior stank of body odor, the windows having been raised to keep out the dust. The half-dozen confiscated civilian vehicles behind the Peugeot carried those cadets who had managed to survive a night of savage fighting in the swamps and on the beaches.

Ramon muttered. "How long can this convoy be!"

Medina felt like shit. His normally starched and pressed fatigues were mud-spattered, blood-splattered and soiled with his sweat, and the stench of the swamp clung to his skin, hair and nostrils. He decided to lower his window a notch. Better the dust than the stink inside the car.

He said, "I would not want to be the American mercenaries who thought they could invade us. They'll get no further than the beaches and this swamp."

Fernandez sighed. He dabbed with his sleeve at the perspiration that made shiny his flushed, round face. "At least our part in it is done."

"Quite so."

"We took bitter losses." Fernandez spoke with flat, emotionless words. "And I thought the fighting would end with the revolution. Now I must personally write the mother of every boy in my command who fell in last night's battle."

Medina tried to muster a sympathetic tone. "Of course, Captain. A terrible thing. As you know, my own command was practically annihilated. But at least we held the invaders confined to the village and the beach. Our men—your boys—died fighting for the glory of Mother Cuba and the Revolution."

Fernandez considered him with somber, searching eyes. "When you were missing for several hours, Major, we feared the worst."

Medina could detect no trace of sarcasm, and so he nodded. "As did I. They had us pinned down. It was...terrible, fighting side by side with my men and seeing so many of them die before the rest scattered in panic. Seeing them cut down...horrible. Ramon and I were so fortunate to survive. Then we wandered, lost for more than an hour in the swamp before we found this road. It's lucky for us that you came by."

Ramon had not taken his eyes from the passing convoy. "Here's the end of it."

Medina tapped Fernandez on the shoulder. "You see, Captain? The fight is in able hands. Let us continue home. Our part is done."

Fernandez started the Peugeot. The vehicles from the academy rattled to life behind it. The Peugeot led the way back onto the road and through the curtain of settling dust.

Medina felt that he was being watched, and realized that the cadet commandant was eyeing him with unwavering, speculative eyes from the Peugeot's inside rearview mirror.

Cosme and Lupita crouched with a small group of people in tangled vegetation along a narrow back road. Their frightened group hugged the ground. There was Lupita's mother, her brothers and sisters and one sister's husband and their infant child. And there was Cosme's mother and grandmother. The single uniformity among them was their grimy, unkempt appearance and the desperation and fear that Cosme could smell like a tangible thing. The sun blazed in a cloudless sky. The mosquitoes were almost unbearable despite regular applications of ointment.

One hundred meters away on the other side of the road was a deserted country store, no more than a clapboard shack with a gas pump in front. The windows were broken out and rows of bullet holes ran across the front of the building. There was nothing else except swampland and the deeply rutted road, sometimes used by hunters. There had been no traffic for the past half-hour.

Giron was in flames. Castro's artillery had opened fire an hour earlier and never stopped.

Cosme and Lupita had returned to the village the night before to find that the landing party had already taken over a bar and set up a radio to start calling in reinforcements. The men of the landing party stood in front of the bar and fired their weapons into the air. Villagers fled their homes without their belongings. Shadows scurried here and there. Chaos reigned. Cosme and Lupita had gone to her family's home first. Finding no on there, they found Lupita's family already with Cosme's family, about to leave Cosme's home. Their families had long known each other and this was a time to draw together for mutual protection. Having reunited, their little group fled to the outskirts of the village, to hide and await the morning, concealing themselves behind this thick blanket of dry sugarcane leaves.

The landing quickly became a full-scale invasion. Hordes of invaders and equipment came ashore to converge on Giron. A defense perimeter was quickly established, though by that time they were safely in the fields overlooking the village. At first there had been heavy fighting when Major Medina's militiamen attacked. Explosions lighted the sky like red lightning, both sides firing at everything that moved. The militiamen were shouting: *Fatherland or death*! as they charged into battle. Then a small convoy of civilian vehicles from another direction had disgorged cadets from the military academy. Later, when the initial fighting had dissipated somewhat, the night was filled with the crack of sniper fire. Automatic weapons chattered in reply from the beach. The cries of the wounded rippled through the night.

With the first light of dawn, cargo planes had flown in and the skies not far to the north were dotted with descending paratroopers. One of the planes had gone down. The others had flown off, not to return.

Cosme's father and Lupita's father had left then to return on foot to the village where Cosme's father had left his family's flatbed truck in a shed where it might still be if neither side had discovered and confiscated it during the night. The men had been gone for more than two hours. Shortly after their departure, the fighting resumed. Tanks were pounding the village, taking stubborn return fire from the entrenched invaders.

Lupita said, "Someone's coming."

"Everybody stay quiet," whispered Cosme.

He crept to where the vegetation bordered the road and looked in the direction from which a lone vehicle could be heard approaching at high speed.

Lupita's mother said, "Is it them?" in a small, scared voice so unlike her usual matriarchal manner.

"No," said Cosme. "Be still, everyone. Please."

A Jeep, top-heavy with Fidelista soldiers, flew past, taking the road deeper into the swamp.

Lupita's brother-in-law said, "It will not be easy, avoiding the fighting."

Lupita said, "It is the only chance we have. We can't stay here forever."

In that moment, Cosme saw a strength of character in Lupita that he had not seen before, or perhaps he had just never noticed it, he thought. He was nervous and afraid inside, and he wondered if Lupita felt the same or if she truly was more brave and steady than he felt in this crisis.

Cosme's mother was fervently pressing her rosary beads to her ample bosom. "I wish they would hurry back! They have been gone for so long. We should have taken the truck and fled last night."

Cosme shook his head, no. He swatted at a mosquito. "My father and your husband know what they're doing, *señora*. To be on the road last night...if the invaders had not killed us, the militiamen would have mistaken us for the enemy and opened fire. We had to wait for daylight."

"But where can they be?"

"Mother, please. We must remain calm."

Lupita placed a reassuring hand upon the sleeve of her future mother-in-law. "They will come with the truck and we'll get away from here, you'll see."

One of her sisters was weeping softly. "But there is fighting every-where!"

Then Cosme heard the familiar engine rattle of the old flatbed truck.

"Here they come!" He tried to keep from shouting. "Come on, everybody. We're getting out of here."

By midmorning, Castro had established a command post in the adminis-tration building of a sugar mill, a decrepit, pastel-green structure located at the junction of two roads that bisected the swamp. The telephone in the manager's office was his direct line to Point One. A grimy wall in the office was dominated by a map of the coastline, dotted onshore and off with red pins.

When an orderly showed in Major Medina and Ramon, Castro

was pacing before the map, holding a pointer, addressing his battalion commanders.

"Our counterattack is going far too slowly." The pointer indicated the map. "Their supply ships have been sunk by our fighter planes. We have cut off their supplies and ammunition. Now we must close in for the kill. I want their heads!"

One general said, "They fight like devils, *Commandante*. Our losses have been heavy. But we're driving them back to the sea. They are in retreat."

Castro gestured with the other hand, which held his cigar. "Not quickly enough, I say. There are side roads, which the tanks could be using. I will draw a map for each of you to take back to your units, and you will redeploy accordingly. I know every road in this swamp. We will bypass Playa Larga and attack it from the rear, then push on to reinforce Giron. I am told the remaining supply ships have turned tail and fled back to the sea. It is but left to us to deliver the *coup de grace* and we will do so with dispatch."

The generals crowded around Castro while he drew the crude maps. This took about five minutes, during which Castro ignored Medina and Ramon, as did the others.

When they were gone, Castro took an exaggerated length of time to relight his cigar. When he had it going to his satisfaction, wreathing his head in smoke, he turned to observe Medina and Ramon as if for the first time.

"Major Medina. How fortunate that you survived last night's fighting."

Medina stood at attention and saluted. "*Commandante!* Yes, Ramon and I are lucky to be alive."

Castro ignored the salute. "Indeed. Sadly, most of your command did not fare as well. They fought valiantly for their homeland. Unlike yourself and your man here," he barely glanced at the hulking black man, "most of your command has paid the supreme sacrifice."

"A part of me wishes that I could have died with them, *Commandante*."

"Well, that's good," said Castro. "Because, Major, you are about to get another chance at doing just that."

Ramon's scarred face twisted with confusion. "What do you mean, sir?"

"Silence, you!" said Castro. He continued speaking to Medina. "You were reported missing last night, before you joined up with Captain Fernandez and his cadets. Where were you exactly during that time, Major?"

"*Commandante*, I have nothing to hide."

Castro blew a stream of cigar smoke into Medina's face, his upper lip curled into a sneer. "Do you think I don't know a coward when I see one? And what of your mission to disrupt the underground in this area that are cooperating with the invasion?'

"*Commandante,* there was the American spy on the beach whom you personally executed, and Diego Vasquez."

"Ah, but you have proven you're unable to capture the leader of the underground, this Felix Carriles. His group is out there right now, as we speak, fighting alongside the invaders. He was your responsibility, Major, and you've failed me in not apprehending him, while on the field of honor, you have no honor. You were out there last night hiding somewhere while better men than you went to their death. Yes, Major, you have failed me. But as I say, I am giving you another chance."

"Another chance, *Commandante*?"

"Yes. I am sending you to join a detachment of infantry, or what is left of them. They took heavy losses this morning in the area of San Blas. Their commanding officer was killed. Your orders are to police the back roads, in the event the invaders try to disperse and attempt to melt into the countryside. And I warn you, Major, this time do not fail. If you do, it would be better for you if you did fall on the field of honor. Now leave my sight, both of you."

Morgan, José and Garcia traveled on foot through the cane field, skirting the swamp south of San Blas. From several hundred yards off to their left, beyond the wall of cane, men yelled harshly in Spanish, immediately buried beneath the angry hammering exchange of automatic weapons fire. The shouting and gunfire abruptly ceased and again there was only the sunny quiet except for the crunch of their footsteps as they hurried along.

Morgan thought, *It's like I never left Nam.* Oh yeah, it was swamp instead of jungle. Cane fields instead of rice paddies. But everything else...a morning of rifle fire from the trees, men around him falling, kicked off their feet by volleys of incoming fire. Returning fire at shadowy targets, clip fired off after clip at an enemy you rarely saw. Sweat. Blood. Smoke. Shouting and the screams of the badly wounded. Movement everywhere. And yet, splinters of time, of tense stillness when you could feel the blood pounding in your ears and your gasping breath seemed loud enough to provide your enemy target acquisition.

They'd parachuted in just as Castro's tanks and reinforcements from Havana came storming into the area. The situation in a nutshell was that they were without air cover. Their invasion force was outflanked and outgunned. The swamps and back roads and cane fields inland from the beaches were littered with the dead. Morgan had seen good men die this day and he had killed in defense and in retaliation. Maybe he hadn't seen the enemy fall but there wasn't much escaping the withering figure-eight fire patterns he'd hosed into those tree lines, into enemy positions, his rifle on full auto fire until the muzzle grew red-hot. But everyone was getting cut to ribbons and the enemy fire just kept coming closer from every direction including the air. Brigade fighters had scattered under the awesome might of Castro's counter-attack. Morgan hadn't expected José's platoon to cave so quickly but that's what happened and suddenly he, José and the big Batista brute, Garcia, found themselves separated from the others and dodging for whatever cover they could find, hoofing it through a cane field.

From somewhere behind them, a tank opened fire with a loud, nasty *boom!* Rifle fire joined in. They threw themselves down to hug the ground. Explosions pounded close and bullets rattled the cane leaves around them.

Morgan wiped sweat from his eyes. "They don't know what they're firing at. They'll move on."

The rifle fire tapered off. The tank boomed twice more, far misses both times. Then came the distant clank of the tank tread grinding up the road, moving away from them.

José said, "We should double back. They would never expect that. We can regroup with the others."

Morgan took a pull on his canteen. "Right about now most of those others you're talking about, the ones who can walk, will be doing what we're doing. Keeping low and off the road and looking for a way out of this killing field."

Garcia spat with a grunt of disgust. "Retreat? José, why should we take orders from this gringo? I will not run away."

Morgan said, "Then call it a tactical withdrawal so we can live to fight another day. I'd call it a successful rout by the enemy."

José glared at Garcia. "How can you want more of the same? You saw the losses we took after that column of tanks and fresh troops poured in. We had Brigade infantry and mortars to back us up, but we've run out of mortars and everyone is low on ammunition."

Morgan said, "That last column of Fidelista troops and tanks came from the west. That's from Havana, and Playa Larga. If they can spare men and tanks from Playa Larga, it means they're close to wiping out all resistance there. They'll outflank us." He pointed in the direction they were heading. "This cane field can't go on forever. There have to be other roads cutting through, for harvest if nothing else. When we find one, we'll follow it and take our chances dodging enemy patrols"

Garcia snorted. "And let them drive us into the sea? We should try to reach the mountains. It's better than being killed."

José said, "It's too far to the mountains."

"Don't try talking sense to him," said Morgan. "He's been popping too many bennies and he's spilled too much blood. That gets to some men. They get crazy from it." He said to Garcia, "What the hell are you going to use for ammunition? Two of our ships have been sunk and the rest sailed out to sea and left us behind."

Garcia looked ready to throw himself at Morgan. "Because your American military didn't give us the support they promised! It's the fault of you gringos that our men have fallen and that we're in this situation."

Morgan slapped a mosquito at the back of his neck. "I can't disagree with you there. But right now I'm trying to keep us alive. José asked me to join this party. If you two want to split up from me and take off on your own separate way, well, just say the word."

José's expression tightened. "Garcia speaks for himself. You know how I feel, señor. You are the only one of us with combat experience. You can get us out of this if anybody can. I'm with you. What about you, Garcia?"

Garcia avoided their eyes. "I will stay with you two, for now."

Morgan rose into a combat crouch. "Then let's move out. Garcia, you take point. Anyone as bloodthirsty as you are, I want in front of me."

CHAPTER 36

A windmill stood at a curve in the road that ran through the cane field, near an abandoned farm. Medina and Ramon sat near the road, their backs against a drinking trough for animals. There had been bombing along here. There were craters in the road. Some dead bodies in fatigues lay in the culvert a hundred yards away and the buzz of feasting flies was a sinister, industrious drone in the steamy heat of the day. Formations of vultures circled over the field of battle. Ongoing firefights could be heard in every direction.

Ramon said, "It's getting difficult to stay away from the fighting."

Medina cupped a hand into the trough and splashed dirty water across his forehead. "We're driving them back. Our side will win."

"While we hide on this desolate road. If Fidel finds out, he'll kill you, Major."

Medina thought he detected a note of satisfaction in Ramon's voice. He said, "Us, Ramon. He would kill us both. You would do well to remember that, my black friend. We must work together, you and I, if we are to come out of this alive. We will stay right here. Our chance will come to bring honor upon ourselves, but on my terms."

Ramon said, "Listen. A truck approaches."

"See if you can identify it."

Ramon parted cane leaves to stare down the road. "A truckload of civilians, coming this way."

"Villagers fleeing the front," said Medina. "We'll let them pass. They can be of no use to us."

Ramon scanned the cane field across the road. "Major. Over there."

Medina followed the direction Ramon was pointing to. He nodded. "Ah, very good."

Three men clad in fatigues, outfitted for combat and carrying rifles, were emerging from the cane several hundred meters along the road in the opposite direction from the approaching truck.

Ramon said, "They're coming this way."

Medina lowered himself behind the trough, out of view of the road, and his finger curved around the trigger of his rifle. Ramon did the same.

Medina said, "Let them get closer."

"What about the people in the truck?"

"What about them? We'll use them for cover, if we have to. All that matters, Ramon, is that we have been handed our redemption in the eyes of Fidel. Let those three get just a little closer, so we can't miss."

Cosme stood in the truck bed, steadying himself as his father steered the vehicle toward a bend in the dirt road. He stared across over the roof of the cab, eyeing the road ahead. The three oldest men—Papa, Lupita's father and her brother-in-law—sat in the cab, leaving him to ride in back with the women and children. But he didn't mind. He wanted to stay close to Lupita.

She sat with her back against the truck cab, both of her arms wrapped around his left leg, her head leaning against his outside thigh as if he were the only person in her world that she wanted to lean on. This filled him with affection that was almost as strong as his apprehension. They were getting away. They were together. They and their baby inside Lupita would be safe, soon.

They'd encountered no one since loading into the truck and leaving their hiding place. From the countryside around them could be heard the sounds of war, but those sounds were starting to diminish, mostly centered around Giron which was falling away behind them.

Cosme wished he had a weapon. His father had an old hunting rifle and that was the only weapon aboard the truck. Soon they would reach San Blas. His father knew these roads and trails. With luck, they could avoid what fighting did continue in the area. He had never cared about politics. He and Lupita would walk through life together, would grow old together, sustained by their love and the love of their families, and when this nightmare passed, they would never speak of politics. He hoped something bad would happen to Major Medina and his scary assistant, Ramon. It would be fine if they were both killed in the fighting. He never should have accepted Medina's offer to spy on the Vasquez family. He was relieved to know that the information he'd furnished Medina had not been responsible for the death of Diego, and he was grateful that circumstances had prevented him from causing trouble for Carmen.

The truck slowed for the curve in the road. Ahead, a windmill came into view. There was a water trough at its base. A short distance beyond the windmill, three men were advancing along the side of the road. They wore fatigues and carried rifles.

Then Cosme saw the two figures were stretched flat upon the ground behind the watering trough, hiding from view of the three approaching men. The ones behind the trough were taking aim with rifles on the men, who had paused and were conferring among themselves. That's when they noticed the truck while remaining unaware of the men about to ambush them.

As the truck rounded the bend, Cosme recognized the men behind the trough. *Medina! Ramon!*

The truck slowed because the men in the cab saw the three men in the road. Cosme saw the ambushers only because he stood in the truck bed, and he was the only one standing. He alone saw the danger ahead, and he began pounding an open palm upon the roof of the cab, shouting for his father to stop.

When they saw the truck easing into the curve in the road, José said, "What should we do?"

Morgan said, "Pull back into the cane so they know we don't mean them any harm. Let them pass."

Garcia snarled and brought up his rifle. "Let them pass? You're crazy, gringo. We'll commandeer that truck and if they don't like it—"

Morgan raised his rifle so the muzzle was touching Garcia's left ear. "I've about had it with you, big boy. Do as you're told. Our fight isn't with the Cuban civilians. This is a war between soldiers. We let them pass."

José said, "Do as he says, Garcia. There's no reason to—"

Rifle fire from very close by opened up on them, the bullets kicking up gravel, snicking through the air like enraged hornets, whistling into the cane behind them, making the three of them duck reflexively. The flatbed truck, carrying civilians, braked to a stop just short of the watering trough and windmill. Morgan saw alarmed faces staring from the cab. In the bed of the truck, people were clambering to their feet.

Morgan saw the rifle flashes coming from behind the water trough. He swung his rifle in that direction.

Garcia shouted, "They're firing at us from the truck!" He skipped away from Morgan and tugged a grenade from his combat webbing, pulled the pin and flung the grenade with a powerful right arm overhand.

"Damn you," said Morgan. He slammed into Garcia with enough force to send them both toppling to the ground.

The white phosphorous grenade scored a direct hit. A thunderclap cut short the shrieks of panic from those aboard the truck and was echoed an instant later by the secondary explosion of the gas tank blowing up.

Morgan pulled free of Garcia, knocking the rifle from his big man's hands. He brought the butt of his rifle against Garcia's forehead with savage force. "You bastard, you're killing innocent people!"

Garcia roared and drew back, unaffected by the blow. He unsheathed his knife and threw himself at Morgan with the roar of an enraged bull.

Morgan tracked his rifle up, saying, "Screw it. That's twice you've pulled a knife on me."

Rifle fire resumed from behind the trough. Morgan shifted his attention to where José was already pressing himself to the ground next to the road. Something hot and liquid splashed across Morgan's face and it wasn't until he was down next to José, bringing his weapon around, that he realized he'd been sprayed with Garcia's blood. The big ex-Batista man lay like a beached whale in the middle of the road, the side of his head blown away, a glistening, pulpy red horror. He wouldn't be pulling any more knives.

The truck had rolled into a tree on the opposite side of the road. Shrapnel from the grenade exploding in the bed of the truck had ripped through the cab, decapitating the three men inside. Smoke rose from the rear of the truck, where arms and legs draped limply over the sides. But there was no movement. There were no survivors. A severed foot, smoldering at the ankle, lay in the middle of the road.

Morgan joined José, making as small a target of himself as possible, rapidly triggering single shots at the trough where muzzle flashes continued to flare. The air whistled with bullets.

He felt a sudden, sharp blow to the side of his head.

"*Shit!*" he heard himself say.

The sky pinwheeled. The ground smacked him in the face and he seemed to keep on going, as if the ground would not stop him. As if a giant pit was opening and he just kept falling into its blackness, leaving the world behind.

At the prattle of weapons fire that could be heard ahead from the direction of the road, Felix Carriles came to a halt and raised a hand. Carmen and Santos drew up alongside him on the narrow footpath that cut through the cane field.

Santos listened with his head cocked like a hunting dog. "No more than three or four weapons. Not a big fight."

Carmen said, "Yes, but it means that someone on our side could be pinned down."

Felix nodded. "They're returning to Giron, just as we are, to help the Brigade hold the beachhead."

Their small group had been intercepted only thirty minutes earlier by a Fidelista foot patrol and the blazing firefight, which had lasted for nearly half an hour, had left Carmen and these two men as the only survivors of their original unit. They had been so full of hope. So full of determination. And now, those others were so dead...

The gunfire dwindled away to nothing.

Santos growled through his beard. "I said it didn't sound like much."

Carmen took a sip from her canteen and spilled some drops due to the tremor in her hand. "What if all of our people are dead? What if the underground has been wiped out except for a scattered few like us?"

"Be strong, little one." Santos spoke in a gentle voice she'd never heard him use before.

Felix said, "We escaped. Why wouldn't others? Quiet now, both of you."

They advanced to where the cane field was bisected by a dirt road. The air here was heavy with a haze of smoke from the wreckage of a truck and with the stench of burnt flesh and death. Charred limbs protruded here and there from the bed of the truck. There was a fallen body clad in green fatigues not far from a bend in the road. Near the truck was a windmill and a water trough, behind which were two men, prone upon the ground with their rifles.

"Medina." Carmen whispered the name like a curse.

Santos growled low and dangerous. "It's about time we paid back these two."

Felix said, "No more talking. Follow me."

CHAPTER 37

The absolute silence had Medina's nerve ends stretched taut.

Ramon said, "It's been five minutes."

"There were two of them left. They could be waiting for us to move."

"We can't stay here forever. What should we do, Major?"

Medina had always known Ramon to be stoic of manner except for the glimmer of pleasure he sometimes detected when Ramon was "interrogating" a prisoner. But Ramon's expression now was drawn with concern; his eyes and mouth were tight slits in his scarred black face.

Medina said, "You take off in one direction for the canebrake behind us, I'll take off in the other. Lay down heavy fire as we run."

"Whenever you say."

"On the count of three," said Medina. "One, two, *three!*"

Ramon darted from cover, firing his rifle as he started for the canebrake, firing a burst across the road. Medina remained where he was, pressing himself even lower to the ground. Rifle fire blazed from across the road. Ramon was kicked off his feet and deposited face down, spread-armed, halfway between the trough and the cane field. His body twitched once, then lay still, a spreading pool of blood darkening the ground beneath him. The firing from across the road ceased.

Medina twisted away from the trough, but not to stand and run. He crawled toward the canebrake. Gunfire from across the road. A round kicked up dirt perhaps a foot ahead of him and another zinged past his ear. He did not waste time returning fire. He was almost upon the canebrake. Someone, concealed from him by the wall of cane, fired a three-round burst at him from his left. He had no choice now, being fired on as he was from two separate directions. He must reach the cover of that canebrake. He must not end up like Ramon. Remaining prone on the ground, he angled his rifle in the direction of this new attack and triggered an extended burst. Someone in there shouted in pain and began thrashing about wildly. Medina slowed, not sure of which way to go. Who was firing on him now? How many were there? Had they outflanked him?

"*Bastardo!*" A woman's voice shrieked at him from his right.

He swiveled his eyes and his rifle in that direction. A woman stood there, holding a rifle, ten feet from him. The shock of recognition, under these circumstances, stunned him.

He said, "Carmen Vasquez!"

The next report of her rifle was the last sound he heard.

Carmen did not wait to watch Medina's body flop upon the ground. She'd winced as the bullet had clipped away the upper half of his forehead. She hurried toward the thrashing and the groans of pain that were coming from beyond her line of vision, within the cane. She could hear a pitiful moaning that she barely recognized.

She heard Felix say in a gurgling voice, "Kill me, Santos. Please, kill me. I'm dying...the pain...I can't bear this pain. Mother of God. Amigo, I beg you...*kill* me!"

Carmen quickened her pace. "*No!*"

A single gunshot checked her forward movement as if she had run into a glass wall. For an instant, the world teetered, but she maintained her balance. The groaning, the thrashing, ceased. Santos emerged from the canebrake, his rifle aimed skyward, its stock balanced against his hip. His bearded face was drawn. His eyes were vacant.

Carmen said, "Oh..." in a small voice and started past him.

His free hand caught her arm. "Carmen, no. Stop. It would do you no good to see."

"You killed him."

"I released him."

"You killed him."

"He was dying. He'd been hit three times by that burst Medina fired. His..." Santos choked back a sob, "...his whole middle was gone. He was practically cut in half. Felix was dying and he knew it. I had to do it, Carmen. I'm sorry. I had to."

"And now there are only the two of us."

Santos jostled her roughly. "Carmen, I had no choice. He begged me to end his pain. I could not refuse him."

"I heard him. I'm sorry, Santos. Yes, what you did was...right."

"That's my brave *meija*. Now you and I must work at staying alive."

She saw something. She raised her rifle.

"What's that?"

A Cuban in fatigues was advancing up the road toward them. He was carrying an unconscious man across his back.

Santos said, "Hold your fire. These are the ones we came to help. Cover me."

He moved forward to assist the man by assuming some of the weight of the unconscious figure who, Carmen saw, was a gringo, also in fatigues.

The Cuban took one look at their civilian clothes, their rifles, and he knew who they were. He said, "I am José Cardena. I am with the invasion brigade. My friend is wounded."

Santos growled like a bear. "We can see that. But he is *Americano*. Have they joined the battle?"

"No such luck. They maneuvered the dead weight of the unconscious man off the road. "But this one is different. And he is a Green Beret."

A flicker of admiration shone in Santos' face. "The best they have!"

Carmen lowered her rifle. She watched the road in either direction. "Are there other Green Berets with him, with you?"

"No. He alone flew in with us. We must get him to safety."

Santos grunted. "We must get ourselves to safety. This day has seen enough blood spilled."

"Thank God," said Carmen.

They struggled to angle the unconscious American into the cane. He was a big man.

"Don't thank God for this," said Santos. "The battle is over, and we have lost."

It was midnight, Monday.

In the Cabinet Room in the West Wing, the President looked exceedingly tired. Deep creases at the corners of his eyes and the drawn line of his mouth bespoke a dark, angry mood in sharp contrast to his attire. He was in white tie, as were the Vice President, Secretary of Defense, Secretary of State and the Director of the Central Intelligence Agency. The President's brother, Robert, also sat at the conference table. The Joint Chiefs of Staff were there too, in full dress uniform, their medals gleaming.

All present had attended the annual reception for members of Congress in the White House. A gala evening featuring a Marine Band in the main foyer, with the staterooms filled to capacity. The Kennedys had established a new precedent this evening. Rather than following the tradition of standing in one room while the guests filed by to shake hands with them, the President and First Lady had instead moved from room to room, mingling with the guests, thus freeing the huge East Room for dancing. The President had spent the evening chatting first to one Senator, then another.

During the day, the Cabinet Room had become an emergency command post. Newspapers and memoranda were scattered across the table. Maps of the invasion area were displayed on easels. Civilian and military assistants had been hurrying in and out via the three doors throughout the day with communications that had been flowing in steadily across the wire service news tickers.

The President and his brother had been in and out all day, monitoring developments as their schedules permitted.

The President began this briefing. "Let me have the bad news first."

Allen Dulles clamped an unlit pipe in the corner of his mouth. His complexion was ashen. "I'm afraid it's all bad, sir. I regret to say the operation has failed. The Brigade fought valiantly, by all accounts, but they made it no further than the beaches and the Zapata swamp. Castro retaliated with a massive force that managed to encircle and overwhelm them. The ammo supply ships never made it out. They were sunk in the bay."

Someone, not the President, cursed.

A general suggested, "It's not too late to send some of our forces in."

An admiral added, "Mister President, you could give the authorization to scramble jets from the Essex."

Another concurred. "Send the destroyers offshore and they could knock the hell out of Castro's tanks."

The President held a pencil, tapping its eraser upon the tabletop. "No. I will not commit American forces. We must continue to maintain minimum visibility. I will not be pressured into committing our military." He seemed to realize that he was tapping the pencil and he ceased doing so.

Dulles spoke from behind a cloud of pipe smoke. "It was bedlam at the monitoring station at Opa-Locka when the exile leaders heard what happened. Three threats of suicide, the rest of them demanding to be sent down and put ashore with the Brigade even after it was obvious how things were going to turn out. The agents on site ought to qualify as psychiatrists, the way they handled those crazy Cubans."

Robert said, "We can't very well blame them, can we? They took a hell of a shellacking. One hundred and fourteen killed, almost twelve hundred captured."

Kennedy took a deep breath and exhaled slowly. "I hate it too, Bobby.

But for us, politically, it will blow over. We promised to try to give Fidel a run for his money. We'll get through this crisis."

The Secretary of State's expression was glum. "Our prestige will suffer considerably."

The President looked down absently at the pencil in his hand. "What is prestige? Is it the shadow of power, or the substance of power? I suggest we proceed on the second proposition." He lifted his eyes to those seated around the table. "This defeat at the Bay of Pigs will be an incident, not a disaster."

Robert looked glum, too. "We're going to take a good kick in the can over the next couple of weeks."

"We can take it," said the President. "Gentlemen, we will not be deflected from our purpose. My main concern is those men of the Brigade caught inside Cuba. I appreciate that I am personally responsible for their situation because of decisions I've made." The pencil snapped in half between his fingers. "And damn it all, I can see what went wrong. All my life I've known better than to depend on experts. I see now how stupid I was to let this operation go ahead. It's beyond me how I could have been so off base."

The Secretary of State's gaze softened. "There's an old saying. Victory has a hundred fathers. Defeat is an orphan."

Robert directed a withering stare at Dulles. "We were depending on men we thought were seasoned, bright officials. It had always been my understanding that the Central Intelligence Agency was not created or equipped to manage operations that were by their nature too large to remain covert, as this operation was. The information we were provided with to make our decisions was grossly in error."

Now the President was drumming his fingertips on the arms of his chair. "We'll get a kick and we deserve it. But we'll learn from this. Vulnerable spots in this administration have been uncovered, especially in the CIA and the Joint Chiefs, and these will be dealt with. We weren't fully organized for crisis planning, and the ones I depended on most exploited that to their own ends."

Dulles began to protest. "Mister President—"

Robert interrupted him. "It's true. Your agency exerted far too much control over this entire operation. Your enthusiasm caused you to reject what should have been clear evidence of Castro's military strength and his political strength." Robert's withering broadened to include the others.

"The Agency and the Joint Chiefs have been more concerned with moving against Castro than with the necessity for caution, not to mention success."

The President sighed. His finger-tapping ceased. "That will be enough, Bobby. For tonight, at least." He loosened his white tie. "I'm more concerned about a Castro spy still working among us with impunity. Whatever happens, we cannot abide that. There's still plenty of damage that can be done. Let us hope that tomorrow brings us some good news."

Someone present muttered, "Not bloody likely."

Dulles was carefully avoiding looking in Robert's direction. "I'm staying until the final word is in. I wouldn't do anything at home except sit up and fret. Might as well do that here."

Several others murmured in agreement.

The President rose. "Suit yourselves. You'll excuse me then."

They rose respectfully, as one. Good-evenings were exchanged.

The President paused at the door. "Has there been any word on Sergeant Morgan?"

Dulles shook his head, no. "He went in with the paratroopers. One of our C-46's went down. He may have been aboard, or he may have jumped. There's no way to be sure at this point. The only thing we are certain of is that he did go in with the invasion force."

"Well," said the President, "considering the way things stand, if the United States is going to have one man inside Cuba, I'd just as soon that man was Graveyard Morgan."

CHAPTER 38

They had stopped on their way from Miami and stocked up on groceries, and had not left the premises since arriving. The pine cabin was ten minutes south of Fort Myers, a one-story, two-bedroom, comfortable getaway, perched on an acre-and-a-half of high ground in a stand of willows, overlooking the Gulf.

Susan Morgan rose from the brown leather couch in the den, where she'd been sitting next to her mother, and switched off the TV when the newscaster finished the lead story on the heated debate in the UN over the United States' role in the failed Cuban invasion.

Susan said, "It's over, then. Thank goodness."

Vera stared out at sailboats that festooned the placid blue-green waters of the Gulf beneath a sunny sky. "They're saying that no American personnel took part in the invasion. That we only equipped and trained the Cubans. At least we know he's safe."

Susan's sleep since their arrival here could hardly be called sleep at all. Every sound in the night—passing vehicles on the blacktop road that fronted the property, a night animal foraging through the underbrush—had alerted her senses to the possibility of a danger that never materialized. For some strange reason she did not feel tired or edgy. The pistol from home was presently under one of the cushions of the couch. She kept the gun near at hand at all times, even under her pillow when she slept. Her initial panic after Maria's death had receded somewhat once they became ensconced in the familiar surroundings of this "hiding place." No mention was made by either of them of Susan's personal involvement that had led to this predicament, and she was profoundly grateful for that. This cabin held many pleasant memories for her; for both of them, daughter and mother. It was where her father had taught her to fish. Where she had first discovered her love of reading when their family came here for the holidays during her childhood, whether Dad was home or not. Mom had taught her to swim here and so reminiscing about those times had warmed the atmosphere between them, balancing the uncertainty of the present...at least until the next newscast.

The television was kept on throughout the day since special bulletins about the crisis were routinely interrupting scheduled programming. The hit-and-run death of Maria Quintana was never mentioned, and so must have been relegated to "under investigation" by the police and all but forgotten considering everything else that was going on.

She so wished that she had not identified herself to the detective, Vickers, at the scene of Maria's death. But this cabin's ownership was not tied to the Morgan name, and she felt that they were safe enough here. She only wished that she could stop seeing Maria's face—animated, glowing, newly married, and alive—every time she closed her eyes.

Out over the water, gulls flitted like windblown pieces of white paper.

Susan said, "I wish I felt more upbeat. I wonder why Dad's not back already."

"His work has always been like that."

"But the government is also saying that all military personnel involved in the operation have been rotated back to the States. That means Dad should be back by now. He'd call as soon as he got back to the States like he always does and when he couldn't reach us at home, he'd call here. Mom, could you call the people he works for?"

"Honey, I'm not even supposed to know anything about what your father does. You know more about that than I do."

Ouch. There it is, thought Susan. The first dig since getting here. Her mother was worried, yes. And she was angry. And Susan wouldn't blame her for feeling betrayed, either. But she was in no mood to talk about that now. She crossed to an armchair and placed the telephone from the end table on her lap.

"Well, we're through just sitting here."

"What are you going to do?"

"It's about time I checked in with the people I work for." Susan dialed the phone and said into the receiver, "Mister McCray, please."

Her editor's voice lowered to a whisper across the line as soon as he heard who it was. "For crying out loud, Susan. I was wondering when the hell you were going to check in. I was afraid," the gruff voice faltered briefly, "...afraid something might have happened to you."

"Something has but I'm alive and well for now," she told him. "Uh,

Mister McCray, I hope you're not sore about this."

"Belay that. Some very important people have been sniffing around here, young lady, and they've been asking about you. If you want my opinion, I'd say you're very high on somebody's shit list, you should pardon my French. This is all tied in with that Cuban refugee article you bugged me to assign you, isn't it?"

"Sir, I have to keep this short. They could have your phone tapped."

That got the crusty old boy's attention. "Phone tap? Say, what the hell? Does this have anything to do with the invasion stunt those Kennedy boys tried to pull?" McCray was a staunch Republican.

"Sir, please. The VIP's who were asking about me. Who were they?"

"Couple of CIA guys. Resnick and Garrett. Garrett was very VIP, from Washington. They stopped by twice."

She thought, Of course. The Feds would ace the local cop, Vickers, out of this completely. She asked, "What were they looking for?"

"Besides you? Anything you might have dug up on a guy named Doctor Ernesto Rivas."

"I interviewed him."

"That information I already possess. The CIA now knows about it too. And you haven't heard the latest on the good doctor because we're breaking it in the next edition."

"What about him?"

"The police are looking for him. They haven't given any details but there's an all points bulletin out for him and they may go public with it. Doctor Rivas seems to have disappeared."

"What about those men from the CIA?"

McCray grunted dissatisfaction in her ear. "When I told them that you'd just interviewed Rivas, they said that if I spoke to you, I was to tell you how important it is for you to get in contact with them. Uh, Susan. They said your life is in danger."

She said, "That's why I'm antsy about phone taps. Sir, I'm going to hang up now. Thanks for the information."

"Wish I could say the same. Okay, kid, you watch your back. The best thing for you to do is cooperate with those Federal boys."

"No thanks, Mister McCray. They're the ones who gave Rivas a clean bill of health for all these months while the invasion was being planned. It's almost as if Rivas has some connection high up that let him slip through to become such an important part of the exile leadership."

She pronged the receiver, set the phone back on the table and became aware of her mother's intent gaze.

"What is it, honey?"

Susan had already brought her mom up to date when they'd first arrived at the cabin. She told Vera now about the CIA agents visiting the newspaper office. "If they're in this, it means Dad was right. Rivas is a Castro agent. He murdered Maria because she was going to give me proof."

Vera looked uncertain. "With the police and the government both looking for him, won't it be safe for us to come forward?"

"Mom, I'm not sure what to do. I think we should give this a few more days to settle. If Dad didn't trust anybody, then neither should we. At least not yet."

CHAPTER 39

In the shade of an oleander in a Miami park, Doctor Ernesto Rivas set aside his newspaper on the bench when a man in his thirties, who wore a crumpled Panama suit and a discolored straw hat, sat down next to him.

"Doctor Rivas?"

Rivas said, "Silvio Morales, I presume, sent from Havana to replace the unfortunate *Señor* Ortiz."

The heat of the day was invading the coolness of morning, even in the shade. There was not much activity in the park this early in the day. Across a pebbled walkway a fountain gurgled, its water glistening like tossed diamonds in the sunshine. At a nearby corner, a bootblack sat at his stand listening to a samba on his transistor radio while awaiting his first customer of the day. Some old men, playing dominos, occupied a bench nearby. A young mother walked past, pushing a stroller.

Morales brought out a pack of cigarettes, placed one between his lips without looking in Rivas' direction, and lighted it.

"Havana has been asking me to contact you, Doctor. You could not be located. I was pleased to hear from you."

Rivas decided that he would have to be very careful. This one was not at all like Ortiz or Hector Solas. Morales was a killer. An assassin. Rivas slipped his hand into the pocket of his lightweight jacket. His fingers closed around the .32 automatic concealed there.

He said, "I should have contacted you earlier. The last time I saw him, Ortiz gave me a matchbook with your telephone number but, well, so much has been happening."

"Indeed."

"I can only imagine Fidel's displeasure with me. He personally selected me for this mission. He trusted me implicitly, yet I was unable to apprise him of the final invasion plans."

"Indeed."

"The CIA agents never told those of us in the exile leadership anything until the Brigade force was landing. I have a," Rivas paused, not wanting to reveal too much, "a highly placed connection but even he was unaware of the precise time and place of the invasion. The Americans kept their information severely compartmentalized."

Morales stared straight ahead at the fountain. "There was concern in Havana once it was learned that you were not sequestered with the other exile leaders during the invasion. Concern increased when it was learned you are the subject of a police manhunt. Ortiz, murdered in his nightclub. Hector Solas, killed in a shootout with the authorities. You are wanted for questioning in the death of your secretary. There is much to be explained."

"Tell me, Morales. Have you been sent to kill me?"

"That," said Morales, "has been left to my discretion." His hand also rested inside his jacket pocket.

"Hector killed Ortiz, following my orders," said Rivas. "Ortiz was jeopardizing security. The Club Paradiso was meant to serve as his cover, yet he was brazenly operating outside the law. Gambling and prostitution. I warned him on several occasions but he grew only more belligerent. I had no choice. Hector, alas, ran afoul of the authorities, as you say, and paid the ultimate price for whatever carelessness on his part that led them to his door."

"What about your secretary?"

Rivas sighed, he hoped not too dramatically. "The Quintana woman's death was my doing, I regret to say. I had no choice. My poor secretary had discovered my affiliation with Havana. She had to be silenced."

"Tell me, Doctor. Given the way everything has gone—the murders, your failure to fulfill your function and provide Fidel with key information—would you at this point consider yourself a liability to our cause?"

Rivas thought, Be careful. Answer very carefully.

He said, "This is another of Fidel's tests, isn't it, sending you here?" He thought of the execution of the American agent on the beach in Cuba and added, "He's tested me before."

"You have not answered my question."

"Very well. Here is my answer. I remain a valuable resource. The exile leadership is bitterly disappointed and will be set back by the failure of the invasion. But they will not be deterred. The Democratic Revolutionary Front has been at odds with itself and fragmented since the beginning. After the fiasco at the Bay of Pigs, there's bound to be a reshuffling and

I stand to benefit by moving into a command position. Would that not make me an invaluable asset? I have already met the President of the United States. Liability? Hardly. My distrust of the others in the Front led me to seek seclusion until this crisis had passed, you see. I am a man of considerable stature in this community. I will be believed." He wanted to say more, but reined himself in. He wanted to persuade, not plead.

"And the police? What of the murders?"

Rivas permitted himself a smile. "This country has a most interesting judicial system. Anyone can be suspected, of course, but may not be arrested, much less charged, without some evidence of guilt. Without *proof.* And of that, the police have none. There is only one person remaining who could supply them with proof. Her name is Susan Morgan, and I am close to learning where she is. And when I do, she will be silenced and there will be no proof. I will be free to serve Fidel and Mother Cuba. No, Morales, I would hardly consider myself a liability."

An elderly Cuban man, wearing city worker coveralls, ambled past using a sharp-tipped stick to spear and retrieve pieces of litter, which he dropped into a sack worn over his shoulder.

When the man had gone beyond earshot, Morales said, "Communications with Havana have been disrupted since the fighting. I could be induced to delay reporting my conclusions."

"Induced? Ah, I see. Of course, I am a wealthy man."

Morales offered a cynical smirk. "I know."

"But foremost, I am loyal to Fidel. Do you truly appreciate that, Morales?"

"I suppose I do."

"Then we can in good conscience proceed with what I have in mind. I would like to engage your services. I cannot reappear until the Morgan woman has been dealt with."

"And you wish me to assist you in doing so?"

"For a price. I will know her whereabouts by this afternoon. Susan Morgan will be dead by dusk."

Morales said, "Very well. Consider me in. But first, Doctor Rivas, we talk price."

Resnick drew his robins-egg-blue convertible to a stop in the No Parking zone in front of the Miami terminal.

"Give my regards to Washington," he told Garrett. "Tell them we did the best we could." His usual easy-going manner was muted, like a sport fisherman who just watched the big one swim away.

Garrett gripped the handle of a small brown leather carry-on suitcase on the front seat between them. "Don't worry, Sam. Heads will roll over this, but ours won't be among them."

"You say. The President is not going to be pleased with a Castro agent burrowing in down here and us letting him slip through our fingers to keep on murdering people."

"You know my main worry. It's why I hate leaving with this undone."

Resnick nodded. His expression was gloomy. "The reporter, Susan Morgan. I'm worried about her too. I've got a daughter that young woman's age. But if we haven't been able to track her down, I can't see how Rivas will."

"Just keep tracking, Sam. I hope we're not too late. I hope she's not dead too."

"We're backtracking on every file we can find on the Morgan family. Something will turn up, a hideaway or something, then we'll have her. Maybe we'll nail Rivas."

Garrett slid out with his suitcase.

"Let the cops work that for now with their APB. They're investigating Ortiz and questioning the Quintana woman's co-workers. That leaves you free to find Susan Morgan. We've got to, Sam. She's got the answers, and her life is in our hands."

"I wonder if Rivas could be dead. Even with Castro the winner at the Bay of Pigs, heads could be rolling on his side too and Rivas could be one of them."

"Uh uh. My gut tells me that our murdering doctor is still in the mix and he's far from done. But Sam, right now I've got a plane to catch."

They shook hands.

"There is one more loose end."

"I know. Graveyard Morgan."

"His name wasn't released by the Cubans as among those captured."

"Missing in action," said Garrett. "Rotten luck for him but play the odds as long as Morgan has, and..." He completed the sentence with a shrug. "I figure right about now Graveyard is nothing but dead meat on some swamp road."

CHAPTER 40

Vera's eyes snapped open and for one disjointed second she did not know where she was, or what had awakened her. She blinked once, twice, bringing herself fully awake.

In the cabin's small living room, she'd fallen asleep, watching television, in the recliner opposite the couch. The ten o'clock news had nothing new on the Cuban situation, and there had been no mention of the manhunt for Doctor Rivas. She must have drifted off during the weather or sports. Presently on the TV screen, Jack Parr was smiling urbanely at an off-color anecdote being delivered by a twitchy, chain-smoking Oscar Levant, Jr. She rose from the recliner and switched off the TV.

Something *had* awakened her...

Susan appeared at the head of the stairs that led up to the bedrooms.

"Mom, I think I heard something." For some reason, her daughter whispered.

They were both dressed for bed, Vera in her ankle-length nightgown and Susan in cotton pajamas.

Without the chatter of the television, the night outside sounded natural enough: quiet, except for the chirping of insects and the knowing hoot of an owl. And yet a sudden apprehension dried Vera's throat.

"What, honey? What did you hear?"

"I'm not sure. I was sitting in bed, reading. It sounded like, I don't know, like maybe a car door closing from the direction of the road."

Vera glanced at a wall clock.

2:20.

She reached over and turned off the reading lamp that stood beside the recliner, pitching the cabin's interior into semi-darkness with only the faintest illumination spilling down from the top of the stairs. She gave in to impulse and picked up the telephone receiver. Was there a reason to call the police? She could request a drive-by from the Sheriff's Department.

Somehow, she knew there would be no dial tone.

"The line's dead."

Susan said, "Oh, my God. It's happening. Mom, where's the gun?"

At a window, Vera parted a corner of the curtain and peered out. Beyond the porch, a lamp, mounted atop a telephone pole, illuminated the property.

The light suddenly went out.

The world became black and silent. Insects ceased chirping. The knowing owl hooted once more, an eerie, ominous sound, then fell silent. Vera let the curtain fall back into place and hurried toward the couch where the .45 still resided beneath the cushions.

"I'll get the gun. Susan, I want you to go out through the back door. Wait in the trees. If you hear anything, run to the next cabin for help."

"But, Mom, that's a quarter mile away!"

"Susan, don't argue."

There came the hurried clump of footfalls on the wooden porch.

She was unprepared for how forcefully they stormed inside. She'd thought they would have tried to gain entry quietly, to surprise them in their beds. Instead, one of them booted the front door off its hinges and they poured in, swooping over her and Susan. Vera opened her mouth to cry out, but a rag was shoved in her face. The smell of chloroform overwhelmed her, and she lost consciousness.

She regained consciousness without knowing how long she'd been out.

They had propped her up into a sitting position on the couch. Her legs were free but her wrists were lashed behind her with what felt like rubberized clothesline. It was not comfortable. Her head was pounding, and regaining consciousness brought pain. Her head hurt, hurt badly. She looked around to get her bearings. Her head swam and black spots passed before her eyes.

Susan was tied with rubberized clothesline to one of the low-backed wooden kitchen chairs, facing the couch. Her eyes were closed, but she was gasping for breath. The reading lamp had been turned to her face and over her stood two men. One of them, in his fifties, possessed a refined air even under these circumstances. He wore a dark suit and a wide, tan print necktie, and sported a well-trimmed moustache. The other was stocky, wearing a crumpled Panama suit and a straw hat. He had mean eyes.

The first spoke with a smile. "Ah, señorita, I see that your mother had decided to join us at last." He bowed in Vera's direction; courtly, Old World. "Señora, I am Doctor Ernesto Rivas." He indicated the man next to him. "Allow me to introduce my associate, Señor Morales."

Her senses were sharpening by the second. She said, "Susan honey, are you okay?"

As she spoke, she became aware of something: the fingers of her hands were between the cushions of the couch. Her fingertips felt what she knew to be the cold metal of the .45 beneath the cushions, where they had not thought to search!

Susan's eyelids fluttered. "Mom." She spoke softly, without inflection. "They wouldn't be telling us their names if they were going to let us live. They're going to kill us."

The man wearing the Panama hat snarled and drew back his hand.

"Shut up, *puta*." He asked Rivas, "Do you want me to slap her around, Doctor?"

"No, that will not be necessary," said Rivas. "Return to the car. Your work here is done. Signal with the horn, should anyone approach."

Morales drew his mean eyes reluctantly from Susan's body, from the curve of her hips and the rounded thrust of her breasts beneath the thin cotton pajamas, accentuated by the tautness of her bound body.

"*Si*, Doctor."

Morales withdrew without a glance in Vera's direction.

While this was going on, Vera tugged her hands back and forth behind her, discreetly testing the play of her wrists, establishing the slightest play in the knotted clothesline. Rivas was obviously the boss. Morales would have been the one to tie them up. That explained the sloppy job he'd done, binding her wrists. The creep had been too busy ogling Susan. The cord grated and scraped Vera's skin. She felt the slipperiness of her own blood. But yes, there *was* some slack, some play.

The hell with being a pacifist. A cool corner of her brain told her to be outraged over her husband bringing this hell into the sanctity of their personal lives. But right now she was damned grateful for the nearness of that .45. It was their only chance. If only she could get her wrists loose and her hands on the gun and if only she could stay lucky after that...

When the door had closed after Morales, she said, "Doctor, please. There's no reason to kill us. The police already know everything. You'll only be making things worse for yourself."

She worked her wrists back and forth, hoping the movement remained imperceptible to him. She could loosen the clothesline, if he gave her enough time. If she could buy enough time. She had no plan beyond that.

Rivas leaned against the kitchen archway, his expression one of detachment, vaguely amused. If he detected any suspicious movement from her, he gave no indication.

"The police may *know, señora,* but do they have *proof* of my culpability? I think not. Yours is a nation of laws. The authorities must have legal proof. I intend to see that there is no such proof for them to find." He cast a glance at Susan. "Your daughter will tell me the names of everyone she has shared information with concerning me. I will backtrack. I will cover my tracks. I will leave this country and return to Havana, but first I will learn who knows what about me and my work here. Your daughter will tell me these things."

Susan raised her chin and Vera could clearly see the physical resemblance between Susan and her father. Anger and loathing burned in her daughter's eyes. She said, "I'm telling you nothing, you pig bastard. You killed Maria Quintana. You can kill me, but you won't make me talk."

Rivas glided a fingertip across the narrow line of his moustache. "Such brave talk from such an innocent child. Have you forgotten, miss, that I am a physician? I know the human body. I know what a cold blade, knowingly applied, can accomplish, especially with a woman. So many vital, tender areas, you see. I could reduce you, child, to a slobbering wretch begging for death. But I have not the time for that. However, I do have a way to make you to tell me what I want to know."

Susan's chin dropped, the bravado vanishing as quickly as it had risen. "There's just no reason to hurt us, Doctor. No reason. No reason for you to kill Maria..."

Vera wanted to rush over and hug her. She wanted to rage at this personification of evil standing, smirking before her, speaking so calmly of the torture of her baby. The threat of death was heavy in the air, yet for some strange reason her mind remained cool. She went on working at the clothesline. The cord was loosening but nowhere near enough for her to tug her wrists free.

She said, "Doctor, you are obviously a man of culture and education. How have you come to this? It's not too late to turn back."

Rivas regarded her for what seemed a very long time. An annoyed scowl ridged his forehead briefly before it smoothed.

"Very well, *señora*. I will tell you a brief story. The story of a humble, country physician of modest means from a backward province in Cuba, who worked his way through medical school in Havana. Upon graduation, he returned to the rural world of his upbringing, where he felt most comfortable. He brought home with him a young wife whom he had met and courted while at medical school, a sensitive, artistic woman of extraordinary beauty and compassion. This woman somehow touched the doctor *inside* in a way that no one else ever had or ever could. She helped him to *understand,* to heal with his heart as well as his knowledge. Her name was Consuela, and she gave to him a fine son.

"Compassion led Consuela to sympathize with the peasant class among whom her husband practiced, often without pay. Eventually, inevitably, though the doctor had always been apolitical, his wife's compassion and the political views of many of his patients came to influence his political sentiments. He came to appreciate the depths of day-to-day human misery that had become a way of life for the underclass, grown worse during his absence, what was then life under the *true* dictator, Fulgencio Batista, who, as you surely know, ruled with a cruel and iron hand, and with the blessing and patronage of your glorious nation."

Vera concentrated on keeping her shoulders immobile, which wasn't easy. She must keep him talking. Keep buying time. Still no indication that he knew what she was up to...

He was saying, "But this compassionate young doctor was a cautious man, you see. He had a son and a wife to support and things could be made extremely difficult for those in the professional class who spoke out against Batista. In fact, the young physician was a coward, afraid to speak his mind or act on principle, on the side of justice. While his wife openly sympathized with the peasants, the doctor refrained from doing so. He had his reputation. He had his fear. Yes, a pitiful coward.

"One day, his wife took their son with her to an anti-government demonstration in the provincial capital. There had been a terrible drought. People were dying by the hundreds, and the peasants marched with the hope of gaining sympathy and assistance from their government. Government soldiers opened fire that day on the unarmed crowd. The doctor's wife died with their infant son in her arms, both of them cut down, butchered by Batista's bullets at a rally for justice."

Vera said, "Such a man would have my sympathy. But right now,

Doctor, I fear for my life and that of *my* child."

Rivas towered above her. He began to loosen and undo his necktie. Susan saw this and made a whimpering sound. Rivas drew loose the necktie from under his shirt collar.

"The young doctor seemed at first to carry on as before. He grieved, of course, grieved deeply for the loss of his wife and son, almost to the brink of madness."

"Almost, Doctor?" She thought, perhaps speaking to him in this manner will stop him. "Doctor Rivas, you can stop what you're doing. My God, is there any glimmer remaining within you that can grasp the useless horror of what you're about to do?"

He continued as if he hadn't heard her. "Our young doctor naturally earned tears of sympathy from all who knew him. He stayed on to continue with his practice in that remote province. But he began to work quietly for the revolution, secretly treating wounded guerrillas who were brought to him under cover of darkness. On two occasions, he met with Fidel and a friendship was forged between them. The physician never gained fame after the revolution. Truly, he was but one of the faceless multitudes throughout Cuba who made the revolution a reality and restored justice to the people." Rivas grasped each end of his necktie in a clenched fist.

Vera's wrists were getting more play. It wouldn't be long. All she needed was a little more time. The clothesline was almost there. Almost loose enough for her hands to break free. Almost. Then she would grab the gun.

She said, "A sad story, Doctor. I'm sorry for what happened to your wife and your son. Now tell me, how can harming my daughter and me assuage your grief, or bring them back to life?"

He lifted his arms, the necktie drawn taut between his closed fists. He stepped slowly forward. A faraway look came into his eyes.

From across the room, Susan watched with despairing eyes. "Doctor, please stop..."

Rivas said to Vera, "After the Revolution, a great opportunity presented itself to me. I was privileged to serve Fidel by infiltrating the Cuban Revolutionary Council in Miami. I have worked long and hard to develop a network of informants throughout Little Havana who have been invaluable to us and will continue to be so. My work here is done. It is time to return to Cuba. I will spend my days tending the graves of my wife and son. But the work of the revolution goes on, and I cannot jeopardize what I have worked so hard to accomplish. You understand? I must take counter-measures so that no loose ends remain. Maria Quintana had in her possession a mere matchbook. Who knows what else I need to know? I intend to find out."

The necktie descended with lightning swiftness, wrapping around her throat. Rivas placed one knee on the couch to lean forward, his body pressing hers back, his breath hot in her face. His face was a mask of grim determination. He began drawing the improvised garrote tighter, slowly strangling her.

"No mercy was shown by my enemies. I am no longer a coward who shirks from his duty." He looked over his shoulder at Susan. "Will you tell me what I need to know? Or will you watch me kill your mother?"

Susan's eyes fell away. "I know nothing. Doctor, stop! I beg you..."

Frenzied panic engulfed Vera. He was killing her! She was dying! She tried jerking her head, tried rocking her body back and forth, but it was hopeless. Her windpipe was about to collapse. Her tongue was swelling, gagging her. Her vision was starting to blur. Pinpoints danced before her. Her eyes felt ready to pop out of her head.

The trace of a smile played across Rivas' lips. When he spoke again to Susan, his voice carried to Vera as if from a great distance. "This is your last chance." His voice indicated none of the physical effort he was exerting. "The woman who gave you your life is dying. Tell me what I need to know and I will spare you both."

Susan sobbed. "Liar. Murderer..."

And the rubberized cord binding Vera's wrists burst free!

She forced out the words, "My daughter said *no*, you son of a bitch."

Using the palms of her hands beneath her to gain leverage, she sent a sharp kick with her bent knee straight to his crotch. Rivas emitted a stunned *oooof!* and his body jack-knifed. The strangling necktie loosened around her throat.

She gulped in air and brought both hands up to place the palms against his chest. She heaved his body from hers, then she clawed under the cushion for the gun. Her fingers closing around the handle of the .45 made her heart soar. Then she was moving fast fast fast, no thought, fighting for survival, pure instinct, kill to live, tracking the gun around in a two-handed grip, one thumb flicking off the safety switch the way she'd been taught while her index finger sought the trigger.

Rivas had recovered enough to lunge, seizing her wrists with both hands. The .45 went off, a clap of unearthly loud thunder. A garish orange muzzle blast, like a pointing saffron finger, stabbed across the room. Rivas was dragging Vera down off the couch, toward him, but she clearly heard the impact, the fleshy *splat!* of a bullet striking flesh, and Susan's sharp cry of pain, followed by the clatter of the chair and Susan's body tumbling sideways onto the floor.

Then Vera and Rivas were struggling side by side on the floor, face-to-face, the pistol between them aiming first here, then there as they wrestled desperately for possession of it. His eyes, inches from hers, grew cold.

"Prepare to die, *señora*."

When the .45 went off again, the blinding blast erased her senses.

CHAPTER 41

Morgan came to and for an instant he thought he was back in his hooch at the Special Forces base camp in Vietnam; that it was time to wake up and head out on patrol. Then the sound of footfalls penetrated his mental fog, and his eyes opened. He became aware of his surroundings.

Daytime. Hot. Sweltering, stifling hot.

He wore fatigues that were soaked with sweat and he was lying flat on his back upon dry ground under some type of crudely constructed shelter. Overhead, three poles met and around them had been wrapped tightly meshed mosquito netting, forming a sort of teepee. The chirping of birds, the rabble of insects and a bug buzzing in his ear, sounding like a big-assed dive bomber, scratched at his consciousness like nails. He had a splitting headache.

With returning consciousness came traces of foggy memory. *The truckload of civilians. The snipers behind the trough. Garcia going crazy. Being taken out during the firefight.* And now...approaching footsteps. A shadowy silhouette came to a stop before the "teepee," the person's features impossible for him to make out beyond the mesh of the netting. The figure pulled back a fold in the netting that was an entrance flap. Morgan propped himself on one elbow and his right hand slapped across his chest, finding the reassuring butt of the .45 automatic in its shoulder holster, right where it was supposed to be, and by the time a head appeared, the pistol was extended at arm's length with the safety off.

José Cardena came to a stop half in and half out, with one arm holding back the flap. From his free hand dangled a line of fish. He did not bat an eye at the muzzle of the .45 aimed between his eyes.

"Señor, welcome back to the world of the living."

Morgan holstered the pistol. "Where the hell are we? What day is it?"

José set the fish outside and stepped in. "It is Wednesday. We are in the middle of a cane field, *señor*, about ten miles from Giron."

"What happened?"

"You've been in and out of consciousness for the past forty-eight hours. Two members of the local underground, sadly the only two of their group to survive the fighting, have brought us to this place. They have a radio. I've been in touch with their CIA contact offshore. We've been told to do nothing and wait for further instructions."

"Where are the ones who brought us here?"

"Gone to the village. They'll be back soon. They're trying to pick up information. A bullet grazed you, *compadre*. We need their help."

Morgan holstered the .45 and sat up cross-legged, Indian-style. He raised a hand and his fingertips gingerly touched a bandage. The headache was beginning to recede.

"Thanks, José."

"You must thank the woman. Her name is Carmen. She cared for you, *señor*."

"I don't remember any of it."

"Ah, the women. They are the healers, the angels of mercy to man, are they not, even when they fight and kill and die at our side on the field of battle. She is a lovely woman. I mean beautiful, like a movie star."

Morgan chuckled and his headache was gone. He liked this guy. "Sounds like you're smitten." Then he grew serious. "José, I need to be brought up to date. Tell me what's happened."

José sighed. "It's all over, *señor*. You and I may be the only ones of the Brigade who the Fidelistas have not tracked down, and this too is thanks to our new friends. Naturally they are in extreme jeopardy, but they heard yesterday that the Brigade ships are gone. More than one thousand of our men were captured and force-marched into Havana. The rest died fighting."

Morgan felt despair well up within him. But all he could say was, "Damn."

"We failed because there was no American air support to cover the landing." José's tone was bitter. "Our supply ships deserted us. Everything went wrong. Señor, we were supplied, trained, brought here...and left to die or fall into enemy hands. So many good, brave men died for nothing."

"I thought the Cuban people were supposed to be on our side. There was supposed to be a popular uprising."

"The CIA overemphasized the anti-Castro sentiment," said José. "Nothing was as our control officers said it would be. There is strong public support in Cuba for the summary execution of those captured. I fear the worst for them. It looks to me, señor, as if we are in some mighty deep shit."

"Yeah. The same old shit. I don't blame you for being pissed off, pal. I'm pissed off too."

"Castro's troops have conducted sweeps through the area twice yesterday and already once today. But our friends know this region. They chose a good, safe place for us to hide."

Morgan's growl came from deep in his chest. "Problem is, José, I don't hide. I'm a soldier. I fight."

The Oldsmobile picked up speed once the motorcade broke away from the congestion surrounding Havana's Sports Palace. Castro rode in the back seat with Che. General Parnov sat in front, next to the chauffeur.

The Russian liaison officer dabbed with a handkerchief at his jowly, flushed features, which shone with perspiration. Parnov was beaming despite his visible discomfort in the tropical heat. "An inspired performance, Premier Castro. You were brilliant."

Castro blew a stream of cigar smoke out through his open window. "That was hardly a performance, General. It was my great pleasure to personally rub their defeat in the noses of those glorious invaders who would free Cuba from my tyrannical rule." He spat out through the window.

"Every seat was full," said Parnov, "and a multitude that couldn't get in. And you, displaying captured documents, using a pointer to retrace on a map your movements during the battle, all of it broadcast from in front of the assembled prisoners."

Castro nodded, smiling. "It is a humiliation the United States will not soon live down."

Che said, "Tanks, mortars, bazookas, grenades, rockets...and their invasion could not even hold a beachhead! I remember, Fidel, when our fight against Batista began. We were twelve men, in a swamp. And we went on to take over a country!"

Castro took a luxurious drag on his cigar. "Their problem was that they did not have a guerrilla mentality, as we do. They acted like a conventional army. We used guerilla tactics."

"We were victorious against the invaders," said Che. "And yet, the people have suffered. Those who died in the fighting, of course, but beyond that, our manpower—our resources, our energies—should be focused on revolutionary construction, not defending ourselves."

"Ah," said Castro, "but let us analyze that. This invasion serves our purpose, my friends. There was a romantic euphoria after we first seized power. But it takes time to improve the daily life of millions of people. This external danger is necessary at this time to keep alive the revolutionary spirit."

Parnov asked, "And what of the men you captured? A harsh example should be made of the lot of them."

Castro arched an eyebrow and eyed the Russian with a bemused glint. "Strong words for one who spent the battle hiding beneath his desk at Point One."

Parnov's back straightened. He started to respond indignantly.

Che said, "Fidel, I did serve in the field. But on this point I agree with the General. Cuban blood has been spilled. The invaders must pay the ultimate price. Immediate execution."

"No," said Castro. "The prisoners are worth more to us alive than dead. Living proof of the humiliation of the mighty USA. They are living proof of the power of our revolution. And they have a more practical use."

Che considered this, then nodded slowly. "Ransom."

"Exactly." Castro gazed out his window at the passing street scene. "The Americans will pay whatever we demand for the release of those men. That would directly benefit our people. I have thought on this. It is the course we will follow. The Americans will pay for what they have done. And I mean *pay*."

"That does make sense," said Che. "It is why you are our leader, Fidel."

Castro was frowning. "I am more concerned with eradicating the remnants of the counter-revolutionary underground."

Parnov continued to mop the perspiration from his face. "They openly assisted the enemy during the battle. At least they should be summarily executed."

Castro threw his cigar stub out of the car window with an irritated gesture. "On that point, we are in agreement. I want every remaining member of every remaining cell tracked down and exterminated." He reached to his breast pocket for a fresh cigar. "And it is time I rewarded myself with some leisure time. The past few weeks have been trying. I have chosen to spend the weekend at my ranch near San Blas. I will be leaving first thing in the morning."

Che said, "There is one remaining matter. There are reports of an American soldier coming ashore with the invaders."

Castro got his cigar going. He said through the smoke, "The Special Forces Green Beret, Morgan. He was not captured, nor is he among the enemy dead."

Parnov frowned. "Are you sure of this?"

Castro glared at the suggestion of doubt. "My source of information is highly placed and has proven most reliable."

Che said, "Morgan will be tracked down, wherever he is."

"But see that he is taken alive," said Castro. "For an American soldier to be trapped inside Cuba under these circumstances there awaits a fate far worse than death. Notify me when he has been captured."

Carmen sat with her back against the trunk of a towering palm that overlooked the road outside Giron. Fields of sugarcane stretched to the horizon in three directions. Across the highway was a chicken cooperative with row after row of triangular concrete coops. She sat partially concealed from view of passersby on the road, a good vantage point from which to observe those traveling the road in either direction. She was waiting for Santos.

The rattle and wheeze of an ancient bus carried to her on the thick, warm air well before the bus came into view from the north, a tail of red dust swirling behind it. The bus passed below her vantage point. She saw farmers in straw sombreros, their wives and children riding to the rear. The roof rack was top-heavy with everything from bicycles to farm produce to crude wooden cages filled with squealing pigs. Rumbling past, the bus began to climb a hill, going slower and slower. Steam billowed from under the hood. Several young men, passengers who had been standing near the door, jumped off to lighten the load. The bus increased its speed but only slightly, inching toward the crest of the hill. The young men, a half dozen of them, began to push. Again the bus appeared to almost gain the crest of the hill, but not quite.

A lumbering, unmistakable bear-like figure topped the hill, walking from the direction of the village. Santos saw the problem and went to assist, placing his broad back against the rear of the bus and pushing in unison with the others.

At last, wheezing and rattling louder than before, the bus topped the hill. The young men, laughing, waving their thanks, hurried after it to catch up.

Santos lifted an arm in farewell. Carmen stepped into the road. He ambled over to her and up close she plainly saw the defeat in his eyes.

She said, "I was beginning to worry. You were gone for two hours."

"I did not wish to appear in a hurry. I had to bide my time, to hear what the people in the tavern and the shops were saying."

"I wish I could have gone with you."

"No. The first person to recognize you would have turned you in and you would end up like your brother and, and..." He stammered. "...like Felix. Me, I'm not from around here. I knew Felix from Havana. It's safe enough for me to move about, I think."

They left the road. They started along a footpath that led from where she had been waiting, through a field.

"So what did you learn?"

He made a rude sound. "I heard part of a speech Fidel gave in Havana. The speech has the people in Giron stirred up. This is where the fighting was heaviest, you know. Civilians were caught in the line of fire, like those poor devils in the truck before you took care of that bastard, Medina."

Carmen said, "Please, Santos. Don't speak of it. I can still feel the recoil of the rifle. I see it in my mind without closing my eyes, what my bullet did to Medina. I took a human life. I know this is war, but—"

"He was not human," said Santos. "Medina was an evil animal. He killed your brother. It was your duty to take his life, *meija*. You should feel honored."

"I only feel revulsion at what I did. Were you able to learn the names of any of those who died in the truck?"

"Yes, and you may have known them. They were trying to escape the fighting. Neighbors of yours.

Her step faltered. "Oh, God...no—"

"Gomez was the name. The whole family was killed, along with some others."

Nausea coiled in her stomach. "The boy, Cosme, and his mother helped me to care for my mother when she was dying." Her voice tapered off. She thought of pregnant Lupita.

Santos said in a small, empty voice, "All I wanted was a good fight, and I end up having to kill my best friend."

"But you mustn't feel that way. It was an act of mercy."

"Yes, but should it be any different for me than your feelings over having killed an enemy? Felix was our brother-in-arms. I had to do it, yes.

But Carmen, there's one thing that I must know. I have to ask. In your heart of hearts, do you forgive me for what I had to do, for taking his life?"

"Oh, my big bear. Of course I forgive you. God will forgive us. We must forgive ourselves." She broke stride long enough to stand on her tiptoes, to deliver him a kiss on his bearded cheek. "What else did you learn in the village?"

He gruffly pretended the kiss had not happened. The sun beat down. It was very hot. The road had fallen away behind them. They pushed on.

He said, "There's a rumor circulating that an American soldier came in with the invasion force. He's still at large. Flyers are everywhere warning people to be vigilant. The Army has checkpoints on every road."

"We may have to move our camp."

"And one final thing." He sent her a trace of the old Santos smile. "I save the most interesting for last, you see. I was a drama student at the University."

"You're cruel," said Carmen with a laugh. "Don't keep me in suspense."

"Our beloved Fidel is coming to his country home near San Blas to recuperate from the rigors of command and, of course, to bask in the glow of victory. You see? *He* is coming to *us,* and without his army. Very interesting, wouldn't you say?"

"When?"

"Tonight." His eyes were beaming, anticipating her reaction.

"Santos, what do you have in mind?"

"Why, what we should have done that day when he came to Giron with the Russian, you remember? Felix wanted to shoot Fidel that day on the beach. You and I should have let him. I would gladly give my life to rid the country of that dictator and murderer. So what do you think of that?"

"I think," said Carmen, "that we should radio this information to our CIA contact at once."

CHAPTER 42

It was a clear-sky day in Washington. The dogwoods were in blossom. The temperature was in the high fifties.

The *Honey Fitz* was moored at a highly secured private dock on the Potomac, less than twenty minutes from the White House. The ninety-six-foot yacht, named the *Barbara Ann* during the Eisenhower administration, had been re-christened in honor of the President's grandfather, John "Honey Fitz" Fitzgerald.

Garrett boarded shortly before noon. Four Secret Service agents greeted him. He had come unarmed and quickly passed the security check of his ID and a thorough pat-down search. Sandwiched by one agent in back and one in front, he was led below deck, down a plushly carpeted, wood paneled companionway to the main cabin.

The President of the United States wore black swim trunks. He lay face down on a chaise lounge beneath the golden glow of a sun-tanning lamp. He was reading a book, which he had placed open upon the floor beneath the chaise lounge.

"Agent Garrett, Mister President."

The agents withdrew, closing the door after them.

Kennedy slipped on a pair of wraparound sunglasses and closed the book, a James Bond novel. He turned over and clicked off the sunlamp. He took a sip of his Daiquiri, and adjusted the chaise lounge to a sitting position.

He said, "A failed invasion. A highly placed Castro spy still on the loose in Miami. Things have not gone well for us, have they, Tal?"

"No, sir."

Kennedy surprised Garrett with a short chuckle. "Don't wear that hangdog expression. You're one of the best men I've got, Tal. You and Morgan were sent to control the damage but you were just too late. Not your fault."

"Thank you, sir."

"You certainly do look worn out."

Garrett's sigh felt like it came from the bottom of his soul. "It's been a rough couple of days. Sorry it shows. Doctor Rivas is still at large. Resnick is on that, but I wish we could've done better."

The President spoke in a bright, peppy voice. "What's done is done. Tal, if you need a quick pick-me-up, I can arrange for you to have one of the vitamin shots I have administered to me by my physician. Perfectly safe, they assure me. Multi-vitamins, steroids, hormones, enzymes, amphetamines. Quite a concoction. Jackie and I both got our shots this morning. We take them four times a week. Makes me feel like a new man. You get more done, more efficiently, and you feel an energy that you wouldn't believe. A real zip."

"No thank you, sir."

"Fine, fine." The fingers of both the President's hands tapped restlessly on the arms of his chaise. "Tal, I sent for you because I wanted to speak with you away from the White House. I've had what I think is a terrific idea. I've discussed it with Bobby, that is, with the Attorney General, and we feel sufficiently enthused to proceed with a covert operation. But what I have in mind will require circumventing the standard channels of operational procedure."

"I understand, Mister President."

A terse smile. "I knew you would. My brother, among others in the Cabinet, suggests that Castro be assassinated. I find that idea abhorrent. The whole notion of assassination is repellant to me. As for reorganizing and re-launching the Brigade, well, I wish I had never okayed the Eisenhower plan to invade in the first place. Right now the fate of more than one thousand Brigade POW's is at risk. Mister Castro is not treating them as prisoners of war, but as hostages. Their confinement in Havana is extremely harsh. He intends to stage a mass trial. He has privately demanded of this government the sum of sixty-two million dollars as a ransom payment to release those men."

"I hadn't heard about that. He's driving a hard bargain."

"On the other hand," said the President, "there may be something that we can do. A positive step that can be taken. But we must move quickly and decisively. Do you see where I'm heading, Tal?"

"Uh, sorry, sir. I'm usually pretty quick on the uptake." Garrett added mentally, *And I didn't have a shot of vitamins and speed this morning!*

The President had what could only be described as a twinkle in his eye. "Don't worry, Agent Garrett, this comes from left field, I'm sure. That's what Bobby said before he had a chance to give it some thought, and he thinks I may be on to something. Tal, I'm tired of consulting the experts. That's what got me into this Bay of Pigs fiasco in the first place. It's time for some innovative action, not a tired, flawed plan inherited from a previous administration. You've been deep cover on this from the beginning, strictly off the record. That's why you and Morgan are the men for what I have in mind."

"Morgan? But sir, we lost him inside Cuba."

Kennedy cracked an impish smile. "Not so. He's alive along with the remnants of the anti-Castro underground that was based in the Bay of Pigs region. Morgan has one of the men from the Brigade with him also. They've made radio contact with us."

"Well, that is interesting."

"Yes, I thought you might find it so. What I have in mind, quite simply, is turning the tables on Mister Castro. You see, Tal, we've learned that Castro is about to take some time off. A well-deserved vacation, no doubt. And he's going to be staying at his country home, which just happens to be very close to where Morgan and the others are encamped."

Garrett blinked when he realized where the President was heading with this conversation. He said, "You intend to kidnap Fidel Castro."

The President clapped his hands once and snapped the fingers of his right hand. "Bingo. A masterstroke of audacity, wouldn't you say? Outrageous? Perhaps. A long shot? Certainly. But it becomes less so when you know the facts."

"Sir, I'm all ears."

"These getaways by Castro are something of a regular habit," said Kennedy. "Routine has set in. He takes with him only a handful of bodyguards. He's well-loved in that area and so there is little real fear for his safety. Security may be a little tighter after the fighting but not much, I'd wager, since their victory was so decisive. It may even be lighter than usual, given the euphoric atmosphere down there and Castro's arrogance. He generally spends several days to a week at this country home, unwinding with booze, women and fishing."

"Put that way, sir, it does sound like a plan with potential."

"Castro is worth far more to us alive than dead. We can beat him at his own game." The President's words shimmered with enthusiasm. "He will become *our* hostage. And the ransom for his release?" Another chuckle. "Why, nothing less than the immediate release of those brave men of the Brigade, what else? Morgan is awaiting orders. I want you to direct the operation from this end. What do you think, Tal?"

Garrett started to speak, not precisely sure yet what he thought, when he was interrupted by a commotion from behind a door to his left, not the one he had entered through.

The door suddenly flew inward, slamming open on its hinges. A young woman—she could have been no more than twenty—sprang through the door with a laughing shriek tossed back over a curved shoulder. Everything about her was curves. She was long-legged with a figure firm yet lush, well-tanned flesh contrasting cascading blonde hair. Naked as a jaybird except for a pair of the skimpiest satin panties Garrett had ever seen. At first he thought she was Marilyn Monroe, so startled was he by the resemblance, by the interruption itself, this display of a naked female at a time and place where he never expected it. She could have been MM's kid sister. She saw the President of the United States in swim trunks and sunglasses, and froze into immobility.

"Oh."

Kennedy appeared unruffled. He sipped his drink with an amused smile.

One of the Secret Service agents, who had seen Garrett aboard, appeared from behind the girl. He had a weight-lifter build with an unusually hairy chest, and he wore only boxer shorts. Latin jazz filtered in from the other room. Another man's lewd chuckle and a feminine, intoxicated giggle drifted in too. The agent grabbed the girl around her waist, hoisting her up in both arms like a groom about to carry his bride across the threshold.

"Uh, sorry, Mister President. Beg your pardon."

Kennedy flashed his famous, toothy smile. "Not at all, Martin. Enjoy."

The couple retreated into the room. The door was drawn shut.

The President broadened his smile at the confusion that must have been apparent on Garrett's face. "Excuse that, please. I'm afraid formality is at times dispensed with when we're away from the Oval Office."

"Uh, I, uh, didn't see a thing, sir."

There would be time to reflect on this insight into presidential nuttiness at a later time. Another matter concerned Garrett now.

Kennedy finished his Daiquiri and set the glass aside. "So then, Tal. Do you think this idea of mine is workable? Morgan affects the kidnapping of the Premier of Cuba. The whole thing is kept strictly under wraps, of course. We can manage that much better with a small-scale operation. We'll have a boat waiting offshore to pick them up. Our overtures to the Cubans will of course be under the table, out of the public eye. A deal will be struck. The Brigade POW's will be set free and returned to the US. I understand Castro. He is ruled by his sense of machismo. That machismo will keep him from ever publicizing his own kidnapping."

Garrett thought, *Ruled by machismo? It takes one to know one, Mister President. He* said, "It could be done if Morgan has good people with him and gets lucky."

Kennedy withdrew a Cuban cigar from a humidor. "Tal?"

"No thank you, sir. I've given up tobacco."

Kennedy winked, in high good humor. "My apologies. This won't make that any easier." He took his time about getting the cigar alight and filling the atmosphere with aromatic smoke.

"Sir, has a strategy been worked out yet for abducting Castro?"

"Not yet. We'll leave that to Graveyard Morgan. It will only be necessary to issue the directive. Advise him of the objective, of a pickup point and a time frame when he can signal us. I'm confident that he will then execute the directive if it is at all humanly possible."

"Very well. I'll set things in motion at the first word from you."

"This is the word, Tal. I want that directive issued at once, without delay. That will be all. Sorry I can't ask you to stay. Perhaps another time."

"Then I'll get started. Good day, sir."

Garrett let himself out the way he had been shown in. His parting view of the President was of Kennedy rising from the chaise and starting toward the other door.

The blade of the combat knife, flung across the clearing, reflecting afternoon sunshine, imbedded itself in the umbrella tree. Its handle quivered square-ly between the eyes of Fidel Castro in a newspaper photograph. Morgan strode across the clearing and retrieved the knife. Carmen watched him.

"Your aim is true. I would not believe that you had taken a wound to the head if I had not treated you myself."

He no longer wore the bandage. "I owe you, Carmen. But it's just one more scar."

This was true. He'd been wounded before in combat. The scab at his temple was tender where the bullet had grazed him, but only a mild ache lingered.

"Sergeant, what do you think will happen next?"

"Damned if I know, but something better happen before I wear out my throwing arm." He pitched the knife again for another bulls-eye.

"Your aim is true. Your reflexes are those of a warrior, ready to resume battle."

He drew the knife from the tree trunk and cleaned the blade, drawing it sideways across his sleeve. "I'm committed to a course of action. I just wish I knew what that course of action was. Frankly, that's damn annoying."

"I sense a deeper concern within you." She sat upon a fallen log in the shade by the edge of the clearing, toying pensively with a shard of cane stalk between her slim fingers. "So much has happened in such a short time."

He returned the blade to its scabbard. "Nothing I haven't seen before. I'm just tired of seeing it. And I left some loose ends back in the States. Castro has a spy placed very high back there in Florida. I was assigned to manage what damage control I could, and letting a spy walk around free to do more damage is not my idea of a job well done. Whoever it is, the son of a bitch is as responsible as anyone for this disaster. The difference is that he's supposed to be my responsibility. I need to nail the bastard. And then there's my, uh, current situation."

The air was warm, though the sweltering heat of midday was beginning to abate.

She picked at the shard of cane. "José and I are driven by a sense of rage. I detest having to hide as if I was a criminal. It is I who have had everything stolen from me! But you, *señor*, you are driven by commitment. There is a difference."

"You're a perceptive woman."

"Sometimes that is a blessing, sometimes a curse. Much like being a woman. There is more than a spy and your mission that trouble you. I can see that."

What the hell, he decided. His brain felt ready to burst, so busy keeping so much inside.

He said, "I've got a family back in the States, in Florida. They seem to be slipping away from me."

She regarded him, a gaze penetrating and caring, waiting for him to continue.

He said, "I left a real mess behind when I came here. Now I want to go home and clean it up. I'm hoping I'm not already too late."

"Yesterday," she said, "when I was waiting for Santos to return from the village, I thought of a day only a short while ago. A beautiful day. I was in my garden. The sun was shining. Birds circled over the bay. I could smell the ocean. My mother was alive. My brother was alive. Felix was alive. Everything was...perfect." She brushed at the corner of one eye with the back of her hand. "Forgive me. That was the day Major Medina came to our house and from that moment to this, a current has swept me along almost faster than I can comprehend. Those I loved are dead now and there is nothing I can do to bring them back." She touched fingertips lightly to his wrist. "Life without love is intolerable. But a love that hurts those we love is more intolerable because the living *can* change if we would but try. You and your family, *señor*, your lives are not over. You have it within your power to change. Let your world change if it must."

He chuckled self-consciously. "Good advice. I'm that easy to read?"

She removed her fingers from his wrist and resumed toying with the shard of cane stalk. "Would it be forward of me to ask why you flew into battle with the Brigade? You might have been taken prisoner or killed. José told us that you disobeyed a direct order forbidding you to accompany the paratroopers. Why did you come?"

"Maybe it's payback for all the poor bastards I've trained around the world for Uncle Sam and then left them to lose on their own." He gave a tight grin. "The eggheads would call it a death wish. But yeah, what happened at your Bay of Pigs turned things around inside my head and now I've got a *life* wish. Guess I had to get this close one more time to really understand."

Santos and José stepped into the clearing.

Santos said, "I made radio contact as instructed, *señor*."

Morgan rose to his feet. "Let's hear it."

"We are back in business. Are you ready for this, my friends? They want us to kidnap Fidel!"

Morgan blinked. "Kidnap?"

"*Si*. And on this very night, too! We are to get him to Cayo Fragoso for pickup at 0300 hours for a boat ride out of the country!" Santos was bubbling with enthusiasm.

Carmen was frowning. "But is that possible? Is it necessary? Cayo Fragoso is five miles from here."

"It's a good idea," said José, "if we don't get killed. They will trade Fidel for the Brigade POWs."

Santos' beard bobbed. "Kidnap Fidel. I love it. What do you think, gringo?"

Morgan slapped at a mosquito feeding at his neck.

"Tonight, you say? An 0300 hour pickup? I think we'd better get started."

CHAPTER 43

Castro's hideaway near Giron was of Spanish colonial architecture, a sprawling single-level stucco house with a tile roof. A ridge ran several hundred yards above the southwest corner of the simple barbed wire fence that surrounded the property. In front of the veranda that ran the length of the house, the waters of a tiered fountain sparkled like pink champagne in the day's final rosette sunshine. The shadows of palm and fruit trees were lengthening. The acreage was well removed from the nearest thatched-roof farmhouse, a half mile away, which was also visible from the ridge where Morgan, along with Santos, Carmen and José, surveyed the panorama.

Morgan was using the binoculars. He swept their field of vision across the property, memorizing the layout—main house and attached garage, guesthouse and assorted outbuildings—while he took another inventory of the visible security force: five bearded soldiers, wearing fatigues and carrying rifles, a few of them smoking cigars. Any one of them could have been mistaken for Fidel from a distance at first glance.

He lowered the binoculars. "Three at the guard house by the main gate, two more lounging on the veranda."

José took his turn with the binoculars. He spoke while adjusting them to his eyes. "That's two more than usual. We keep an eye on this place, of course. There will be more. Santos, you were right. Fidel is expected."

A breeze picked up off the sea, the scent of fresh salt air brushing across the ridge, pushing inland the oppressive heat and the stench of the nearby swamp.

Carmen said, "The guest house is where the bodyguards stay. My brother and I have watched from up here other times when Fidel came here. One bodyguard in assigned to stay with him overnight in the main house. But if Fidel has a woman, my brother told me that then he insists on privacy and no bodyguard is allowed in the house."

Santos spat. "We should kill him, not kidnap him."

José glanced at him earnestly. "We must obey orders. You're the one who took down the radio message. You know the instructions."

"I'll do as I'm told, but I don't have to like it."

Morgan said, "Isn't that true of everyone here? I don't want to deal with you anymore, Santos, if you've got too much emotion tied up to be part of our team. If that's the case, I want you on the sidelines."

Santos was taken aback. "*Señor*—"

"Be honest with me and yourself. You hold Fidel Castro personally responsible for what happened to your friend, Felix, and to Carmen's brother and to all the others, and you're right. But right here and now, all that concerns me is the mission and getting that man to the pickup point on time. So quit screwing around. Are you with us or not?"

Santos actually blushed. "I'm sorry, amigos. I'm with you. You can count on me, I promise you."

"Okay then," said Morgan. "We'll wait here until dark. We're going in soft."

José nodded. "Yes. Penetrate their security without them knowing, like commandos."

Carmen said, "And what then?"

"Beyond a certain point," said Morgan, "we make things up as we go along. There's a high risk factor no matter how we play it."

Santos regarded Carmen with affection, and concern. "What is it, little one? You hesitate?"

She said, "There's been enough killing. It will be four of us against those sentries plus the bodyguards Castro brings with him from Havana. And even if we get inside, Fidel won't just walk out with us. The Premier is a giant of a man, strong as an ox. He will not be easily taken unless by complete surprise."

Santos said, "We have the element of surprise. There's shrubbery and trees down there for cover. If we exchange fire, it will be their lives, not ours."

Morgan said, "We don't have much choice. We have a directive to kidnap Castro. It sounds hare-brained to me too, but I've been placed in charge of this operation by my people and by you. We can't walk away from this. The fate of those Brigade guys in Havana hangs in the balance. They've already taken the shaft. They deserve better. They deserve the best that we can give, and that means taking on any odds."

Carmen's eyes swept the three of them. She leaned her rifle against a tree. "Then you must forgive me, *amigos*. I cannot go down there with you tonight, prepared to kill more people." She removed the bandolier she wore of spare ammunition and draped it across the rifle. "I cannot kill anymore."

She turned and walked away.

They watched her go.

"Now what?" Santos wondered aloud. "We're short one."

"Doesn't matter," said Morgan. "We maintain surveillance. If Castro shows up, we're going in."

Two hours later, near dusk, an open Jeep carrying Fidel Castro traveled the road to Giron. He sat alone in the back seat. He wore fatigues, with a pistol holstered at his hip. He puffed leisurely on a cigar. Next to the driver, a bearded soldier rode with a rifle. A black Oldsmobile trailed the Jeep, which was rounding a curve for the final approach to their destination when the driver tapped his brakes, arresting Castro's attention.

A beautiful young woman sat beneath a tree on the side of the road, on a grassy knoll. She wore a peasant blouse with a scooped front that left little to the imagination. She filled the blouse nicely, Castro thought. She wore gold earrings and her long, untamed hair was the black of a raven's wing. A print skirt flared out from a shapely waist. She sat with an elbow on each knee, taking bites from a succulent slice of mango. As the Jeep drew closer, even in the diminishing light of day, Castro saw that her full lips glistened with the juices of the ripe fruit.

He said, "Stop."

The driver had anticipated the command. The Jeep coasted to a halt directly before her.

"*Hola*, dear lady."

"*Hola*, Premier Castro."

He gestured expansively with his cigar. "A lovely evening, wouldn't you say?"

"A very lovely evening." Carmen took another slurping bite of the mango. "I hope you don't mind me being here, so close to your property, but I heard that you were coming for a visit and I—" She paused, her eyelashes lowered demurely. "I think you are a great man, sir."

Castro's eyes twinkled. "Now whyever should I mind hearing something like that coming from the moist lips of a beautiful woman? Fidel loves to surround himself with beauty, my dear, and you certainly embody that."

"Thank you, Premier. You have done so many great things for our country. I live near here. We owe you so much."

"Approach me."

She rose and flung aside the mango and left the grassy knoll and swayed forward with an almost indolent air to stand beside the Jeep, hands clasped before her, for Castro's blatant inspection. She stared into his eyes and did not flinch, then modestly lowered her gaze.

He reached out and traced a fingertip across her cheek, then ran his fingers through her hair with bold familiarity. She tilted her head, leaning into his caress like a kitten who adores being petted.

"What is your name?"

"Juanita."

"I must insist, Juanita, that you forgo the formality of addressing me as Premier. I am Fidel, and you will address me so. I insist."

"Yes, Fidel."

"So you wanted to see me in the flesh, eh? Well, you seem an adventurous young lady. If you would care to join me and continue on with us, I think I can promise you not only a look at your Fidel in the flesh, but a night that you will never forget. What would you say to that, eh?"

"I would like that very much, Fidel."

The solder with the rifle stepped down, assisting her into the backseat. Castro did not move over to make room for her, and so she tried to make herself comfortable in the less than adequate space. The curves of her body pressed closely against Castro.

"Proceed," he instructed the driver.

From the ridge, Santos witnessed this with stunned disbelief. "God in Heaven, what does she think she's doing?"

The Jeep, followed by the Olds, continued on to be waved through by sentries at the front gate, onto the property, without slowing. Carmen was staring straight ahead. Castro held her hands in both of his. She was laughing at some remark.

José said, "She's been through too much. It's affected her mind. If Castro finds out who she is, that she's one of us—"

Morgan said, "Fidel's a healthy red-blooded male. He isn't thinking with his big head. Carmen is using a woman's oldest trick to get a man where she wants him. I only hope she's not too smart for her own good."

José's sigh was purely Latin. "You've got to admit, amigos, she looks mighty fine all dolled up in that pretty outfit."

Santos' eyes glowed like fanned embers. "If one of those sons of a diseased dog takes liberties with her, including Fidel—"

Morgan said, "She hasn't flipped. She played a long shot, hoping to intercept Fidel, and it paid off. What Carmen just did is based on the knowledge that we're up here, watching. She's going to offer herself up as a diversion and get next to Castro so there won't be a bodyguard inside the main house, and she's right. That's a hell of a lot more effective than sending her in with a gun. Okay. We proceed with the mission."

CHAPTER 44

"You may speak freely, Tal. I'm on the red scrambler."

"Yes, Mister President. You asked to be notified when Morgan radioed for pickup."

"Ah. Good."

"The boat's on its way from Key West. We're using one of our regular freelance contractors. Guy named Riley. There's, uh, just one thing."

"Yes, Tal, what's that?"

"Graveyard has moved up the timetable by three hours, to midnight."

"Why would he do that?"

"I don't know. There must be a mitigating circumstance."

"There'd damn well better be. There's far too much riding on this to take on additional risk. I want you to stay on this for me, Tal. I want an hourly update. If this leaks, it will be my ass. My administration could go down."

"Yes, Mister President."

Morgan led the way with his .45 automatic drawn. Santos and José followed at combat intervals, their rifles carried at high port. The night was pleasant under a starry sky. They crossed the road, well away from the gatehouse, and traveled along the barbed wire fence until they reached a corner of the acreage. The barbed wire was easily negotiated and they were inside the property line.

Light shone from the main house. The garage beside the house was dark. A single light over the guardhouse showed a cluster of men with shouldered weapons, standing about, idly conversing. A laugh drifted on the breeze off the bay, the murmur of conversation in Spanish.

Morgan whispered, "I see two Jeeps parked alongside the guesthouse, but I don't see the Olds. It's got to be in the garage next to the house."

Santos said, "To hell with their transportation. We've got to find Carmen."

"She'll be with Fidel," said José, "in the main house...without a bodyguard." He sounded more hopeful than certain.

"Down," said Morgan.

They sought cover, flattening themselves upon the rocky ground behind an inky outline of shrubbery. A sentry patrol, carrying shoulder-slung rifles, passed within several feet of them. These men were conversing idly and when they saw the group loitering before the gatehouse, they quickened their pace to join them. Their footfalls faded away.

Morgan made a *move out* gesture and they resumed their advance across a neatly trimmed expanse of lawn. The breeze rustled the fronds of palm trees. They gained a side of the guesthouse that was beyond view of the men by the gatehouse. Morgan made another motion to indicate that José and Santos should fan out to his either side and cover him, which they did, while he spent less than a minute silently raising the hood of each Jeep. He slashed the distributor cables with his knife, effectively disabling the vehicles.

They advanced on the main house, approaching it from the rear. They passed the closed doors of the double garage. The gravel of the driveway was white in the darkness. They gained an open screen door at the rear of the house. The door was unlatched.

Morgan peered through the screen, into a kitchen. Somewhere in the house a radio or a record player was playing calypso music. There were bottles of wine and brown paper sacks with groceries strewn about the kitchen counter, yet a stillness of non-occupancy permeated the house despite the music. Morgan nudged the screen door open and went in. Santos and José joined him inside the house. An archway led to a spacious dining room with an unlighted chandelier.

Carmen stepped into view. Framed by the archway, she wore the same peasant girl blouse and skirt she'd had worn on the road. She was barefoot. When she saw them, she placed her hands on her hips and smiled.

"Well, *mis tres amigos*, it is about time. I was beginning to worry that something had happened to you."

Santos lumbered forward. "Thank God. Are you all right, Carmen? That pig, Castro, did he—"

"Relax, big bear. Our Premier is no match for the ways of a woman."

Morgan said, "Where is he?"

"In the front room, passed out on the couch."

José said, "We were worried. You're very lucky, Carmen."

A brief twinkle came into her eyes. "Not so lucky. We knew what he would do, and he did it. He left strict orders that we were not to be disturbed. I led him to expect that...wicked things would happen. He told his sentries to keep well away from the house."

Morgan went to one of the curtains, parting it to peer out, finding nothing beyond the window but the night.

"They obeyed their orders. That's why it was so easy getting in. Good work."

Santos said, "And nothing, er, uh...nothing happened?"

"He was too busy ogling me," said Carmen, "to notice what I put into his drink."

Morgan couldn't help but be impressed. "And what was that?"

She said, "After I left you on the ridge, I went to the home of our family druggist who filled prescriptions for my mother. A kindly man. He had no idea what I was going to use it for, but he gave me a dosage of something to put into Fidel's drink, to render him incapacitated for another," she glanced at her wrist watch, "another two to three hours."

Morgan said, "Let's see him."

The front room had a high vaulted ceiling, marble flooring, and a cold, unused fireplace in a wall of stone facing the couch and a bar with a television set behind it, tuned to a Cuban baseball game with the sound turned off. A wall of drawn draperies concealed windows that, during daylight hours, would present a spectacular view of the bay. A mahogany stereo console stood in one corner and from it came a series of clicks. The record ended. The calypso music abruptly ceased.

Castro snored heavily. He was fully clothed in his fatigues. His boots were still laced up. A dead cigar, only three quarters smoked, rested forlornly in an otherwise clean ashtray upon a table next to the couch, inches from where his furry head rested upon an arm of the couch. Carmen had crossed his ankles, making it appear as if Castro had merely fallen asleep.

José considered the unconscious figure. "He is indeed one big *hombre*."

Santos positioned himself at the archway leading to the dining room and kitchen. He eyed their withdrawal track, rifle up and ready for target acquisition, his finger ready to squeeze an automatic burst at the first sign of trouble. He made Morgan think of a walking time bomb, seconds away from exploding. In this case, that could be a good thing. Morgan wondered how far they could press their luck.

Santos said, "What do we do now?"

José snapped his fingers. "The Oldsmobile."

Morgan nodded. "Fidel and the lady will go for a moonlight ride."

Carmen nodded with a trace of eagerness. "Castro is well known for taking off on such jaunts from here, always spontaneously."

Morgan said, "Okay, then. We get him out to the garage and into the car. If there aren't any sentries near the house, and with the garage attached to the house, we stand half a chance of pulling this off. We'll prop him up in the back seat so he's sitting next to Carmen. José, you'll have to ride in the trunk."

José smiled briefly. "A minor indignity to suffer for a worthy cause."

"Santos, with your beard you could pass for one of Fidel's boys."

"Thanks a lot, gringo. So you're saying, you want me to drive?"

"Right. I'll crouch down in the back seat to help steady the big guy for the ride. We'll have to be ready to shoot our way out if it goes sour." Morgan glanced an unasked question at Carmen.

She said, "I won't let you down."

"I'll take your word on that," he said without hesitation. "We'll get Fidel to Cayo Fragoso and radio for the boat to come in for the pickup."

Santos was grinning heartily. "And Fidel will be in the custody of the United States government."

"It sounds easy enough," said José.

Morgan said, "Let's find out."

Ten minutes later, the black Oldsmobile exited the garage and sped away from the house, gaining speed on the crushed gravel driveway leading to the front gate. Sentries scurried to swing the gate open in time. The Oldsmobile raced through without slowing. The figure of Fidel, riding in the back next to the woman, passed briefly beneath the light above the gatehouse. Then the car was gone, rapidly gaining speed away from there.

Twenty minutes later, Che Guevara and General Parnov sat in the Russian military advisor's office at Point One, studying a map. Major Almeida hurried in, his face flushed.

Parnov looked up. "Yes, Major, what is it?"

Che said, "You look as if you've run all the way from the Communications room."

"I've just received a phone call from the captain of the guards assigned to Fidel for the weekend."

Che's expression hardened. "What happened? Is Fidel all right?"

"Yes! At least I think so."

Parnov said, "Out with it, man. What have you to report?"

"Uh, it seems that Fidel is, uh, missing."

Che stormed to his feet. *"What?"*

"He left earlier tonight with a woman," said Almeida. "He hasn't been seen since."

Che said, "But there's nothing unusual in that. That is our Fidel."

"There was a chauffeur driving the car as they left," said Almeida. "The captain of the guards assumed it was one of his own men driving, but a short time ago every man was accounted for."

Parnov remained seated. "You could be right. Are they certain he's gone?"

"They are. There is the very real likelihood that the woman was a decoy. If that's the case—"

Parnov finished the sentence for him. "Your leader has been kidnapped."

Che strode to a window and stared out at the darkness. "This is the gringos' work. The man—what was his name, Graveyard...Graveyard Morgan. You remember?"

Almeida nodded. "The gringo who is still at large."

"Fidel joked about him," said Che. "He's the one behind this, with the help of the underground. They have Fidel."

Parnov thumped his desk with a fist. "We must act." He instructed Almeida, "Order a full alert in the area."

Che added, "And order gunboats to patrol the coastline around there. See to it, Major. The gringos must be stopped."

"They *will* be stopped," said Almeida, and he bolted from the office.

CHAPTER 45

The chrome of the black Oldsmobile glinted like silver in the moonlight. This close to the beach there was the trace of the swamp on the heavy, muggy air. The night crackled with its symphony of night birds and insects and with the eternal whisper of the sea lapping the beach, a narrow strip of black sand fifty yards from the stand of pines where the Olds was parked.

Santos leaned against the car, finishing off the last of a pint bottle of rum. He flung the bottle over his shoulder and heard the sound of its shattering.

The sound was lost beneath the sibilant surf to the three people who stood at the shore. Morgan, Carmen and José were conversing, limned in moonlight, facing away from him, watching, and waiting for a signal from the pickup boat. Everyone was edgy. Yet none of them turned, which meant they hadn't heard the sound of the breaking bottle.

Good, thought Santos.

He was alone with the prisoner. Castro had stopped his infernal snoring during the drive but he remained unconscious; an ungainly, practically impossible-to-move mountain of dead weight. They had managed to load him into the car for transport. They had brought him here. And now Fidel lay stretched upon the ground near the car, facedown upon a carpet of ancient and recently fallen pine needles at the base of a tree. Castro was handcuffed to the trunk of the tree, and the key to the handcuffs resided in Santos' breast pocket. He had been instructed to inform the others when Castro regained consciousness. But as yet Fidel had not uttered a sound.

Santos drew his sleeve across his mouth, wiping away rum that moistened his beard from his last, sloppy sip from the bottle. He relished verbal and physical confrontation, but tonight had been about stealth, the penetration of Castro's defenses, about being made to pose as Castro's chauffer in order to get Fidel off the property. It was not his nature to be stealthy. His nerves were near breaking, though he had concealed this behind his facade of stoic silence. He'd waited until the others were gone before uncapping the rum. But then he drank too much, too fast on an empty stomach. Everything took on a razor's edge, as if his blood was liquid fire coursing through him.

He'd intended the rum to dull his emotions, but instead a kaleidoscope of images would not stop hammering into his brain like an ice pick. *Felix. Diego. The loss.* The pain. The savage inhumanity that had unfolded during these past days, an unending nightmare for even the survivors, permanently scarred. What had any of them done to deserve this? Nothing, that's what! They fought for freedom, personal freedom, personal dignity; to subvert a revolution that had replaced one totalitarian government with another; the iron rule of a military dictatorship replaced by the sociopathic rhetoric of a charismatic devil, selling their beloved island out to the most totalitarian thugs in the world, the communists. To prevent that, many had died. And, thus far, all in vain. *And the single human cause for all this suffering was handcuffed to a tree, at his feet...*

Santos snarled under his breath. "Bastard." He drew back his boot and put every bit of his anger and savagery into a swift kick. He heard a snort, a grunt, and peered down at where the gloom was Stygian because the surrounding trees blotted out the moonlight. "Welcome back, *Señor* Dictator. You've been neatly taken, do you know that? I'm going now to fetch the gringo in charge. You will not like what they have in store for you but it's not bad enough, to my thinking. I'd like to kill you."

Castro's brown eyes were wide with dawning awareness. He sputtered, struggling to regain consciousness after the heavy sedation.

Santos unsheathed his combat knife and squatted beside the bearded giant. He placed the blade to the exposed throat beneath Castro's beard.

"I won't kill you, but I want you to feel the cold kiss of my blade, you communist scum. I want you to know how close you are to getting what you deserve. Well, *Señor* Fidel, what do you think? How does it feel?"

Castro pivoted his huge body, using his weight. His thick, long legs swung around. The blow from both boot heels caught Santos along the side of the head, toppling him. The knife flew from his fingers. He landed on his back, his senses reeling, stunned by the fury of the sudden, unexpected counter-attack.

Castro's thick legs snaked around either side of his neck and Santos knew that he had been a fool. He was a drunken fool. He clawed at knees that were as solid and strong as bricks, bracing him like a collar, tightening like a vise. He should have listened to Morgan. He should have left the prisoner alone. Fidel would kill him and find the keys to the handcuffs. The car keys were in the ignition. *Fidel would escape!* He must not let this happen. Castro crossed his ankles for added leverage. The others, so close by, could not hear their struggle. Santos could not find his voice. He pummeled with his fists. Castro laughed a low, guttural growl. Then his legs shifted. There was a distinct *crack!* like a dry twig snapping.

Santos went limp and made no further movement. His head drooped from his neck at an unnatural angle.

Castro maintained the vise-like grip of his knees, using leverage of the tree provided by his being handcuffed to it, and the considerable strength of his leg muscles. He managed to shift the burly body about, scuffing his fatigues and scraping his skin raw in the process. But soon the dead man was positioned just so, allowing Castro to search his pockets for the key to the handcuffs.

"Where is the boat?" José wondered aloud. "Why haven't we seen the signal?"

Morgan said, "Relax. Time drags when you're waiting."

Carmen was watching Morgan in the moonlight. "It will not be long, then you'll be gone."

José added, "Along with our fearless leader, the mighty Fidel." He snickered.

"There's room on the boat for the two of you and Santos if you want to come with me," said Morgan. "I owe you that. My country owes you."

José said, "America owes me nothing. I fight for a free Cuba. You are taking Fidel off our hands. That is enough. *Muchas gracias, amigo.* As for Santos?" José chuckled. "He will never leave this island. At last count he has two wives and seven children and he loves them all. It is for them that he fights."

"And you, Carmen?"

She said, "My family is buried here. This is where I belong. Santos called me brave. I'm not brave. But I'm not afraid, either. The ones who have suffered and died, their souls cry out. I will stay and carry on. We must reorganize, perhaps go deeper underground. But the fight will continue. Your invasion failed because you underestimated Castro. Do not underestimate us, *señor.*"

"There," said José. "The signal."

Morgan lifted a flashlight, which he clicked on and off, returning the signal. "Let's go see if Fidel is awake. It's time to bring him down here for loading."

Behind them, the engine of the Oldsmobile gunned to life. They whirled as one. The car's headlights came on and the Olds accelerated away, kicking up clumps of vegetation and dirt in its wake, the headlight beams revealing the burly form that sat unmoving against the base of a tree. Santos' head lolled at an impossible angle from his shoulders.

José cursed in Spanish.

Carmen cried out. *"Santos!"*

Morgan and José opened fire after the departing car. The repeated bark of Morgan's .45 was nearly lost beneath José's assault rifle firing on semi-auto. But the taillights only winked at them and grew smaller like red little eyes in the night, mocking them. The Olds topped an incline and disappeared from view.

The night had become quieter. Insects and night birds were silent. There was only the timeless, sibilant whisper of the surf.

CHAPTER 46

The speedboat was a sleek sixty-three-foot V20 bearing no name or markings, barely visible from the beach, riding the calm black waters a dozen yards from the shore. Morgan made out the vaguely defined shape of a .50-caliber machine gun mounted in a gun pit amidship and two figures waiting for him beside a squat wheelhouse.

Carmen gave him a gentle embrace. She whispered in his ear, "Thank you for everything you have done."

"I'm sorry it wasn't enough. And thanks for telling me things I needed to hear about what I've got to do when I get home; about my family. I don't want to lose the ones I live for."

"Good luck to you, Sergeant."

Then he and José were exchanging a handshake and *abrazo*, the Latin embrace of macho friendship.

"Vaya con Dios, señor."

Morgan said, "Good luck to both of you."

There was nothing more to be said. There was no more time. He had experienced hundreds of such farewells during his time spent in the war zones. He waded into the thigh-deep water, to the boat. One of the men extended a muscular arm to hoist him up; a refrigerator-sized black man wearing a skipper's cap at a jaunty angle.

"Welcome aboard, Graveyard Morgan. Don't usually get celebrities on this run. Name's Riley."

They shook hands. Riley had a meat grinder handshake.

"A pleasure to meet you, Riley, and you can believe that. Now how's about showing me what this baby can do on the open water?"

Riley's gold-toothed grin split his ebony face. "With pleasure, my brother, with pleasure." He started to turn away.

The other man spoke. "Hold on a minute. Morgan, where's your prisoner?"

Morgan recognized this voice. He stepped in closer until he could discern the lean, dark complexioned features. "Well, well. My old pal, Conklin. Haven't seen you since Happy Valley. What the hell are you doing here?"

"I was in the wrong place at the wrong time. I haven't even been debriefed and the Man gets this wild hair. Where is Castro? You're supposed to have him here for pickup."

Riley said, "Excuse me, gents, but as Mister Conklin knows," there was a trace of derision in the word *mister*, "we had to wait out a patrol boat before slipping in. You fellas ought to straighten out this mess after we're out of here. I've known them patrol boat boys to double back."

Conklin sneered. "Shut up unless you're spoken to. You're just an errand boy, Riley. I'm running this show." He glared at Morgan. "Now, where's the prisoner? And who the hell are those people?" He indicated where Carmen and José had been standing on the shore. But they were gone. "Hey, where'd they go?"

"That was José Cardena. He was with Brigade 2506. And Carmen Vasquez, with the underground."

"So where the hell is Castro?"

"Carmen slipped him a mickey that didn't work for as long as it should have because he's a goddamn giant. I should have known."

"Castro got away?"

"That's about the size of it."

"I thought you call yourself a professional."

"I've been calling myself a lot of things."

Conklin punched a fist into his opposite palm. It sounded like the report of a small caliber handgun. "I don't believe this!"

"Okay, you've made your point."

"Have I? What the hell are you doing on this boat? Your job isn't done."

"I gave it my best. I've got a ride home and I'm taking it."

"The hell you are." Conklin's voice was pitched low. "I've been waiting for a showdown with you since Nicaragua, you goddamn boy scout, and this is it. You were issued a directive to effect the abduction of Fidel Castro. I'll be back to pick you up when you've carried out your mission."

"Screw that," said Morgan. "And screw you. No one is going to carry out that mission. Not for a while. Not after tonight. Castro's going to triple his security and no one will get near to him. He won't let news about tonight get out but he won't take any more crazy chances, either. Tell you what, Conklin. You're so gung ho for a suicide mission? You stay. How's that?"

Riley, who had not been paying much attention to their conversation, said, "Uh oh. That patrol boat is back."

Then Morgan heard it too. The mutter of a motor from somewhere out there in the darkness, carried across the water to their starboard side. The patrol boat was prowling with its running lights off. Morgan thought, *I should have been listening with Riley, not yapping with this damn CIA guy.*

He whispered to Riley, "You're going to outrun them, right?"

Riley's bulk shifted in the shadows. He towered over the controls. "Can't nobody outrun bullets. But if they spot us, I'll open up this mother and, partner, we will haul ass."

The silvery lance of a searchlight stabbed its beam outward from the patrol boat, sweeping across the smooth surface of the cay, initially panning well away from them.

Riley said, "Aw, shit."

Conklin snorted. "They're just dumb spics. We'll blast our way out." He lunged for the .50-caliber machine gun.

"No!" snapped Riley. "We can pay those boys off. I've done that before."

But Conklin was already behind the big gun, swiveling it around.

Morgan leaped at him.

"Conklin, don't be a fool!

The hammering of bright golden muzzle flashes when the M-50 opened fire turned the calm glass-like water red and the sea seemed to shimmer, the night exploding into flying fragments with nothing but the *blam!-blam!-blam!* of the heavy machine gun pounding away.

When the firing stopped, yelping of agony and startled shouts from the direction of the patrol boat could be heard. Then their machine gun opened fire and Morgan was throwing himself flat upon the deck, hearing the ugly popping sounds of heavy caliber bullets smacking apart Conklin's body. He whipped around in time to see Conklin being hurled away from the machine gun, stumbling backwards in a dead-man's-walk that ended with Conklin tripping over the side and the splash of his body hitting the water.

Morgan flung himself behind the M-50. He braced himself and reluctantly depressed the trigger. His body shook with the recoil of a quick three-round return burst that extinguished the patrol boat's searchlight. There was more shouting in Spanish from aboard the patrol boat, then it swung about and made a hasty retreat. Within seconds, its sounds disappeared beyond a distant point.

Riley drew himself up from where he'd hit the deck. "They'll be back with backup." He nodded at where Conklin had gone overboard. "What about the spook?"

Morgan said, "The hell with him."

Riley said, "Damn spy boys. That punk almost got us killed until you sent that patrol boat scattin' out of here. Reckon I'll pay you back, soldier, and tell you some scuttlebutt I heard that you ought to know. Key West, here we come."

The black Oldsmobile braked to a stop at the main gate. The captain of the guards had positioned himself squarely in its path, raising a gloved hand, his other hand on his sidearm. Behind him, sentries stood poised, their rifles aimed at the car. The captain stepped to the driver's side. When he recognized the lone occupant of the car, he quickly motioned for his men to lower their weapons. He snapped to attention, rendering the driver a curt salute.

"*Commandante*, it is wonderful to see you safe! Thank God. We thought there had been foul play."

Castro laughed without bothering to remove the cigar that was clenched between his teeth, protruding from the corner of his mouth. "Foul play? That's absurd. I've been out sampling the local nightlife, my dear Captain. Perhaps you were not aware of it, but this area is renowned for the beauty of its women."

"But, *Commandante*...the man driving the car when you left, and that woman—?"

"Silence. You dare to interrogate *me*?"

The captain stepped away from the car as if he had been slapped. "Certainly not, *Commandante*. But I regret to report that Havana has been notified of your, uh, disappearance. They're searching for you. There was a fire fight with a patrol boat near here, at Cayo Fragoso."

"Notify Havana to cancel the search, and order your men out of my way. I've had a strenuous evening. I'm in no mood for inconvenience."

"Si, Commandante."

CHAPTER 47

At the CIA headquarters in Miami, in the drab apartment house on Segovia Street, Tal Garrett answered the telephone on its first ring.

"Industrial Imports International."

Resnick said, "Welcome back to Miami."

Garrett grumbled. "It's like I never left."

He'd managed exactly four hours of fitful sleep since his surreal "conference" with the President aboard the *Honey Fitz* in Washington. But Resnick's voice told Garrett that he wasn't the only one feeling ragged around the edges. If the Miami OIC's sportsman personae had seemed muted during their previous conversation at the airport, Resnick now sounded downright gloomy.

"Where are you, Sam?"

"Key West. I'm still at the dock."

"What the hell are you doing there? Don't tell me Riley just landed! I know all about the snafu with Castro, and about Conklin, but you're supposed to be on your way here with Morgan."

"Uh yeah, Tal. But, uh, we've got a problem."

Garrett sighed. "You know, Sam, I really wish I wasn't back in Miami. I really do. I wish I had a cigarette and I wish I was anywhere but up to me adenoids in this."

Resnick said, "I know the feeling, believe me."

"I believe you, Sam. So let's have it."

Resnick paused, took a deep breath and exhaled quickly. "Graveyard gave me the slip."

"Goddamn."

"He gave me the slip, easy as it is to tell you about it. Said he had to use the head. There was a public one by the dock. I should have gone in with him. There was a window on the other side and out he went."

"Did you tell him which hospital his wife and daughter are at?"

"Yeah, I told him."

"The hospital where his wife and daughter are...meet me there, Sam. Fast as you can make it."

The two-bed room stank of that stuffy, universal mixture of illness, detergent and medicine. Beyond the closed door, this wing of the hospital was humming with morning activity. Beyond the window, cumulus clouds against a pale sky held onto the rosette warmth of the sunrise. Miami was beginning a new day.

Susan Morgan was bandaged like a mummy from her neck down to where the bed sheet was drawn about her waist. An array of intravenous tubes connected her to an assortment of bottles and plastic bags. A machine monitored her breathing and heartbeat. She was asleep.

Morgan sat at Vera's bedside. The sight of her made his heart ache. Vera sat, propped up in bed with pillows, and seemed to be staring at their daughter despite the gauze bandages that covered her eyes. Vera had been blinded by the close proximity of the gun blast to her eyes in the cabin shooting. The doctor was pretty sure that her eyesight would return in time. *Pretty sure...*

She said, "They made special arrangements for us to have the same room. An Agent Resnick saw to it." Her face was swollen, badly bruised.

"Vera, I'm sorry."

"For what?"

"You know for what. For everything."

"No, I mean where are you going to start? How far back do you think it was when you made the wrong turn and I ended up here like this, and our daughter with a bullet hole in her?"

"The doc said she could expect full recovery too. The bullet went through the flesh of her shoulder."

"The doc sounds like a cockeyed optimist. Susan may recover physically but things like this do things to a person, Graveyard. Or didn't you know that?"

"I know it. Please don't call me Graveyard."

"Why not? It's your name."

"It's what *they* call me, not you. Vera, how are you?"

"I'll live. The blast was so close to my face..." She lifted her fingertips to touch the bandages. "They've got me on pain medication. It hurts like hell, but not as bad as when I gave birth to Susan."

"You're better off than Rivas. I hear your bullet took away most of his face and the top of his head."

"I don't know how I made it to the neighbors'. Something drove me. I heard Susan's breathing before I left. I knew I had to get us medical attention. That's what sent me through the night."

"I love you, Vera."

"I'll tell you the truth, Mike. I'm not sure that's enough. I have a lot to think about."

"I know, and you'll have plenty of time to yourself when they come for me, which should be any second now. But I had to see you two. I had to tell you that I'm not going to wait anymore for the world to settle down. It never has and it never will. But you and I can settle down and take charge of our lives. What we've been through, what we have, Vera, it's worth that."

"But you're a soldier. A man's got to do what a man's got to do."

"I don't *have* to be anything. I don't want to lose my family. My life isn't some writ-in-stone military position that has to be defended no matter what the cost. Life is a journey. The scenery changes. Sometimes we have to change with it. I've been a soldier long enough."

This brought her face around to his for the first time. "Do the people who are coming for you know that, or the people they work for? Have you told them? How about your friend, the President?"

"They're about to find out. Then it's you and me, honey, and Susan makes three. I've done my time in hell. I mean, I'm almost done."

"Almost?"

"It's almost over."

"I wonder, Mike. Can you change?"

"You'll see." He instantly regretted the choice of words. He reached across and lightly caressed the bandaged eyes. "Vera, I'm so sorry."

She drew back with a wince.

"Don't apologize for what happened to me. I'll write it off to the price of an education, what happened at our cabin. Our pristine getaway. Ha. That blast seared my eyeballs but it also seared some smarts into me about what's bullshit and what's real." Her jaw lifted. "I may be a pacifist, but I'll kill the son of a bitch that tries to harm my daughter."

"You proved that," said Morgan. "Magnify that to a world scale and you've got the rationale that's kept me going all these years."

"Okay. So now I understand. God knows what you've done over the years in those places they sent you. There will always be some dark side to you that I won't be able to touch."

"I *can* change."

"That's not what stands between us, Michael. It's you drawing Susan into it. No mother could forgive that."

"I'd give anything to go back and change what happened."

"But you can't, can you?" Vera regarded him from her bed even without seeing him. "To think, I was ready to end our marriage because I thought you brought the *taint* of your dark evil world into our lives, into our home. But then, my God, you bastard, you hand those savages your own daughter and it's only because of me that she's safe and we didn't both die. How could you have done something like that? *How?* Even when I can see...I don't think I ever want to see you again. Go away."

The door burst open and the room became filled with people.

Resnick and Garrett went for Morgan, each grabbing hold of him and pinning his arms behind him. A middle-aged nurse rushed in to make a fuss about Morgan being there while in the doorway, with a pistol in his hand, stood the uniformed cop Morgan had earlier conned to gain entry, having shown the officer his credentials, claiming to be there on CIA business. The cop now looked mad enough to use his gun. The nurse was taking over, fussing over the patients and shooing everyone out.

Garrett and Resnick strong-armed Morgan from the room without giving him and Vera another chance to speak. Waving off the policeman, they hustled him past a nurses' station, to a bank of elevators. They released their hold on his arms.

Resnick said, "Thanks for making me look like a jerk. I thought you were a right guy. Did you think we wouldn't track you straight here?"

Morgan said, "I didn't care." He flexed his shoulder muscles. He didn't like being manhandled. "I had to see my family."

Garrett said, "The President is in Miami. He wants a complete briefing from you in person, right now."

"Great," said Morgan. "I want to see him too."

CHAPTER 48

As he had during his previous visit to Miami, the President met in secret with the Democratic Revolutionary Front exile leadership at his father's Palm Beach estate. Robert Kennedy and General Atwater were also present. The President declined to discuss the matter of Doctor Rivas. He was asked about his future commitment to the Council and La Causa.

"Despite the tragedy of how the invasion ended," he told them, "my commitment and that of my administration stand firm behind the struggle for Cuban freedom."

There was a smattering of polite applause.

He was reminded by one of the members that the invasion had failed because of a lack of control of the air, which the Brigade thought it had been guaranteed.

"The Bay of Pigs was a bitter lesson in the limits of secrecy," said the President. "I must accept the consequences of that lesson. But be assured that I am determined above all else to prevent the execution and seek the liberation of the men my government has helped send to their imprisonment. Believe me, my friends, I share your grief. This is nothing I take lightly. Remember, I have seen combat. I lost a brother and a brother-in-law in the war. I know something of how you feel."

The meeting lasted thirty-five minutes.

Robert accepted a telephone call while President Kennedy, Atwater and some of their staff were seeing out the exile leaders. When the President returned, the Attorney General requested a moment alone.

"Garrett just called. They've left the hospital. They're on their way here with Morgan."

"I'll see them in the library," said the President. "I'll want you there, Bobby, and General Atwater. I could use a drink. Ask the General to join us."

No children played this morning beyond the glass of the French doors.

Low, ominous gray clouds made the air warm, though it was not yet midday. A light mist had begun to fall, streaking the glass, rendering the expanse of lawn and cypress beyond the patio a blurred vision, shaded a rich emerald green.

Morgan, Garrett and Resnick remained standing, Morgan between them, facing their Commander in Chief.

John Kennedy sat in a rocking chair, attired more formally than during Morgan's previous visit. The President wore a conservative tailor-made suit of somber blue. He introduced the Attorney General and a stern-faced man with five stars, introduced as General Atwater, who occupied a pair of armchairs.

Then the President said, "Sergeant, it's good to see you again. You've been through quite an ordeal."

"Mister President."

"There's been a run of bad luck and you've suffered for it, as has your family. I was saddened to hear about what happened to your wife and daughter, but gratified to know that they are receiving the best of treatment and are expected to recover. You're to be commended for a job well done, soldier."

"Sorry to disagree with you, sir, but Castro got away."

Robert Kennedy frowned darkly. "We're going to bury this one *deep*." His hands flittered with nervous energy as he spoke. "No word of this, uh, 'kidnap' fiasco must ever surface."

Atwater growled agreement. "What happened at the Bay of Pigs was bad enough. But the abduction of a head of state? My God, the press has been friendly for the most part. They'd eat us alive if this stunt ever got out."

Morgan added, "So would the history books."

Garrett and Resnick each sent him a look.

The President said, "I want from you at this time, Sergeant, as concise a report as possible, solely from your perspective; your evaluation, your observations and conclusions, on what went wrong."

Morgan gave a rude snort. "What went right? You were betrayed, sir, by the men you trusted."

Atwater bristled. "Watch your tone, soldier."

Robert Kennedy bent forward in his chair. "Those are harsh words, Sergeant. What are you talking about?"

"You want harsh, Mister Attorney General? Try this. That racist SOB

Conklin damn well got what he deserved." Morgan indicated the man standing to his right. "Garrett here is the only honest, straightforward CIA man I've encountered since I was brought into this."

Resnick cleared his throat. "Hey, what about me?"

Morgan's eyes grew cold. "It's time for some long overdue housecleaning. Yeah, Castro's got a mole inside the CIA operation in Miami. And Sam, you're it. That's the only way the pieces of this puzzle fit together. You're a traitor who let the enemy get inside the President's inner circle."

A startled pause. Every man in the room stared at Resnick, whose mouth tightened into a hard line. Little bunches of muscle formed knots along the side of his jaw.

"What the hell are you talking about, Morgan? Are you crazy?"

Morgan said, "I expect you to hard-line. That's okay, go ahead."

"You're in shock, that's what it is," said Resnick. "What happened down in Cuba, then coming home and seeing your wife and daughter like that in the hospital. Me? You're forgetting about Doctor Rivas."

"I forget and I forgive nothing," said Morgan, "but I can almost forgive Rivas. At least he was Cuban. He was the enemy. The CIA idiots who betrayed the President, bungling the training and their support of the invasion, that was incompetence, political fervor, ambition. But you, Sam, you're the lowest of scum. You sold out. They bought you."

Perspiration glistened along Resnick's upper lip, and formed beads on his forehead. "You're talking garbage. If you've got some crazy idea that you can pin anything on me, you'll fall flat on your face because there's nothing to pin."

Tal Garrett said, in an uncertain voice, "Easy, Sam. Let's hear him out."

"Hear him out? Tal, you're supposed to be on my side." Resnick's eyes swept the men seated before him. "This is outright lunacy."

Morgan said, "Doctor Rivas ran a spy network in the exile community, but Havana had only one man planted inside the Central Intelligence Agency. They'd like to see Rivas take all the heat. A dead man makes a good fall guy. Then they'll still have likeable Sam Resnick right where they can keep on using him. Rivas was guilty as sin. He strangled that nightclub guy, Ortiz. Rivas and Resnick made it look like Hector Solas was a spy and a killer."

Garrett watched Resnick with narrowed eyes. "You tailed Rivas that night, when he and Solas went to the *Paradiso* the night Ortiz was murdered. You worked real hard to convince me that Hector Solas was the Castro agent responsible for the Ortiz murder."

Resnick took a deep breath and exhaled like a man doing his best to restrain mounting indignation and righteous wrath. "Tal, do not let this son of a bitch make it personal and turn you against me. We've worked too many hours together. Yeah, I tailed Rivas and his boy Hector to the alley behind the club. I saw Hector Solas go in."

"Uh-uh," said Morgan. "You're an accomplice to murder. You sat in your car and knowingly let it happen, knowing that you'd help Rivas hang a frame on a poor dumb-ass. You boys must have had quite a laugh when you had to pay Rivas an official visit to 'question' him about Solas."

Garrett was nodding. "The hit and run of Maria Quintana fits into this. We haven't sorted that out yet, but she's the connecting link." He said to Morgan, "And your daughter was involved. It's why she and your wife went into hiding. It's why Rivas tracked them down."

Resnick said, "But I wasn't involved, and I don't have to listen to this."

The President said, "I'm sorry, but you do. I asked Morgan for his report and I will hear him out."

"But Mister President, everything he's saying is a lie. I mean *everything!*"

The President said, "Continue, Sergeant."

Morgan said, "They had Hector Solas all set to take the fall. Solas not only trusted Rivas, he idolized him. When Resnick and I 'discovered' Ortiz's body, I heard Resnick call it in. But later, when I was out of earshot, he called Rivas and they set Hector's frame-up in play. Rivas telephoned him and told Solas that we were on our way. He fed him some lies that pushed Hector over the edge and made him run blindly for his life, which resulted in an agent named Masden being shot down in the street. That wasn't in their plan, but it didn't hurt. The plan was for Resnick to shoot and kill Solas and he would have gotten away with it, except a city bus came along and that was that. So Hector Solas takes the heat and Rivas is free and clear until my daughter shows up and starts asking questions. Susan will have plenty to tell us when she's able."

Atwater glowered. "Those are mighty strong accusations."

Robert leaned back in his chair, his fingertips steepled beneath his chin. "They are," he agreed. "And so before we proceed any further, Sergeant, let us hear your evidence."

Resnick said, "Begging your pardon, sir, but I've served in the Agency since its inception. My record does not have a blemish on it, not a one, and this will damn well not be the first."

Morgan locked eyes with the President. "Sir, as the Officer in Charge in Miami, Resnick is the one who processed the background security checks on Rivas that got Rivas admitted to the exile leadership." He said to Resnick, "You told Rivas about my cabin at Fort Myers. That was my safe house, set up for me by the Agency in Miami long before you were assigned here. *You* had access to that information, damn you. If it hadn't been for you feeding that information to Rivas, my wife and daughter wouldn't be laid up right now in a hospital. I owe you, you son of a bitch."

The President said, "Sergeant, we must have proof."

Resnick smiled. "I'm relieved to hear you say that, sir. I swear on a stack of Bibles that none of this is true."

Robert was bent forward again, his young-old face severe. "What do you say, Morgan? What proof do you have?"

CHAPTER 49

Morgan said, "I think I can produce all the proof you need."

Resnick sneered. "There. He *thinks* he can. Does that sound substantial? Nothing but wild fabrication."

Morgan said, "There's a loose end named Morales who's on the run. He was tied in deep with Rivas. Tag Morales and he'll sweat out the answers you need. And there's another loose end."

Garrett muttered, "One more loose end and I'm taking up smoking again."

"That Brigade guy, Perez, who died in the practice jump. Was he a pawn like Solas, or was he a spy inside the Brigade? I don't think we'll ever know." Morgan grimaced. "I hate loose ends."

Resnick said, "Get back to me. If there's a mole inside the Agency, why does it have to be me? Why not Tal, here? He fits the bill as well as I do, even more so because he outranks me. Why are you so gung ho about digging *my* grave?"

Morgan said, "Screw gung ho. I don't have one bit of enthusiasm for this. Castro needed a man deep inside here in Miami, not in Washington where Garrett was stationed. Miami is where everything was happening."

Garrett said, "It wasn't me. The information leaks have been ongoing. I was just assigned to this after that agent, Lehman, bought the farm on that beach in Cuba."

"Well," said Resnick resolutely, "it wasn't me, either."

The President observed Morgan with a cocked eyebrow, mirroring a skepticism, combined with a willingness to believe, that was conveyed by the others.

Morgan said, "What if I got this turncoat to confess and hand over the hard evidence we need?"

Resnick sneered. "Confess to what? I haven't done anything, so why the hell should I confess?"

"Because if you don't, I'll kill you."

Someone blurted, "Hold on a minute—"

The Attorney General rose to his feet. "I'll remind you, Sergeant, that this is a nation of laws."

Resnick sneered. "You're crazy. What would you kill me with, Graveyard? They frisked us before we came in here, remember? No one gets this close to the President with a weapon except for the Secret Service. I'm not afraid of you."

Morgan said, "Well, you damn well ought to be."

The President straightened in his rocking chair. "There will be none of that. We will follow the letter of the law."

Resnick was gaining confidence by the second, sensing the tide turning in his favor. He started to address the President. But before he could speak, Morgan, with an almost nonchalant grace, placed a foot behind one of Resnick's ankles and proceeded to drop Resnick to the polished wood floor without the least effort. Resnick shouted in surprise, caught completely off guard. Morgan dropped atop him, pinning Resnick with a knee to the chest, wedging his throat from below and above between his forearms. Resnick struggled, but found himself securely pinned. Without releasing his hold, Morgan brought Resnick about into a sitting position.

Resnick snarled, "Let me go, damn you! I'll have your head for this! Let me go!"

"I have *your* head," said Morgan.

The seated men leaped to their feet. Everyone was taken aback.

Atwater ordered, "Sergeant, release that man."

Doors flew open. Secret Service agents poured in, pistols drawn, unbelievably fast, blocking the President from the others, weapons tracking toward the men on the floor.

President Kennedy ordered, with curt authority. "Lower your weapons. Morgan, if Resnick is guilty, we surely don't want him dead. There is much he can tell us."

Resnick snarled at the President, "I'll tell the press everything I know about the kidnap attempt on Castro. They'll crucify all of you."

Morgan said, "I wouldn't go that route, bub. These men don't like to be threatened." Then he was addressing the President. "Sorry, sir, but I want you to hear it from Resnick's own mouth." He tightened his vise-hold on Resnick's throat. "Come on, traitor. Tell the truth. Let's hear you say it."

Resnick's face was darkening from lack of oxygen. He clawed at Morgan's arms.

Garrett stepped forward to rest a hand on Morgan's shoulder. "Graveyard, stop. Man, you *are* crazy!"

"You guys knew I didn't play by the rules when you brought me in." Morgan leaned into a twist that would break the neck. "You know I'll do it, Sam. I'll do it and it'll feel good no matter what they do to me, because I'll have popped this mad-on I've got after what you did to my family. But that won't mean squat to you, because you'll be dead. Nothing but worm bait. So talk and fast. Tell the truth or I'll kill you, I swear I will."

Secret Service agents eyed the President for direction. He waved them back.

"Let them be."

Robert said, "But, Jack—"

"Let this play out. Morgan's right. We've screwed up every step of the way. Let him set this right."

Resnick heard that and panic filled his reddened face. "*Don't!*" He was gasping. "*Don't kill me!* It was me! I *was* the one! Don't kill me!"

"How much did they pay you?" said Morgan. "What was the price of your soul?"

"Twenty-five...twenty-five thousand dollars...they promised more... stop, can't breathe..."

Robert said, "But that won't stand up in court."

Morgan grinned. "Hear that, traitor? We need hard proof. What have you got? I'm giving you the three-count, then you're going to be nothing but a bad memory. One."

Atwater said, "Mister President—"

Resnick squealed.

"Two."

Robert said, "Jack, for Godssakes!—"

Garrett was yelling, "Stop this, Morgan! Goddmmit—"

Morgan said, "Three," and started to twist his forearms.

Resnick screamed. "A diary! I kept a journal!" His raspy, gasping voice was unrecognizable. "A log to blackmail those spic bastards after they got into power. All the laws we broke! I kept it. I keep it in a safe in my house. Okay? *Okay?*"

Morgan held him like that and looked at the President.

"Do you believe him, sir?"

No hesitation. "Yes, Sergeant. I believe him. We'll confiscate the diary. Now let him go." Kennedy indicated the hovering agents. "These men will take him into custody."

Morgan did not budge.

"I'm not ready to let him go, sir. You guys really want him alive now, don't you? Sammy boy can tell you everything once he gets his voice back. But I can still break his neck with no trouble at all."

Garrett said, "Uh, Graveyard, reason this thing through. You're digging your own grave, man."

Atwater said, "That's your Commander-in-Chief you're disobeying, soldier."

"What, precisely," asked the President, "is it that you want from us?"

"From *you*, sir. I need assurance from you, one soldier to another. That's the only thing I'll trust. See, I want out. I'm done. I quit. Write it off as battle fatigue. Fix it any way it can be fixed. But I want out when I walk through that door, and I don't want any strings attached. No vendetta. I don't want any 'help' from the Agency. I don't want anything from anyone. I just want gone. My word of honor that I will never confide anything to anybody about what I know. Allow me to walk out of here and take my family and disappear...and you get Resnick alive."

Garrett laughed. "For the love of God, he's blackmailing the President."

Again, no hesitation.

John Kennedy said, "After what you've been through, Sergeant, I can see where a man would feel the way you do. And after this Bay of Pigs disaster, I can't say as I blame you. I agree to your conditions. You have my word."

Morgan released Resnick, who practically collapsed, barely conscious. Secret Service agents bolted forward to catch him, roughly supporting him on his feet. Resnick was coughing, breathing raggedly. The President made a dismissive gesture to the team leader and Resnick was escorted from the room. Morgan felt like a specimen under a microscope, the way everyone's attention shifted to him.

When it was quiet again, Robert said, "But this is wholly unreasonable!"

"No, it isn't," said, the President. "I've read the Sergeant's file." A fleeting smile. "In fact, I read it three times. It reads better than a James Bond novel, only not as believable."

Atwater grumbled, "It's true enough. But that doesn't justify," he stammered in exasperation, struggling for the right phrase, settling gruffly for, "whatever the hell Morgan is up to!"

"I beg to differ, General. Morgan has served admirably, performed heroically, over and above the call of duty, every time he's been sent out. In this affair, despite his failure to abduct Castro, his service to our cause was invaluable. His sacrifice has been formidable, pitching into combat when every other American, including myself, was deserting those men of the Brigade; and the endangerment of his family at the hands of a maniac. Frankly, Sergeant, part of me would have preferred to see you snap Resnick's neck."

Robert groaned. "Jack, no..."

The President returned to his rocker. "But you're right, Graveyard. We need Mister Resnick alive. That traitor did not get what he deserves, but you shall."

Atwater blinked. "Sir, you're not letting him get away with this?"

"Gentlemen, I've given this man my word. Michael Morgan will be allowed to walk away from this and vanish from sight and from history if that is his wish."

Garrett eyed Morgan with a clouding stare. "Guess I never had you figured for a quitter."

Morgan ignored this and spoke to the President. "Sir, I say this with all due respect. Castro is holding the men of the Brigade for ransom. We tried to hold Castro for ransom. And damn me if I can't see the point of each side. But we're supposed to be better than our enemies. We should start acting like it."

The corners of the President's mouth crinkled in a humorless smile. "I did ask for your observations and conclusions, didn't I?"

Morgan's focus took in the others. "And I'm not quitting. I'm just getting started. I'm going to put my family back together again if I can, if it's not too late, and I don't need any distractions. This soldier is going home. This Graveyard is closed for business."

He delivered a smart salute, which the President returned in kind.

"Whatever the future may hold, Sergeant, good luck to you."

Morgan executed an about face and left the library.

No one tried to stop him.

He had not noticed while inside, but outside the rain had stopped. Shafts of sunlight had broken through the clouds and birdsong filled the air. The morning wore a new, fresh scent. Morgan walked down the driveway, toward the front gate, and he did not look back.

EPILOGUE

Following an elaborate mass trial in Havana and lengthy negotiations, the Cuban government agreed to release the prisoners of Brigade 2506 in exchange for fifty-three million dollars worth of food and medical supplies provided by the United States.

ABOUT THE AUTHOR

STEPHEN MERTZ has written novels that have been widely translated and have sold millions of copies worldwide. His thrillers *The Korean Intercept* and *Blood Red Sun* are ebooks available from Crossroad Press. As "Jack Buchanan," he also produces the popular MIA Hunter series. Stephen Mertz lives in the American Southwest, and is always at work on a new novel.

Curious about other Crossroad Press books?
Stop by our site:
http://store.crossroadpress.com
We offer quality writing
in digital, audio, and print formats.

Enter the code FIRSTBOOK
to get 20% off your first order from our store!
Stop by today!

CPSIA information can be obtained at www.ICGtesting.com
Printed in the USA
BVOW03s0012300913

332469BV00002B/8/P

9 781937 530549